Take My
HAND

Endorsements

It's "curtains up" on Ane Mulligan's delightful story, *Take My Hand*. Talk about setting the stage! Theater. Food. Romance. Intrigue. Adorable kids. What more could you ask for in a great book? Filled with innovative twists and turns, this story will captivate your imagination and keep you hanging on till the very last (amazing) scene. Highly recommended (and not just because I'm a theater buff)!
—**Janice Thompson**, author of the Weddings by Bella series

How many obstacles must one woman overcome to finally achieve her dreams? Ane Mulligan's ability to create delightful Southern characters makes it fun to find out. Ane's books never fail to entertain.
—**Linda W. Yezak**, award-winning author and freelance editor.

Small town, check. Romance, double check. Bad guy who messes things up, yep, that too. Like the characters in a cozy Hallmark movie, *Take My Hand* is a story that will give you all the feels because Marleigh and Gabe are sure to win your heart. Author Ane Mulligan pens yet another tale that will leave you smiling.
—**Michelle Griep**, Christy Award-winning author of *Man of Shadow and Mist*

Take My Hand has all the feels ... a sister raising her

precocious little brother, a chef trying to escape his malicious family, and a dream that puts a community at odds. Another sweet, sassy, heart-warming story from Ane Mulligan!

—**Tara Johnson**, author of *To Speak His Name*

Take My
HAND

ANE MULLIGAN

ELK LAKE PUBLISHING INC

PUBLISHING THE POSITIVE
Plymouth, Massachusetts

A Christian Company
ElkLakePublishingInc.com

Copyright Notice

Take My HAND

Cover and Interior Design: Kelly Artieri, Deb Haggerty
Editor(s): Peggy Ellis, Cristel Phelps, Deb Haggerty

PUBLISHED BY: Elk Lake Publishing, Inc., 35 Dogwood Drive, Plymouth, MA 02360, 2024

Library Cataloging Data
Names: Mulligan, Ane (Ane Mulligan))
Take My Hand / Ane Mulligan
344 p. 23cm × 15cm (9in × 6 in.)
ISBN-13: 9798891342491 (paperback) | 9798891342507 (trade paperback) | 9798891342514 (e-book)
Key Words: romance; Southern; small town; friendship; women's fiction; heartwarming; community theatre
Library of Congress Control Number: 2024947329 Fiction

Dedications

For Aysha Jerald and Jordan Powell, our best theatre interns ever.

I couldn't imagine writing a story about theatre without you two in it.

Thank you for all you did to help make Players Guild at Sugar Hill a success.

Acknowledgments

No one writes a novel alone. There are a multitude of people behind every author who offer encouragement and answer questions. A million questions. Though I am managing director at a community theatre, there is so much new technology I don't know how to operate or understand.

A huge thank you to Lee Morgan, Technical Director for the Eagle Theatre at Sugar Hill. He answered many questions about rigging, lighting, and sound.

I'm grateful for friends like Wade Williams, who in real life, is Atlanta's premiere exotic car mechanic. He chose Gabe's Ferrari model and year for me, plus he makes a cameo appearance.

An eternal thank you goes to Boo Kirsch Hynes for allowing me to use her first name. I fell in love with her name when I met her, knowing I wanted to use it in a book. She graciously gave me permission. Boo is a nickname from childhood which stuck with her into adulthood, giving you a glimpse into her fun personality.

Another name from real life is Kathryn Baskin. Her active involvement in Gwinnett County's and the City of Sugar Hill's historical preservation society helped me with my research. She's become a good friend and allowed me to use her name. She also makes a cameo appearance.

Appreciation is due David Lawler's family law practice for helping me with Marleigh adopting Elijah.

Sugar Springs

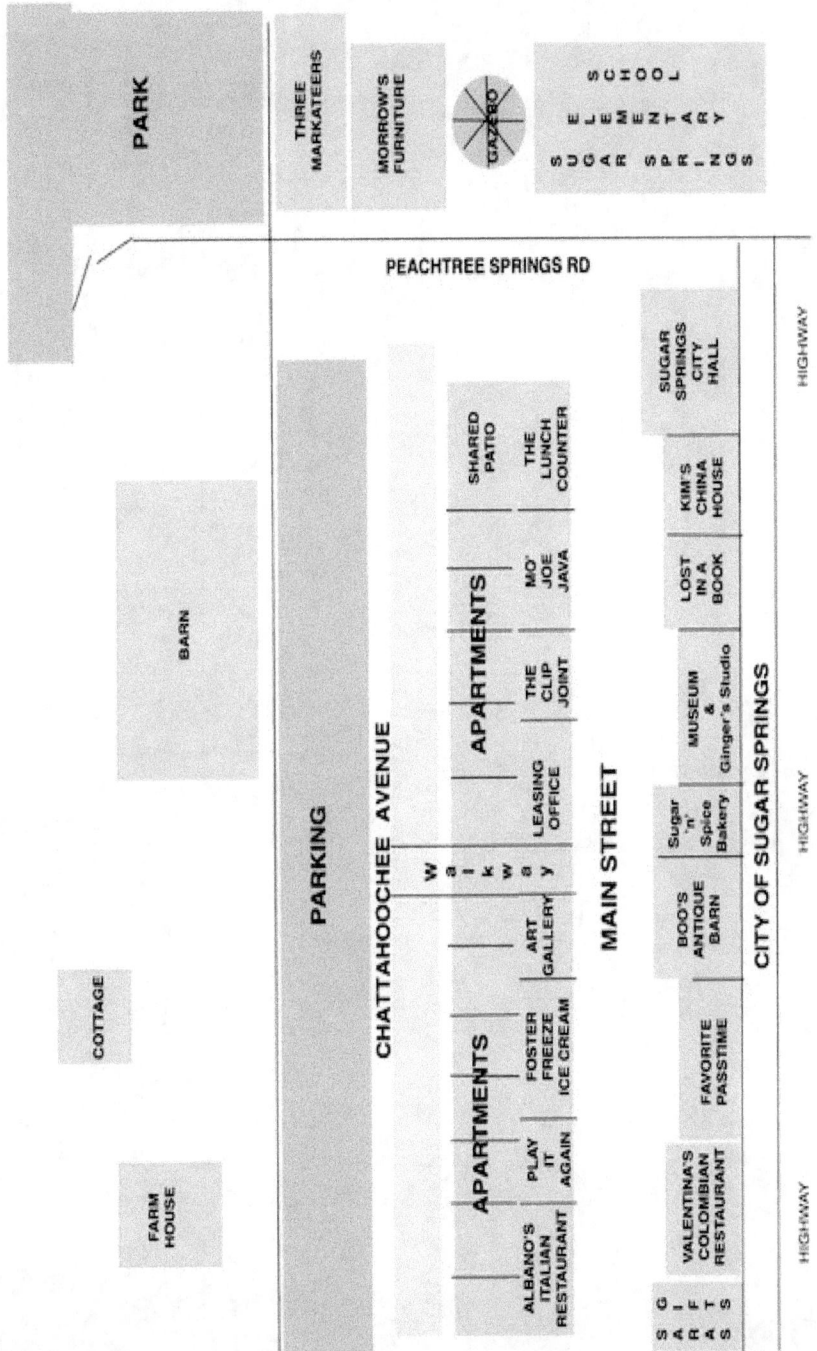

Glossary

AD: Artistic Director

Back of house: all areas behind the proscenium arch (below).

Batten: a horizontal rod or pole hung above the stage from which scenery, lighting, and other equipment is tied and can rise or lower.

CAD (Computer Aided Design): a program architects and building industry people use.

Fly: suspend scenery from the battens via battens.

FOH (Front of House): All areas in front of the proscenium arch.

Gaffer: head of the electrical department and the chief lighting technician for the show.

Green room: a room backstage where the actors can relax when not onstage.

Grip: in charge of all the rigging in the theatre.

House: where the audience sits.

IMDB (International Movie Data Base): a database where all equity actors register.

Proscenium Arch: the arch around the front of the stage.

SM: Stage Manager.

Strike: to remove an item (or set) from the stage.

Rigger (also the grip): one who works on ropes, booms, lifts, hoists, battens, etc., for a show.

Rigging: a term generally describing how equipment on a stage is suspended and/or moved. Rigging can be dead hung and manually operated or can be a motorized system of battens that raise and lower to hold backdrops and set pieces.

Wrap sheet: ticket sales report for the entire run.

Chapter 1

MARLEIGH

A crash explodes onstage, followed by a string of muffled words—cursing, if I know the grips working today. I cringe, hoping Cruella de Vil didn't hear it, and leap from my desk. I open my window overlooking the theatre house and stage. Work lights illuminate the stage. Battens are down. So is Mitch. Before I can ask if he's hurt, Cruella screeches from her office door across the hall from mine.

Yup. She heard. She can hear a pin drop at fifty yards. She hears a breeze before the leaves rustle. She hears through walls.

"What are you idiots doing?" Her shrieking grates on my ears.

Angel's deep bass floats from onstage. "Sorry, ma'am. We forgot the horse was still flying."

The headless horseman's horse from *Sleepy Hollow*. I face-palm myself.

"Well, be more careful. Those cost money, y'know. You break it, it comes out of your salary." Cruella doesn't ask whether anyone's injured.

I wait for the slam of her door. "Are either of you hurt?"

Angel reaches down, grasping the rigger's arm to help him stand. Mitch slips a hand beneath his overalls' strap and rubs his bare shoulder. "Came close to gettin' beaned. I'm fine, though."

I make mental notes to be sure all items flown are struck after a show. The stage manager's job is to make sure an entire complete set is struck right after closing—not left for a couple of days. I'm sure Cruella will find a way to blame me. She always does.

"Good reflexes, Mitch. Glad you're okay, but y'all be careful.

Back at my desk, I lift my coffee mug to my lips, getting nothing but air. If I ever needed caffeine, it's now. I pop a French vanilla pod into an off-brand coffee maker, set my cup on its platform, then lower the handle. The top pops, and lifeblood flows into my mug. While it fills, I run our coming season's shows through my mind, coupling each play with the director we've chosen. One script isn't what I call stellar, but its author is a friend of you-know-who.

This season is more challenging than normal. I add cream to my coffee, then mosey to my office's other large window overlooking Atlanta. While nice, I prefer the view of a certain old barn in Sugar Springs.

A sigh escapes me. My dreams live inside that barn. Dreams I haven't told anyone ... yet. Well, other than my roommates. But if Cruella de Vil doesn't change her ways—

My door flies open.

Speak of the devil.

My boss and Artistic Director of Atlanta's Apollo Theatre—to whom I'm assistant AD—Candace DeMille, swoops in. Her striped palazzo pants give the impression she's ten feet tall. With dramatic flair, she drops into a chair.

"I don't know what I was thinking when I let you talk me into this play selection for next season."

Talk *her* into it? Right. When my choices are great, she takes credit, presenting them to the board of directors as her own. So far, I haven't made a bad one—other than accepting this job. Cruella, uh, Candace, a very distant relative of movie mogul Cecil B. DeMille, thinks the American theatre owes her. She's the great-grand niece of his *adopted* daughter, legally changing her name to DeMille when she learned of the nebulous connection.

It's unfortunate she couldn't adopt his instinct for great theatre. She tosses a script—plus a newspaper—onto my desk with a scowl. I glance at the title, then back at her. Ahh, understanding dawns. *Calen's Dilemma.* The one script she bulldozed through.

"Has the board said they don't like this one?"

She lights a cigarette and exhales a perfect smoke ring. Who smokes nowadays? I spin my chair and open a window behind me, then turn on the overhead fan.

"They wouldn't dare. Uncle Cecil would haunt them."

I make a valiant effort not to roll my eyes—not too hard since I feel more like blinking from the sting of smoke. She never met Cecil B. DeMille. He died decades before she was born, but she talks of an intimate relationship.

"So, why are you worried?"

She pushes a copy of the *Atlanta Journal* toward me. "Have you seen the review of Majestic's production of *Calen's Dilemma?* It's brutal." She groans.

"Our production will not be a flop. While it's not the greatest script I've ever read, I think Ruby Dumas will do a credible job directing it." Ruby can turn this flop into a blockbuster—well, maybe not a blockbuster, but we'll get decent reviews, which will drive up ticket sales.

She leans forward. "Do you really think so?"

"She's a Shuler Award winner." She's also *my* choice.

Cruella regards the nails on her right hand, then quirks one eyebrow as she departs the chair. "I wasn't worried." She sails out my office door, curtains shimmying in her wake. Rounding the corner, she tosses over her shoulder, "I'm going out for a manicure."

She had a mani/pedi on Tuesday. This is Thursday. I need to find another job. I've been here four long years, but what thanks do I get? I want to influence lives, especially those of young actors. Talking Cruella off another ledge isn't part of my dream.

I flip open the newspaper to its employment pages, searching for entertainment. My eye stops at a listing for an Artistic Director at Jeremy Ridge Academy of the Arts. This isn't quite my desired goal but close enough. At least it's a step up. I wonder where Daniel Myers went. He's been AD at Ridge for several years. I open my computer and send my résumé.

My phone rings. There's no way he could have read my email by now. "Hello?"

"Hey, Marma! I'm home." My heart warms with the sound of my baby brother's voice. "Miss Boo an' Aysha an' me are feedin' the goats."

"Hey, sweet boy. How was school?"

"Cool. I made a hundred on my test. I gotta go. Bambi's waiting for his dinner."

Elijah's in kindergarten. Who gives kindergartners tests, not to mention grades them?

"Okay. Remember to be good for Miss Boo. Love you."

"Love you more." He clicks off, gone to play with the goats.

If I could get a job closer to home. If—I sigh. I keep telling Elijah he can be anything he wants. Last Friday night, he asked me why I couldn't.

"I can, sugar."

"Then, why aren't you runnin' your own theatre?"

How does one explain resources to a five-year-old?

My computer dings as an email comes in. It's from the Managing Director from Ridge Academy. I open it.

> Hello, Marleigh,
> I'd like to meet with you to discuss this position.
> Can you come by tomorrow at 3:00 pm?
> Manny Dupont

I look at my calendar for tomorrow. The only thing scheduled is lunch with Nola and Willow. I can eat with them, go to the interview, then be home to have supper with Elijah. Tonight, there's a board meeting I have to attend since Ms. de Vil refuses to go. She claims board meetings give her hives.

Agreeing to the interview, I hit send.

I push a piece of bell pepper to the edge of my plate. They tend to upset my stomach, and my interview is in a couple of hours. "Nola, what does the Lyric have going next season? I haven't heard any scuttlebutt." Nola is the CPA for three theatres.

"They're announcing next month, but they have a great line up." Her grin tells me it's an exciting one.

My ears perk. "Anything with a part for Elijah?"

Her smile fades. "No, I'm sorry. They don't have anything for kids this year."

"Oh, foot. I'm trying to find one where we can both get parts." I spear a tomato. "He came alive last year as an orphan in *Annie*." Juice squirts between my teeth when I bite down. Oh bother. A quick glance at my blouse reveals no stain, but just in case, I blot my chin.

Willow leans toward Nola. "I've never known another little boy who doesn't care if he plays a girl's part. Both kids should audition for something."

"Aysha says she's waiting until Marleigh opens her theatre." Nola twirls her fork once and points it at me. "Then, she'll be in a show."

A tomato seed escapes with my laughter. I'm so glad I'm sitting with my besties. "Your daughter's a mess. They're so stinkin' cute when they put on plays for us."

"I was relieved when you and Aysha moved in." Willow nods at Nola. "Y'all saved my sanity. Elijah used to ask me to 'play-play' all the time." A mischievous grin twitches her lips. "Now he has Aysha." She flaps her linen napkin open and lays it over her lap, covering her Van Gogh printed skirt.

And yet ... Willow saved *my* sanity when Mama and Aunt Susan died. She moved in that same night, leaving her parents' mansion for my old, rented farmhouse. She's the *Wikipedia* definition of friend—or at least should be.

Nola fiddles with her pinkie ring. "Do y'all remember the hissy fit my mother-in-law pitched when we moved in?"

Oh, do I. She accused me of hypnotizing normally normal Nola. "I'll never forget what Elijah said the following week. He told me, 'Since Aysha and Auntie Nola moved in, there aren't any rooms leftover for crying.'"

Nola leans forward with a conspiratorial grin. "Well ... *my* mother's glad of how everything worked out. Her whole attitude on life has changed."

"Do tell!" Willow rests her elbows on the table, lacing her fingers beneath her chin. "And don't leave out any details."

"After all this time, she has found someone."

An old memory strolls across my mind. We were nineteen. Nola was afraid her college education would be buried with her daddy. Much to our surprise—not to mention her mama's—her daddy had a large life insurance policy. Nola received her education and a good savings account.

My heartstrings quiver. "Your mama has waited a long time." How long will sweet Nola wait before embracing love again? It's been three—no, four years since her husband died.

"She didn't purposely wait." Nola pushes her empty plate away. "She never found anyone who could compare with Daddy."

I'm a sucker for a good love story. "So, who is he?"

"Daddy's former business partner, Walter North. He's been taking care of Mama's financial affairs since Daddy passed. Then, his wife died two years ago. I guess they began to see each other in a different light. Anyway, I'm happy for her." Nola grabs her napkin, managing to cover her nose before she sneezes. The large face on her watch screams two-fifteen.

Yikes! I yank a twenty-dollar bill from my wallet, laying it on the table. "Let me know if I owe you more. I need to hustle. I have an interview at three. See you tonight."

Thirty minutes later, I walk into Ridge Academy, coming close to being trampled in an unchoreographed tornado of students leaving the building. By their own volition, my fingers touch a scar in my left eyebrow, the result of my own tornadic exit from school when I was fifteen.

In Manny's office, his secretary greets me. "Ah, Miss Evans. Manny is ready for you." She motions to a closed door behind her. "Go on in."

The office is decidedly dull. Brown on brown. A utilitarian desk, recycled sofa, and worn chairs testify to donations going into student programing and not the director's comfort.

Manny's eyes light up when he sees me. "Marleigh, this is such a pleasure. Sit, please." He gestures to a grouping of threadbare chairs away from his desk. Its fabric looks like nervous students have picked at its threads, unweaving them.

I take a seat. Before he joins me, he asks if he can get me anything.

"No, thank you. I just finished a late lunch. Nola and Willow say hey."

"How are they?" Manny sits, crossing his legs, one ankle resting on his knee.

"Both are doing well."

"Good to hear. Willow is the best stage manager in the Southeast." He chuckles, then becomes all business. "I was surprised to get your résumé. I didn't know you were looking, or I would have called you earlier."

"I hadn't given another job much thought until I happened to see your ad."

A knowing smile crosses his face. "I have to say, you've stuck with Cruella de Vil longer than anyone. You've incorporated some innovative ideas." He leans back in his chair. "Don't look surprised. Everyone in this industry knows Candace. She doesn't fool anyone but herself."

I admit I'm relieved to hear it, but I never talk about people in our business, unless it's complimentary. I let the subject drop. "If it's not inappropriate to ask, where did Daniel go? He's been here for years."

Manny's smile fades to melancholy. "He's been snapped up by Georgia Southern. We will miss him, but he was born to head a collegiate theatre department."

My alma mater. "The students will love him."

"Let's talk about you. I know you work well with kids. Is the Academy somewhere you'd like to land?"

He wants a long-term commitment. I don't know if I can give him one. His gaze doesn't leave mine. Manny's one of the good guys. I can't be less than transparent with him.

"I have a dream of owning my own community theatre, but I don't know when that will happen."

With a smile, he settles back in his chair. "Tell me about it."

For the next half hour, my dream flows from a hidden place in my heart. Only Nola, Willow, and the kids know about my dream. Nobody else. Manny's intense concentration encourages me. When I finish, his smile is wistful.

"Like Daniel, you were born to make your dream come true, Marleigh. Offering you this position would be a disservice to you." He rises. "Best of luck. Call me when you're ready to begin. I have a couple of people in mind, who I know will want to invest with you."

At first, I'm a little disappointed I didn't get the position, but then I realize how grateful I am he allowed me to voice my dream. Just speaking the words seems to bring it a step closer. I thank him for his time.

As I head to my car, reality hits like a hammer to my head. I'm still working for Cruella de Vil, raising my little brother, and trying to grow his college fund.

My dream is fast evaporating like mist in a desert.

Chapter 2

GABE

Water from my shower's rain head sluices over me. After a sleepless night, I need caffeine to wake me. What a day for my coffee machine to die. My shower doesn't do the job of coffee.

I squeeze shampoo on my head, giving my hair a brisk scrubbing. Dad's newest target for acquisition robs my scalp of enjoyment. Sometimes, I wonder if he's getting too old. He's what, sixty-two? His mind should still be sharp, but this new property—a strip mall *behind* Main Street? It's crazy. Preposterous. Not like dad a bit. *Always get the most bang for your buck.*

After I'm dry, I step into black elastic-waisted chef pants printed with flying pigs. When I landed in this chef gig, the idea of wearing what almost constitutes pajamas was its saving grace. Now, besides loving what I do, I appreciate the comfortable clothing. My phone rings. Whoever it is can leave a message. I pull a black chef coat, embroidered with "Wild Azalea," from the closet, button it, then grab my briefcase. The first item on my agenda is coffee.

An SUV pulls out of a parking spot right in front of Mo' Joe Java. I zip the Ferrari into its space and jump out, ignoring a few Lookie-Lous, who think they have to touch to see—"Hey, kid, don't touch. But I'll give you a buck if you watch my car for me."

The street-wise boy eyes my car, then me. "Make it five bucks, and nobody'll get close enough to breathe on it."

Inflation on all fronts. I point at him. "You gotta deal, kid." My phone rings again. I don't even look. My sights are set on coffee.

When my phone rings for a fourth time, I know it has to be Dylan. My brother never leaves voice mail. I open the door to Mo' Joe's, then tap the button on my Ear Pod. "All right, give me a minute, will ya? I'm getting coffee."

I give the clerk an apologetic shrug. "French vanilla, medium roast, largest." Why can't coffee places use small, medium, or large for their sizes? They all compete for clever names we can't remember anyway.

I point to the pastries. "Any will do. You choose." After hovering her tongs back and forth, she selects one. I hand her a twenty. "Keep the change."

Walking to a small table in a back corner, I ask Dylan, "What's up?"

"Do you have any info on that brewery yet?"

"I sent my file over last night." I take a sip of my coffee. He also prefers to be told rather than read a report. Now he'll ask—

"What's in it? Anything useful?"

Do I know my brother? What I don't know is why I bother with spreadsheets. I pull out a chair to sit. "Plenty. The owner's in financial trouble."

"How bad?"

"The brewery is ours for the taking. No one else knows." I take a bite of pastry. Pretty good. I unfold the napkin to see what I bought. A bear claw. I take another bite.

"Good work. Now, do the same with the—"

"Dylan, hang on." I swallow the bite. "You forget. I don't work for you." Some dude at the next table scowls. I grab my coffee, heading for the door. "I don't have ti—"

Curses fill my ear. "Find time. If you weren't playing Guy Fieri—"

"That was *your* idea." *Get a job as a chef, Gabe. Then, you'll be on the inside to help us.* "Live with it." I click off and straight-arm the door, tossing a "sorry" over my shoulder at a chick, who gets in the way of my exit. I don't look back. *Never look back.*

Dylan takes every opportunity to dis my chef status. Ha. Without me, he wouldn't have his insider. That grinds on my brother. He wanted a minion. Dylan never thought I'd take to cooking like eggs to a soufflé.

I balked when he first suggested I should go to culinary school, become a chef to find them restaurants ripe for takeover. I'd never cooked anything other than a grilled cheese sandwich. Well, not only did I survive, I thrived. Anything is preferable to working under Dylan's supervision.

I hand a fiver to the kid watching my car. With a grin, he snatches it, taking off. I don't watch him leave. I never look back. I've been trained since birth to never look back—focus forward, eye on the goal, build the empire.

A dog with his tongue lolling out of his mouth plops on his haunches in front of me blocking any forward movement. Rover cocks his head to one side.

I look at my pastry, then the mutt. "You want this?" Poochy smiles. I shrug and toss the remaining bear claw to him. "Enjoy." He devours his tidbit in one gulp. I show him my empty hands. "All gone, buddy." He saunters over to the door to wait for another handout. I gulp down the last of my coffee. Before getting in my car, I execute an overhead cup-toss toward a trash can. Score.

The engine fires, and the Ferrari purrs—my reward for a restaurant I delivered to them last December. They're still waiting for me to deliver Wild Azalea, but they're delusional. Chef Mateo, besides being a friend, is a smart businessman. His restaurant is a huge success.

I turn down Sweetwater Lane. Dad is a degree off his game. Not enough for anyone else to notice, but I see it. Why, I'm not sure. Dylan is too focused on the end to care whose lives he disrupts—or ruins—in the process.

Unless a strip mall is Dylan's idea. I chew on his plan for a moment but change my mind. My brother wouldn't go for that. Not enough money in it.

I press on the Ferrari's accelerator. I won't walk the proposed land today. I'll drive by it on my way to Buckhead, though. Scope out any possibilities.

Tomorrow, I don't go into work until late afternoon. I'll walk it then.

MARLEIGH

Of all mornings to be out of coffee, this is the worst. I don't dare be late to work, or I'll have to listen to Cruella gripe all day. Willow did our grocery shopping this week, but my tea-loving friend forgot coffee pods.

My objective, Mo' Joe Java, is one more step. I reach for the door, but it bursts open, slams into my shoulder, knocking me sideways. My ankle rolls, my high heel breaks, and I scrape my elbow on a table as I fall into a chair. The jerk who caused my tumble tosses a meaningless "sorry" over his shoulder but doesn't even look back. What a beast. A moment later, a fancy sports car zooms away from the curb with him at the wheel. Figures—rich and rude.

I pick up the amputated four-inch heel to my second favorite pair of stripper-slippers, looking for the silver lining in this disaster. My morning devotion said to be joyful in all things. As illumination strikes, I snort a chuckle, "Okay, thank you it wasn't my favorite pair."

The guy at another outdoor table laughs. Did I say that out loud?

"Are you okay?" he asks.

"Yeah. My pride—along with my left shoe—took a hit, though." With a shrug, I limp inside Mo' Joe's to get a cup of java.

Coffee and severed heel in hand, I hobble home to change my shoes. I'm glad I live right behind Main Street. I call into work as I take the covered walkway between two shops. I stifle a groan when Cruella answers the phone.

"Candace, my heel broke. I have to change my shoes. I'll be about fifteen minutes late." With my phone between my shoulder and ear, I unlock the back door.

"Ya gotta be kidding. I have an appointment in ten."

Inside, I grab the first pair of shoes my hand touches from a stack by the door—a sassy pair of high heeled sandals.

"I'll be there as quick as traffic allows." I bend down to buckle the ankle straps, blessing Nola for wearing the same shoe size. I hope she doesn't need them before I get home. I'll send her a text to explain.

"How did you say your heel broke?"

I didn't. With a sigh, I tell her what happened.

"You should sue him."

Cruella's delusional. "You can't sue for a broken shoe." Besides, I never saw his face. He could be Shakespeare's brother for all I know.

With my shoe stuffed in my bag to take to a repair shop at lunch, I lock our back door.

"Oh, your *shoe*. I thought he broke *your* heel. Not your shoe's. I'm leaving for my appointment. I'll have Chloe sit Front of House until you get here." She clicks off.

An intern for FOH? Sweet mama flapjacks, she has no idea how our ticketing system works. So, in other words, get there fast. Cruella wouldn't care if my foot's heel were broken. I need to find another job.

When I arrive at the theatre, Chloe is nowhere to be found. Mitch and Angel are in the scene shop, working on a set. Mitch is assembling a revolving stage for our next show. I find Angel mixing paint for a backdrop.

"Have you seen Chloe? She's supposed to be watching the FOH."

"Green room." Angel smirks.

Mitch lays a wrench on the worktable. "Too bad Jordan graduated. She was the baddest intern we ever had."

Jordan was a gem. My best hire ever. A theatre major, she spent her spare time here, not just during scheduled hours. Now, she's at NYU studying technical theatre. That's the joy in this business—training kids. I miss her, and I'd give my eye teeth to have her back. Nobody since has measured up to her. Maybe, one day ...

When I open the door to the green room, Chloe is on a sofa, sound asleep. She doesn't twitch when I clear my throat—nor when I touch her shoulder.

If she's high ... "Chloe?" I shake her.

She doesn't jump like I expect. She stretches, yawning. "Yeah?"

I sit on a low cabinet across from her. "Tell me why I shouldn't fire you right now."

"What? Why the heck would you want to fire me?"

She doesn't have a clue. "For starters, you're supposed to be watching the FOH, not sleeping. Have you taken something?"

"No. I know your rules." She rolls to a sitting position. "I got bored. Nobody came in."

"You have a list of jobs on Ms. DeMille's task board. I suggest you get to them before she returns." Jordan never would have allowed herself to stop until her task board was empty. She had pride in her work. I pluck a piece of lint from my skirt and stand. "Consider this a warning."

Using a hot pad, I carry a sizzling pan of fajitas to the table. Tonight's my turn to cook, so I chose a favorite. I call over my shoulder, "Come an' get it." Elijah and Aysha race into the kitchen, skidding on stockinged feet into their places. My roommates are close behind.

Nola inspects each kiddo's hands, nodding at their cleanliness before she sits. Suppertime is a boisterous affair in our farmhouse. Willow removes a bowl of warm tortillas from the microwave. Once I have the rest of our meal on the table, I join them.

Elijah, being "man of the house," asks the blessing. At his "amen," we all fill our plates. Nola and I help our kids roll their fajitas. This is my fam. Only one is a blood relative, yet each is chosen. Cherished.

"Who wants to go first?" I take a bite of beans.

Aysha's hand shoots up, but her cheeks bulge with food.

"You can have a turn when you swallow what's in your mouth," Nola says. A frown accompanies Aysha's chewing. Tears of frustration well.

"We'll wait, won't we, Marma?" As usual, Elijah is a peacemaker. I don't know how or why this little boy is so patient with everyone. There are times I think he's from another world.

After a moment, Aysha swallows her mouthful. "How come you always call Marleigh 'Marma'?"

When Elijah grins, his eyes crinkle up like an elf, making his nose wrinkle. "I know she's my sister, but she's the onlyest mama I have now, so I call her Marma. It's 'cause she's my sister-mama."

Aysha digests her buddy's words for a few seconds. "That's gucci. I like it." She looks at Nola. Her little face scrunches. She's trying to figure out how to combine Nola with "mama." I bite back chuckles and smother them with beans.

At length, she shrugs. "Bambi climbed on top of the doghouse, an' Scrappy followed him." Both kiddos giggle.

After the kids tell us their day's goat escapades, they go to the den to watch TV. We linger at the table over tea. Willow is quieter than usual, which raises my curiosity. She has something to tell us. Her attempt to act casual doesn't fly. The way she dunks her tea bag in fast, short dips gives her away.

"Okay, girl. Spill."

"I met a new guy."

Nola and I trade glances. How many times have we hoped for the man she's met to be a keeper? A gazillion, starting back in high school. How many have stuck? Zero. Poor Willow. She's so pretty, but a little naïve when it comes to men. Most are losers. I can't understand why.

Nola pours steaming tea into her cup. "So, tell us about him. Where did you meet him?"

"Today's auditions."

Another actor, looking for an "in." I hate to be so skeptical, but it's a repeat of the last guy she met.

Nola stirs three spoonsful of sugar into her tea. How she can remain thin while using so much sugar is a mystery. If

I used as much as she does, I'd be fat and diabetic. "Tell us more."

"When he handed me his résumé, he didn't let go right away. He kept staring at me." Willow sighs. "His smile is so beautiful, his eyes hypnotic."

Well, yeah. It's a trait I've seen a lot of actors develop. I don't want to burst her happy heart, though. "What else have you learned about him?"

She folds her hands beneath her chin. "His résumé says he's a college grad with a theatre major." She glances between us. "Oh, I know, every actor we know uses those words. But his minor was in business admin, so he could work anywhere."

I put a check in my mental good column for him. "Did he get on the callback list?"

She picks up our plates and carries them to the sink. "He did. He's the best actor I've seen in a long time. Very professional onstage." Squeezing soap into the basin, she turns on the faucet.

Nola and I help her with cleanup. Under normal circumstances, whoever cooks doesn't have to clean up, but I don't want to miss anything. Nola clears the table, while I pull a dish cloth from a drawer.

Willow continues to extol his virtues. His ability grows while we finish the dishes. Still, I can't help but wonder if this guy's so professional onstage, why his come-on to Willow. Could it be her reputation as a crackerjack stage manager? Then again, she's gorgeous. His reaction may have been a natural one. I hope. Oh, I hope so.

Chapter 3

GABE

I drag my feet crossing City Hall's parking lot. A network meeting of businessmen is the last place I want to be. However, it's precisely where I need to be. Before I enter the room, I pause on the threshold of want-versus-need to survey the crowd, which appears to be around forty. Not bad for a small-town chamber of commerce. This might yield a few good connections. I step into the fray.

Voices from several conversations blend in an indistinguishable hum. Perfume and aftershave vie one another to overshadow the aroma of beer. A man about my height with a toothy smile, walks toward me, hand extended. In his other hand, he holds a bottle of dark ale. "Hey, there. Tom Metford, president of Sugar Springs Chamber of Commerce."

I shake his hand. "Gabe Sadler."

He gestures toward a counter where name tags and a sign-in sheet await. "First time with us?"

"Yes." I fill out my information to keep from saying too much too soon. *Keep your cards close to your chest.* "I'm ... considering a business in the area." Beer bottle in hand, another man peers over Tom's shoulder. He looks familiar.

Tom slaps my back. "Great. We welcome new business, don't we, Ross?"

Ross? *Ross Morten*. He's a restaurant investor. Dad's biggest competitor.

"How are you, Sadler? What brings you here?"

Not on your life. "I live in Sugar Springs. You?"

"Looking for investments, as always." He scrutinizes me. "How's—"

Tom slaps a beer in my hand. "I want to introduce you to a couple of people. Excuse us, Ross." Like a tugboat moving a freighter to the pier, Tom steers me toward a table of appetizers. "You know Ross?"

"I do." I select a large shrimp—31 to 35 per pound size. Not bad for a small-town event.

"What's your line of work?"

Wait till he hears I'm not an investor like Ross. "I'm *chef de cuisine* at Wild Azalea in Buckhead."

And quick as a blink, Tom loses interest—doesn't see me as a mover-and-shaker. His former schmoozy smile turns plastic. The door opens, ushering in a new batch of people. Tom excuses himself, heading to greet newcomers.

Ha. A compass always finds north. Like my dad and brother, Tom views relationships through a lens of greed—accrue the most members. The largest network. The biggest customer base. The most money in the bank.

Eye on the goal. Win at all costs.

I turn away from the door. Across the room, a woman chats with friends, at least I assume they're friends. She looks relaxed. Dark blond hair falls over her shoulders. I can't see the color of her eyes from here, but she's beautiful. I'd sure like to know her.

"Bud Pugh. Welcome." An older man steps between me and my view of Beauty. His eyes squeeze to mere slits with his smile. He has more hair in his eyebrows than on his head.

With one last glimpse past his shoulder at Beauty, I grasp his hand. "Gabe Sadler. Thanks."

"Good to meetcha. If you need toys or a hobby, come see me. I own Favorite Pastime."

"Clever name."

"I think so, but I can't claim its creation. My great-grandaddy named it back in 1937. My grandson will take over soon—but," his eyes twinkle, "not too soon."

Impressive. My family hasn't *owned* a single restaurant or any business for more than six months. *Turn around, don't look back.* What would life be like to have Mr. Pugh's kind of legacy?

"I'll be sure to stop by to take a look." Neither Dylan nor Dad has a hobby unless you count Dad's car collection. For him, his cars are strictly for show. He doesn't tinker with them. He doesn't drive them either. They're strictly for show. *Always project the image of success.*

"So, how is the business climate in Sugar Springs?"

Mr. Pugh's brows draw together. "I thought I heard you say you live here." He pops an entire Ritz cracker with cheese into his mouth. Beauty moves to the bar.

I snap my gaze back to Mr. Pugh. "Ahh, yes. I do, but I work in Buckhead, so much of my time is spent there."

He nods and swallows. "Business is good. You thinking of a start-up here?"

I don't want anyone to get wind of this until it's a done deal. If I do, Ross has enough networks around this region to find out. He'd swoop in, trying to take it. I don't want him or Dad involved. This is my dream. "Maybe."

Mr. Pugh chuckles. "You couldn't find a better place than Sugar Springs."

A man hands Beauty a glass of white wine. She doesn't drink any. When he turns his back, she sets the glass on a table.

"Mr. Pugh—"

"Bud."

I smile. "Bud, do you know that young woman?" With a discreet gesture, I point over his shoulder.

He doesn't turn around. "Known her all her life. Marleigh Evans. Works as assistant artistic director in a theatre in Midtown."

Theatre? I wonder if Willow knows her.

Bud's bushy eyebrows waggle. "Want an introduction?"

A little obvious, Sadler? "Yes, I would. Thanks." Marleigh. The name suits her. I don't know what an "artistic director" is, but I'd like to find out.

"May I have your attention?"

Tom stands in front of the room. Next to him is Sugar Springs's mayor. So much for an introduction to Marleigh, but I can wait. I glance at Bud.

"Would I be rude asking the history behind our mayor's name?"

He leans close, lowering his voice. "A childhood nickname that stuck. I've known Boo since she was in diapers."

Marleigh is a mere few feet from me, her attention focused on the mayor. It's difficult to turn my attention from her to Tom and Boo.

"I want to thank all of you for your support in this past election. I know y'all put me over the top. My first objective will be to bring more business to the downtown corridor. I'm working on some ideas and want to call on all y'all for your suggestions."

I may have one or two I could give her. I like her approach. If I can realize my dream—even better. I glance to see Marleigh's reaction. She's disappeared. As far as I know, she isn't a business owner, at least Bud didn't say she is.

I turn a three-sixty but don't see her anywhere in the room. I sure hope our paths cross again. I haven't had anyone spark my interest like her since my freshman year in high school.

MARLEIGH

Bending, I kiss Elijah's cheek. "'Night, buddy. I love you. Sweet dreams."

"'Night, Marma. Love you more." He turns over, pretending to snore.

I giggle as I close his door. It's our nighttime routine. He'll grab his flashlight, looking at a picture book for a while, thinking he's getting away with it. Funny little bunny. I guess he's boosting his sense of independence. If reading late is the worst thing he ever does, I'll count myself lucky—no, blessed.

Nola blows a kiss to Aysha as she shuts her door. With conspiratorial grins of "it's our time," we head downstairs to the front room. Nola pours glasses of sweet tea, while I plate cookies for us. Willow is out on a date with her newest boyfriend. Nola and I have a bet on how long this one will last. I give the romance another week.

When I plop onto one end of the sofa, Nola has the remote in her hand, aiming toward the TV.

"Anything good on?" I pluck an oatmeal raisin cookie from the plate. Sweet raisins and smokey cinnamon burst on my tongue. "These are good. Did you make them?"

"You're joking, right? You know I didn't inherit a single cooking gene. Willow baked them before she went out. Her new boyfriend gets two dozen. We get leftovers."

I pull my legs up, folding them underneath me. "You can't blame her."

"Oh, I don't. Just an observation." She clicks off the TV. "I'm concerned about this guy, though. It's been what? Two weeks since she met him? Every night, she's going for a ride with him. Do they ever do anything except drive around town?" Her brows dip, her mouth drawing downward. "She never talks about a movie they've seen or a play they went to. Not even a stop for co-colas."

I take a mouthful of tea to wash down my cookie. "I've wondered the same thing. It's beyond odd. Do you remember Michael?"

"Yeah. When did you last see him?"

"Not for several months. He found the love of his life who lives in Arizona. I bring him up because when I dated him, I wasn't looking to get married. Willow couldn't understand why not."

Tea spurts out Nola's nose when she giggles. "I remember her asking you, 'Why go out with him, then?' to which you replied—" she gestures to me to finish as she munches a cookie.

"'Because he's funny and has money to take me to all the shows.' That's my point. This guy—we still don't even know his name—doesn't take her anyplace. They just drive around, stopping to talk to people."

Nola wipes tea from her upper lip. "Well, we can't change her mind right now, and it's time for 'Grey's Anatomy'." She clicks the remote, bringing the TV to life.

"Speaking of anatomy, I forgot to tell you I borrowed your sandals last week. Some dude tore out of Mo' Joe's, knocking me over. I broke the heel on my shoe. I grabbed your sandals to wear to work. I haven't had mine fixed yet. It's hanging out in my office for when I get a minute."

"I never mind you borrowing."

Twenty minutes later, our front door bursts open hitting the wall. Red-faced, Willow storms inside. "Never—ever will I go out with another actor. Or any man." She throws her handbag into a wingback chair, then flops onto the floor. "Do you know what happened tonight?"

Nola and I stare at each other, wide eyed. I shake my head. "We don't have a clue."

She jumps up and paces. "He's a jerk, I tell you. A total jerk."

Most of the guys she dates are jerks. Poor Willow doesn't have a good database from which to draw. Her dad left her mom as soon as she announced her pregnancy. Her stepdad is a good guy, but he didn't come along until later.

"I'll bite. What happened? Why is he a jerk?" I'm already running scenarios through my mind—he got fresh or he's an egomaniac or—

"He's dealing drugs."

Nola turns white. My heart stops. My thoughts fly to the kids. Nola already has trouble with her mother-in-law wanting her and Aysha to live with them.

I want to shake some sense into Willow. I cross the room, but she spins away, stopping by the window. She throws her arms out wide.

"He's not even a *real* actor. You want to know where I've been for the last three hours?"

I'm afraid to ask, but knowledge is a weapon. "In this order, sit, then tell us."

"I can't sit." Her pacing borders maniacal. "I'm too ticked off."

"Then, at least tell us what happened." I've never seen her this mad. My stomach pitches.

She stops, facing me, arms akimbo. "I've been in jail."

"What?" If the authorities suspect her of being involved, DEFACS will swoop in. They could take the kids from us. I grab Nola's arm.

"Oh, no." I'm putting two and two together, coming up with Willow in major trouble. "Do they think you had anything to do—"

"At first, yes." She giggles.

Giggles? Doesn't she understand the enormity of this?

"There's a new rookie cop on the force. He doesn't know me or the fact my uncle's his boss."

I need her to give us the bottom line. Is my baby brother safe? I steer her to the sofa. With a gentle push she lands, nestling into the cushions. "So, he arrested you?"

"Once we arrived at the jail, Uncle Henry saw me and asked if I'd done anything wrong. I replied an emphatic, 'NO!' Then, I had to explain I was out on a date. A date with a jerk. If I hadn't been so angry, I would have laughed."

I'm having trouble following her. "Laughed? Willow, this isn't funny. We could have the kids taken away from us."

Willow scowls. "I know. Why do you think I was so mad? I knew I wouldn't be arrested, but I didn't want anything leaked to DEFACS." Her gaze swings between us. "You can relax. A social worker was there, but Uncle Henry explained James to her."

Another knot in the story. "I'm confused."

"Me too," Nola says. "Who's James?"

"James is the drug dealing jerk. He's also delusional. He thought I'd plead his case with Uncle Henry."

The first wave of relief turns my knees weak. I drop onto the couch. Nola sits beside me. She's still shaking.

Willow picks up a cookie. "I can't believe I didn't see it."

Nola stares at her like Willow's from outer space. In a way, she is. At least, her head is always up in the clouds. "There were clues."

"Like what?" Willow licks a cookie crumb off her lip.

"Like he never took you anywhere but his car. A car ride isn't a date."

She waves my argument aside. "I meant he isn't an actor. I looked him up on IMDB. He's not even listed. Any actor who wants a career onstage or in film registers his history on IMDB. You know that. Turns out his whole résumé is fake." She snatches another cookie from the platter, stuffing the whole thing into her mouth. "Nefe agon. Weminphs ot po—" she swallows. "Remind me not to date any man for at least ... ever."

Nola and I hold up our fingers for the number of weeks we think she'll last. I say four. She's pretty upset. Nola thinks two. We'll see. There's a five spot at stake.

I turn to our dear friend. "Sugar, please be careful with any guy you date. We can't risk DEFACS taking our kiddos."

Willow strolls toward the bathroom. "I'm going to take a shower. Don't worry, I'm swearing off men forever." The bathroom door clicks shut.

Right. It's like poor Willow has a sign on her back telling the world she's naïve. She'll believe anything.

Chapter 4

GABE

I open Wild Azalea's back door to a kitchen full of smoke. My heartbeat kicks into overdrive as I grab the nearest fire extinguisher. "Where's the fire?"

"No fire, Chef."

For no fire, there's a lot of smoke. After a second glance around, I hang the extinguisher back on its hook, my pulse inching closer to normal.

"Turn on the fans, Ramon."

"Right away, Chef."

I drop my briefcase in my office and return to the kitchen. The smoke is already clearing. "What happened?"

"The new guy." Ramon flaps a towel over his shoulder. "He walked away from his station while he had bacon in the pan."

What incompetence. Why was finding good help so hard? "I hope you fired him."

Mouth quirked, Ramon nods. "Faster than a Yankee talks."

Good man. Though most of the smoke is gone, my throat feels scratchy. Ramon's has to be raw, poor guy. I clap him on his back. "I'll hire a new line cook right away. Anyone else coming in to take up the slack?"

"Yeah. I called Josh. He'll be here anytime." Ramon attacks the burnt pan with steel wool.

"Okay, good job. Thanks for handling it." With things in the kitchen back on track, I head to the office I share with Mateo, Wild Azalea's owner. First order of business is to hire a new line cook. Then, I'll check our menu for today's specials. Finally, I'll create a new recipe for tomorrow's special.

Two hours later, everything is completed. I'm pleased with my idea for our special. I made my Granny Hamilton's fried chicken one time for the staff. Mateo had never eaten true Southern fried chicken. When he asked what made the meat so juicy, I told him the brine is buttermilk. With a few extra spices to change things up, Granny's chicken will be exceptional for tomorrow's special.

My phone rings. If that's Dylan ... I glance at my screen. Huh. Willow Raines. I haven't talked to her in a couple of months.

"Hey, Willow. Good to hear from you. Whatcha been up to?" I met her, what—ten years ago? We were in a play together at church—a one-time event. Scared the snot outta me. I'll never go onstage again. I went out with Willow once, but I wasn't flashy enough for her. Despite my lack, we became good friends. She's the little sister I never had.

"Work. No dates. I've sworn off all men. Except you, of course."

I've heard the same tirade every time she breaks up with some guy. "Why?"

"Why you or why I've sworn off men?"

"Yes. Both. Either." I pick up Granny's recipe. Garlic. I'll add more garlic for one thing. Hmm, maybe a little rosemary could work.

Willow giggles—she never chuckles. "I've sworn off men because of the last louse I dated. He was dealing drugs."

What? My protective hackles rise. "How did you get involved with a drug dealer?"

Her sigh whistles through the phone. "Auditions."

"Willow, what have I told you?" Not rosemary—sage. I'll add a half teaspoon. Rosemary would take the flavor in a different direction. Not a bad one, but not Granny's.

"I know. I know. I try, okay?"

"Please be more careful. How about you bring any new guy you meet by here for me to look over?" I smirk at my own words. It's amazing how she brings out the big brother in me.

"You're a pal, Gabe. Girls should always have at least one male pal. Which is kind of why I called. You know my roommate Marleigh, right?"

"I've heard you talk about her, but I've never met her." Wait. Marleigh is not a common name, and Bud said she works in theatre. So does Willow. "Is she an artistic director by any chance?"

"Yeah. I've told you about her, right?"

Not enough. I set down my pen. "You've mentioned her, and what's the other one's name? Nora? Something like that, anyway, but you never told me anything beyond their names." *Stay cool, Sadler. Don't sound too eager.* "What about her?"

"I ... uh ... she ... well, she isn't dating anyone right now. I ... uh .... Oh, never mind, this is a bad idea. So, what have you been up to?"

"Not so fast. It's not a bad idea. To tell you the truth, I saw her at a Chamber of Commerce meeting the other night. I wanted to meet her, but she left before I had a chance. Can you set up something?"

"I sure can." Her voice smiles over the phone. "How about we come to Wild Azalea for lunch next week? What days are you working?"

I pull up my calendar on my phone. "We're closed Mondays. I'm off Thursday."

"Tuesdays aren't a threatening day. Let's settle on a week from Tuesday."

Threatening? "Okay, I'll bite. What determines a threatening day?"

"Because, silly, if it were a Friday or Saturday, one would think 'setup.' But a Tuesday is safe. Anything after hump day is threatening."

I gave up trying to follow her reasoning a long time ago, but she's a super gal. "Ah, I see. So, Tuesday next week." I enter it on my phone's calendar.

We spend a little more time catching up, then say goodbye.

In the kitchen, I get out my ingredients to tweak Granny's chicken, while I count the hours until I meet Marleigh.

MARLEIGH

I swanny, any high-pitched buzz coming from our stage means progress on a new set, but the noise gives me a headache. I rise to shut my window overlooking said stage, pausing for a moment to see what they're building—a giant shopping buggy for the Shembo Express scene in our next production, *Cats.*

Our master carpenter, Kyle, is so talented, he can make a wooden structure look like metal, complete with wheels. He lifts a piece of wood from his saw, spies me. He waves as he turns. I give him a thumbs up, then close the window.

Back at my desk, I pull out the final production stats for our last show. I want to recheck all numbers before I send my report to the board. Candace's financials don't match our ticketing company's wrap-up report. I know for a fact we sold out all but two performances, yet her rendition indicates a single sellout.

What is she trying to do? We can't give fake numbers to the board. They'll figure it out in a hot minute. She's not going to like it, but I refuse to go along with her erroneous figures.

My door flies open, hitting the wall. I don't bother to turn around. Could only be one person. Cruella. Then, a newspaper lands on my desk with a plop.

"What are they trying to do, ruin me?" Her dagger-like fingernail taps a story on the entertainment page. Those things could do some serious damage to a person. "We don't need another theatre."

I glance at the article. Old news at best. Doesn't have anything to do with us anyway. "This is a *community* theatre, Candace. Not a professional one. I don't know why you're so bothered."

She flops dramatically into a barrel chair, spinning as she drapes her arms over its sides. "Do I look bothered?"

I hand the paper back to her. "Yes, you do. Why do you think an amateur theatre could ruin you?"

Her lip rises in a sneer. "They can't. But I want to be the only theatre in town."

Where did the board find her? "Have you never heard about competition being good for business?"

Candace stands, an evil grin stretching her lips. "Nonsense. I'd like to see all others sink." She examines her blood-red fingernails. "I'm having lunch with my boyfriend, then I have a manicure appointment." She stops, staring at my file cabinet next to the door. "Why are you displaying a broken shoe?"

"It's the one from my coffee shop debacle. I still haven't taken it to be fixed."

A man sticks his head inside my door. "Hey, Candace. You ready, babe?"

He's her boyfriend? With his thick neck and huge shoulders, could he be a professional football player? He resembles one.

She plucks up my shoe along with its heel. "I'll drop these off at the repair shop on my way to the salon."

Whoa. An act of kindness from Cruella? Is she trying to impress her boyfriend, or is it a diversionary tactic to throw me off the reports?

"Uh, thank you."

Needing to get to the bottom of the report difference, I break down her numbers to find where she deviated from our ticket company.

Even more important, why?

When I get home, an Acura is parked beside the farmhouse. Nola's mother. I haven't been able to congratulate her yet and can't wait to see her. This will take away any gloom my day cast over me.

The back screen door bangs open as I get out of my car. Aysha and Elijah run to greet me.

"Guess what Marma? Mimi Jess'ca's here."

"I wanted to tell her." Aysha's lower lip sticks out so far, a hummingbird could perch on it.

"I'm sorry. I was e'cited. I don't have a mimi. All I have is Marma."

I drop my briefcase, gathering both kiddos into a hug. Using two fingers, I lift up Aysha's chin, so she sees me. "He's right, baby girl. Elijah and I don't have anyone but each other." Factual, but scares the fire out of me. I have to be here for him. "But I saw her car when I drove in, so I already knew she was here."

As usual, Nola's daughter gets over her funk in a flash—all smiles again. "You can share my mimi, 'Lijah."

The kids whiz off to play with the goats, as I head inside. The instant the door opens, my mouth waters from a heavenly aroma engulfing me.

"Marleigh? Is that you, dear?" When Nola's mom speaks, her words float. Elijah said it first, and he's right. There's a musical quality to her voice. Once, I took him by my office to pick up something—I forget what. After he met Candace, he said, "That lady's words drop to the floor like rocks."

"I'll be right there, Jessica." I can't wait to see what she's cooking. I sniff the air. Garlic. Another sniff. Beef. Yum.

Glancing at my stack of mail, I spy one from my agent. I rip open its envelope. Inside is a sweet residual check for a little over a thousand dollars. A nice addition to Elijah's college fund. I slide the check into my purse, tossing its envelope into the waste basket along with some junk mail.

After hanging my shoulder bag on our hall tree, I saunter into the kitchen to see what Nola and Jessica are doing. Tonight is Nola's turn to cook. Since her mom's here, I'm sure I won't be disappointed. I walk through a rich aromatic cloud to a large casserole dish of Aysha's mimi's famous Cottage Pie waiting in the center of the table.

A few minutes later, the dinner bell rings. Aysha and Elijah race inside. After washing their hands, they carry a basket filled with crusty loaves of French bread to the table. My sweet boy asks the blessing before we dive into supper. When we do, it's every bit as delicious as its aroma promised.

"This is yummy, Mimi Jess'ca." Elijah grins as he shovels in another spoonful.

"I'm glad you like it, sugar. I'll have to give your Marma the recipe. Now, tell me how school was today."

Aysha swirls up her spoon through her mashed potatoes in the middle of her plate. "Me an' 'Lijah got into trouble 'cause I pushed Timmy Morrow down." She shoves a bite of potatoes into her mouth, then stirs again.

My gaze snaps to Elijah, while Nola reaches over to stop her daughter's stirring. "Meat. Take a bite of meat, then tell us what happened."

"Who's Timmy Morrow?" Jessica asks while Aysha chews.

"Morrow's Furniture," Nola replies. "He's Pete's grandson."

"Oh." Jessica nose wrinkles like she's caught a whiff of dirty socks.

"It wasn't Aysha's fault. Timmy's a bully. He was bein' mean to a new girl. Aysha's a hero."

Jessica beams at her granddaughter. "I remember Timmy's grandpa from when I was in school. Looks like the apple didn't fall too far from the tree."

Aysha and Elijah look at each other, neither understanding what an apple tree has to do with anything. I purse my lips to keep from chuckling. "What did you do when Aysha pushed Timmy down?"

I keep my gaze on his eyes. If he looks away, he's not telling the whole truth. He stares me straight in the eye.

"I sat on him."

Funny little stinker is proud of himself. I fork a bite of Cottage Pie into my mouth to keep from laughing out loud. These two keep Nola and me on our toes.

Closing her eyes, Nola schools her face. "I see. So, you both got into trouble. What did your teacher say to you?"

In a sing-song voice, Aysha repeats their teacher's admonition. "To come an' tell her an' don't push nobody down an' don't sit on nobody."

"Anybody," Nola reminds her.

By her wrinkled nose, it's obvious Aysha thinks Mrs. Davis's advice is ineffective. I hope Tom Morrow's grandson was disciplined.

"Elijah, what happened to Timmy?" If he didn't receive any punishment, I'm going to have to go to school to have a talk with the principal.

"His mommy has to come meet with Mrs. Davis." Elijah's giant grin stretches wide, plumping the apples of his cheeks.

I'm so glad I requested Lindsay Davis as Elijah's teacher.

"Did you both learn a better way to handle a problem next time?" Nola asks.

"Yeah, but if we went an' tolded her, Timmy would have pushed Debbie off the swing while we were gone." Aysha lower lip trembles. "An' that's worser than gettin' in trouble."

"You have to admit she's right, Nola." I tweak Aysha's ear. "Some offenses call for heroic action, as long as you two don't start becoming bullies yourselves."

The horror on their faces assures us they won't.

We ladies linger over coffee while the kids run off to play. After a moment of silence, Jessica clears her throat.

"I have a request." She blots her mouth and lays her napkin beside her cup. "For the most part, this is aimed at you, Marleigh, but I'm sure Willow can help you. I'd like you to be my wedding planner."

"Me? I've never planned a wedding." Then, again, maybe it won't be too hard—a small event, since it's a remarriage. Should be simple.

Willow, who ignored our school discussion, now comes to life. "A wedding is like directing a play, Marleigh. Think how you block action, plan props, and feed the cast. In a wedding, you don't even have to work on characterization." She flips her wrist. "You orchestrate people every day. With me to help you, we'll have a blast."

Nola and I share a wink. Maybe having fun this way will keep Willow preoccupied for a while. After all, what could happen?

Chapter 5

MARLEIGH

Sunshine streams through my bedroom window, teasing my eyelids open. Light glints off narrow, gold leaf stripes in moss-green wallpaper. Yawning, I stretch. Saturday mornings are my favorite. Both kids are old enough to get their own cereal, as long as one of us has milk in a small pitcher for them. They like to eat in front of television watching cartoons.

After lingering a moment longer, I throw back my covers, then slip into overalls and a T-shirt. I told Nola and Willow that I'd show them my ideas for the barn.

Downstairs, I stop to say good morning to the kiddos, then head to the kitchen. Eyes half-mast, Nola sits at the table. She's still in her robe.

"Morning." I grab a mug from the cupboard.

Nola yawns. "Is it?"

"Trouble sleeping last night?" For a change, I pop a hazelnut pod into the coffee machine.

"Didn't the thunder wake you?" My friend drains her cup. "Soon as yours is done, put in another dark roast for me, please." She holds out her cup.

"I never heard a thing." The machine gurgles. I pull out my mug, slipping hers into place. "My brain was worn out from wedding plans. I dreamed Cruella was baking a wedding cake with sales reports coming out its top."

"That's just weird." Her nose wrinkles, but her eyes remain shut with her hand still outstretched for coffee. She's a hoot.

I wrap her fingers around her filled mug. "Not as much as you'd think. Are you awake enough for me to pick your brain?"

As I expect, her eyes pop open. "Fire away."

"Okay. I'm pretty sure Cruella is cooking the books."

"What leads you to think she is?" She blows on her coffee, takes a sip, then a mouthful.

How she can drink her coffee so hot is a mystery. "I prepare a report every month for the board of directors. Cruella said she'd already done this month's report."

One eyebrow rises. "She never does reports. You've told me several times. Why now?"

"I'd like to find out myself." I savor a sip of coffee. Ahh. "So, I pulled hers. Nola, she changed all her numbers." I set down my mug with a thunk. Coffee splashes onto the table. "What I don't get is she knows I receive our ticketing company's wrap sheet with their payout. It's part of my job." Nola wipes up my spilled coffee with a napkin. "Thank you. I'd already sent the wrap sheet to the comptroller, along with all the expenses for the production. I swanny, she has grits for brains."

"What are you going to do?"

Aysha runs in, jumps into Nola's lap handing her a hairbrush.

"Morning, sunshine." She kisses her daughter's rosy cheeks and builds her a pony tail. Aysha's ash blonde hair is the exact same shade as Nola's. But when she wears a pony tail, her little ears stick out, a legacy from her daddy.

Elijah carries in their bowls. Then, he hops onto my lap. I love the warmth of his little arms around my neck.

"Morning, Marma. Can we go play outside?"

Nola and I both nod.

"We'll come outside after a few minutes. But be quiet near Auntie Willow's window."

"'Kay." The screen door bangs in punctuation to their tandem voices.

"Back to my dilemma." I grab a frying pan and four eggs from a bowl on the counter. "I found where she changed things. She inverted numbers in several places. It's not a huge amount of money—a couple of thousand. Easy to explain if she gets caught, but why is the question."

"Doesn't she realize a lot of changes would be noticed? Over easy, please. Has she done this before?"

I flip the eggs, plate them, and bring our breakfast to the table. Nola has toast ready—one thing she can do well.

"To be honest, I don't know. Maybe I should go back to before I started doing reports."

Nola drops a forkful of egg onto her toast. "You still haven't told me what you're going to do about it." She bites into her eggy toast.

"I'll tell her I found a mistake. If she freaks, I'll remind her our reports need to match. The board—not to mention the comptroller—expect it." I dip a corner of toast into my egg yolk. "We'll see what she says."

"I don't envy you. She's such a witch."

We finish eating. I'm anxious to show Nola my ideas for the barn—if Boo ever decides to sell it to me. I haven't even asked her yet. I hurry through washing our dishes.

"Let's go look at the goats."

Nola tilts her head. "Why?" She likes goat cheese but not so much goats.

"So you can envision my plans."

"Oh, right." She hangs her dish towel over the sink front.

When we step outside, we're hit with a strong gust of wind—the tail end of last night's storm. My hair whips around my head, stinging my cheeks.

Nola swipes at a strand stuck to her lips. "Wow. The wind blew away my ideas."

Standing beside her, I nudge her shoulder. "No worries. I have enough for both of us."

Laughing, we run to the barn, jumping over a small, skittering tumbleweed.

Both kids are by the goat pen. My sweet boy runs over. "Are you here to play with the new baby goat?"

"There's a new baby? I didn't know Bambi was pregnant." I glance at Nola. "Did you?"

"Nope."

"Bambi's not its mama. Miss Boo 'dopted Lickrish. She's a girl goat." Elijah grabs my hand. "Come see her."

The new edition is well named. I can't see a speck of white on her. "She's adorable. You two be gentle with her."

Elijah plants his fists on his little hips. "I know how to handle baby goats, Marma."

Oops. "I'm sorry. I forgot you are a master goat herder."

He grins, forgiving my *faux pas*.

"Auntie Nola and I are going to look around the barn. You two can play here until we go shopping."

I walk Nola around, pointing out where various components of a theatre would go—stage, sound booth, control room, etc. The aroma of sweet hay and pungent manure accompany our tour. I like hay but hope the odor doesn't linger after I turn this into a theatre.

"First thing would be to build a new, smaller barn for the goats. Elijah wants a mini donkey too."

"I can see the kids with one." Nola turns in a complete circle. "What are your tech plans in here?"

"The barn has the height we need for rigging."

She crosses her arms, gazing up. After a moment, she nods. "It's going to take about fifteen to twenty-five thousand to get motorized rigging—more if you want programmable."

I knew rigging was expensive, but twenty-five-k is more than I planned. "I've given a lot of thought about a manual versus programmable counterweight systems. But if we can get enough investors, I'd love to go with a computerized one."

"Have you calculated the entire cost of rehabbing all this?"

With a sweep of her hand, my gaze takes in the scope of my dream. I gulp. It's huge, but I can't stop dreaming. I feel like it's what I'm supposed to do. "If we go with a programmable rigging system, then we can offer internships to technical theatre students. Those would enable us to obtain grants. Education is a big part of those. Besides, my heart lies in training up new talent."

"I can submit applications for grants. I think we might be able to come up with what we need. I already know we can get approved for a construction loan."

I gaze at my dear friend. "Are you positive about investing in this?"

Her decisive nod is my answer. A rumble of thunder proclaiming another storm drowns out any words she adds.

I love a good thunderstorm in spring. "Come on, kids. Let's head inside."

Within five minutes, thunder booms louder. The storm is on us. A tree limb breaks off, falling to the ground. At its demise, a thought strikes me.

What if Cruella insists my report matches hers?

GABE

With everything set at Wild Azalea, I plan to visit the property today. Yesterday, when I called Mayor Higgins to see if I could stop by, I mentioned I was interested in her farm. If she thinks I'm looking for advice on a small farm, well, I guess some of my dad has worn off on me. Guilt is a bitter breakfast. I want to set the record straight—although I wouldn't mind some farming advice from her. She's done well for herself.

I park in a lot on Broad Street behind some apartments. From this vantage point, I can view the property, with a large barn to the right of a two-story farmhouse. There's another small cottage-type building between them.

I cross the parking lot and the bordering grassy knoll. Standing by the barn, Mayor Higgins greets me. "Morning."

"Good morning."

There's a good-sized gravel yard in front of all the buildings. If extended, the area could serve for parking. The rustic setting doesn't call for a paved lot. Similar to The Bluegrass Barn in Suwanee, where folks park in a meadow.

"I believe I saw you at the chamber meeting. Sorry I didn't get a chance to meet you then. You are ...?"

I shake her outstretched hand. "Gabe Sadler."

With blatant curiosity, her eyes travel over me like a tourist surveying the height of the Empire State building. "What can I do for you?"

How does one say 'sell me your land' when there isn't a 'for sale' sign? Her gaze demands honesty. I can give her no less. "My dream is to own a farm-to-table restaurant located on an urban farm. Your property has everything I'm looking for."

She doesn't speak for a moment. Have I been too honest? Did I sound greedy? I lick my lips, jamming my hands into my pockets.

Then, she smiles. "Young man, Gabe, your interest is … interesting." She shakes her head. "My husband and I have been talking about retiring from farming, either buying a condominium in town or a house on the lake. We're at an impasse. I prefer the condo. He wants to fish."

The prospect of my dream being realized is so close I can taste it. "Is there anything I can say to persuade either of you?"

She shakes her head. "How about I show you what you'd be in for if you bought this place."

"I'd love to see everything."

"Well, come on." We start walking. "The house is leased, so it would be unavailable until the contract renews in eleven months, nonnegotiable. Some very special people live there."

I'm not telling her I know one of them. She'd think Willow set this up. I didn't know this was where she lived, when I first noticed Miss Boo's property. "That's fine by me."

"Okay. Here's our barn."

The door stands open. The barn is huge. The space would be fantastic for a restaurant, but maybe it's too big. I glance over my shoulder to study the farmhouse. I'd prefer something its size. Five acres would support that size restaurant. But this …? However, this space could be a great event venue. Food for later thought.

"Wow, it's large."

Two kids run into the barn. I glance at her. Are they her grandchildren?

"Miss Boo—" I guess they aren't hers. They skid to a stop. The boy grins. "Who are you?"

The mayor steps between us. "Manners, Elijah." She turns them around. "Go see Mr. Herb and get a snack. He baked brownies this afternoon."

Can't blame them for losing interest in me. They scramble out the door. "Cute kids."

She ignores my comment. "The cottage is where we live now. Those are all our buildings—main farmhouse, barn, cottage."

She steers me toward the car. My tour is over. I hope I haven't done anything to warrant her change of demeanor.

"Ma'am—"

"It's all right, Gabe. I'm protective of those children. I'll talk to my husband and let you know our decision as soon as we come to one. Do you have a card?"

"Yes, of course." I remove a card from my wallet, jotting my cell number on its back. "Thank you for showing me around."

She nods with a smile, then heads toward her cottage. On my way off the property, I glimpse gardens behind the buildings. There are at least a half-dozen raised beds within sight, each filled with healthy foliage.

This property is exactly what I need. Now, I just have to hope and pray they decide to sell it to me.

Chapter 6

MARLEIGH

Cruella is on the warpath. She always is on board-meeting day, hating to attend. Every time, she finds a way to send me in her stead. Her doctored report looms large in my mind. I'll have to out her if she presents hers to the board. Then, what? What happens when one tells their board of directors one's boss is cooking the books? She has a couple of friends on the board—at least that's the scuttlebutt around here. Are they still there?

With a sigh, I revisit the budget in front of me. I initial my "okay" on our stage manager's prop list. This upcoming production is properties heavy. I had asked him to get with the director to see if all items were necessary. They cut their budget list by a third.

Cutting costs.

Cruella's report.

Board of Directors meeting.

Heartburn sears my throat. Our meeting is at three o'clock. It's now ten-fifteen. I pop an antacid.

My phone rings. Can I pretend I don't hear it? I answer on the third ring.

"Ms. Evans? This is Nancie at Elijah's school. He's had an accident."

My heart stops, and I jump to my feet. They don't call parents for skinned knees. "Is he all right? What happened?"

"Timmy Morrow pushed him off some playground equipment. I'm afraid Elijah's arm is broken. In addition, he has a nasty gash on his forehead. He may have a concussion. He's being taken by ambulance to the emergency room at Northside Hospital Forsythe. We called Mayor Higgins, since she's on your contact list. She was here before the ambulance arrived and rode with him."

Thank you, Lord, for Miss Boo. "I'm on my way." With my pulse racing, I snatch up my shoulder bag as I yank open my door.

And run smack into Cruella.

I grab the doorjamb to steady myself. With a huff, she straightens her suit jacket, eyeing my purse under my arm.

"Where do you think you're going?"

"Elijah had an accident at school."

"Well, don't they keep extra clothes for kids? Why do you need to go?"

Grits for brains. "Not *that* kind of accident. He fell off the monkey bars. He's been taken to the hospital." I turn to leave.

"He'll be all right. I'm sure it's nothing. You need to get your report finished before noon. It must match mine."

"Cr—Candace, my brother, the child I'm raising, has been taken to the emergency room with a broken arm and a concussion. I'm leaving. Now." I stalk down the hallway.

"Get back here." Her screeches fill the corridor. "If you don't, you're fired. *Come back here.*"

I don't slow my steps or bother to answer. I open the door.

"You're fired. You'll never work—" The door cuts off her final words.

Cruella is a vindictive woman, but I can't think about her right now. Elijah needs me. A normal drive home takes forty-five minutes. The hospital is ten miles beyond, but I pull into emergency parking in fifty-one minutes, thanking the Lord for no freeway accidents and all green lights.

I hurry inside where a gray-haired gentleman greets me. "May I help you?"

The smell of disinfectant causes my nose to twitch. "Yes, my little brother was brought in by his school. Elijah Evans."

He looks at his list. "Where are his parents?"

Why now? "Deceased. I'm his sister. His legal guardian. Where is he, please?"

He accepts my response and escorts me to a door, waving his keycard over the entry monitor. The doors whoosh open. "Through those doors, third cubicle on the right. The mayor is with him."

In a cubicle, Elijah lies on a gurney, eyes shut. The sight takes my breath away. Miss Boo holds his little hand, but it should be me. She smiles. Motioning me closer, she steps back.

I brush the hair off my baby's forehead. A line of five stitches closes a gash over his right eyebrow. My poor baby. When Elijah doesn't open his eyes, I throw a worried glance at Miss Boo.

"He's all right, Marleigh. They've given him a sedative. He's just sleeping."

"Thank you for being here." Guilt thicker than sawmill gravy swallows me. My boy blurs. I want to scoop him up into my arms and cradle him. "I hate to not be here for him when he needs me."

"Sugar, look at me." Miss Boo lays her hand on my arm. Her sympathetic smile holds no judgment. "You can't be with him twenty-four seven. He needs providing for too."

And I can't do that either—not without a job.

"And you do an admirable job providing for him."

"I try, but I can't help feeling like I've let him down. I'm all the family he has." My throat closes. How I miss Mama and Aunt Susan.

"You also created a family for him in me, Herb, Nola, and Willow."

"Marma?" Elijah's sleepy voice pulls me out of my pity party.

I lean down, wrapping my arms around him, careful not to jar his broken arm awaiting a cast. "Yes, sugar?"

"I's sorry." His eyes slide shut. Then, they flutter.

"There's nothing to be sorry for, baby."

"'Kay. My arm hurts."

I kiss the side of his forehead without stitches. "Go to sleep. You won't hurt when you sleep. I'll be right here."

"I wuv you." His words slur.

"I love you more."

The doctor enters our cubicle. "Miss Evans?"

"Yes?"

"I'm Dr. Shrader, pediatric orthopedist. I've X-rayed Elijah's arm. He has a clean fracture and won't need surgery. Only a cast."

"Does he have a concussion?"

"We don't believe so. His pupil activity doesn't indicate one, but I have instructions with signs to watch for over the next twenty-four hours."

An hour later, with Miss Boo's help, I take my five-year-old home.

My five-year-old.

He's been mine alone since he was two. I need to look into adopting him. I want to be his mama, not just his sister. Can a person adopt their adopted brother?

When we get home, Elijah insists he can walk. "I didn't break my leg."

I can see him proudly showing off his black eye, which will be a beauty by morning. "No, but you did get a nasty bump on your head, so at least hold my hand." I let him lead me to the house.

"Miss Boo, want to come in for some coffee or sweet tea?"

She follows me. "I won't say no to sweet tea."

We settle Elijah on the sofa with a pillow to keep his arm elevated while cartoons keep him company. "Do you want anything to eat, sweetie? You missed lunch."

His little mouth scrunches as he thinks about it. "A banana. When will Aysha be home?"

"In an hour." After I take him his fruit, I join Miss Boo in the kitchen.

"Thank you again for being there for Elijah. I know he was in good hands."

"Ahh, we adore him and Aysha. Our grandchildren don't live close by, so we borrow yours and Nola's kids." She swirls the ice in her glass. "What will you do with Elijah for the next few days? He should stay home until next week, according to the doctor. I have a meeting in Savannah, or I'd take care of him."

I don't want to tell her I've lost my job, yet. She might worry about our rent. "I'm able to stay at home."

"Oh, good. A few days off will do you both wonders." She drains her glass. "Well, I have animals to feed." She sticks her head in the front room. "Bye, Elijah. Get well quick, sugar pie."

After closing the door, I sit next to my boy. "Hey, buddy."

He snuggles close and clicks off the TV. "Do you have to go back to work today?"

I never had to think about Mama going out to work. "Nope. I'm all yours."

His face lights up. "Can we play a game?"

"Sure. What would you like?" As if I didn't know.

I open a hidden drawer of our coffee table and pull out his favorite game as he hollers, "Candyland." As the word flies out of his mouth, he winces.

"What hurts, sugar?"

"My head. I guess I should've used my indoor voice."

I remove the list the doctor gave me from my pocket.

"Whassat?" Elijah touches the paper.

"The doctor's instructions on how to take care of you for the next few days." I glance at the clock—too soon to give him anything. "Why don't we whisper so your head doesn't hurt?"

We play for a half-hour, then Aysha comes home. She skids to a stop, staring at his arm. "Wow." She comes over and touches Elijah's cast. "I'm gonna beat up Timmy Morrow."

"No, sweetie. There's no need." I tuck an errant strand of hair behind her ear. "Timmy's been handled by your school."

Aysha climbs onto the sofa to look over his wounds. "I didn't see what happened. I was inside."

Elijah spins his tale for her, embellishing his rendition a little. To keep from laughing, I slip into the kitchen. It's Willow's night to cook, so I call her to fill her in on what's happened.

"Since I'm home already. I'll go ahead and start supper. What do you have planned?"

"Enchiladas. Everything is there. How's my little buddy doing?"

"As well as can be expected." I fill her in on the details.

"I'll bring home some get-well balloons."

GABE

"Chef?"

Wild Azalea's new server, Cindy, taps on my office door frame. "Yes?"

"Your brother's insisting on seeing you."

A sigh rips out of me. Of all the times to come, he had to pick now?

"Okay. Thanks for checking with me first." She's intuitive—not like Brandi. We replaced her when she let a food salesman wander into the kitchen by himself.

I set my menu aside. My brother has his back to the kitchen door, surveying our busy dining room. Mateo has a thriving business Dylan wants. I can't believe he thinks he could do better.

I approach him. "Dylan. What's up?"

"I want you to do some investigating on a property I found."

I glance around. Too many customers. Why he has to pick noon to come is beyond me. "Let's go into the office."

As we pass through the kitchen, Dylan doesn't react to any aromas coming from the stoves. He doesn't belong in the restaurant business.

In my office, I motion to Mateo's chair. "Have a seat."

Looking down his nose, he takes in the room. One corner of lip rises. "Kind of drab for a successful business office, isn't it?"

"We don't spend a lot of time here. Our real office is in there," I point to the kitchen, "where I'm needed, so what do you want?"

"Always to the point. I like that about you, little bro. Okay. I want to expand beyond restaurants."

Good, then he'll leave me alone. Still ... I frown. "What does Dad think?" He's always been a restauranteur.

"Dad's old. He's retiring."

Retiring or pushed out?

"I want you to come back. Work for me."

Not on your life. "Is something wrong with Dad? He's a little young to retire."

"Sixty-four isn't too young. Anyway, you can leave all this—" he runs a finger over a desktop—"grease. You could be my junior partner." He won't leave until he tells me everything. Then, I'll ask for time to think.

"What do you want me to do?"

"Research. Development. I want to build strip malls, multi-use apartments. The future's in those."

He has a point there. Big malls aren't the draw they used to be. Besides, with so many large stores closing, he may be onto something—but without me.

"You know what? I've discovered I love what I do."

"You have to be kidding. Standing in a malodorous kitchen, cooking?"

"I rarely get to cook. A Chef de Cuisine is in charge of all activities related to the kitchen. I create menus, recipes, manage our kitchen staff, order all our supplies—."

He waves me off. "This will be better for you. As my brother, you'll have a stake—own a portion of the stock. You'll make millions."

And hate my life.

I shake my head. "You don't need me."

"Yes, I do. I've discovered a property I want. You are better than me with talking to hillbillies."

"These people you call "hillbillies" aren't chasing the almighty dollar. Have you no shame?"

He can't keep a sneer from invading his voice. "They're closer to my description than you think. They'll take less than market value and think they've hoodwinked us."

My brother has zero human kindness. Somewhere along the way, somebody milked it out of him. "If you've already met them, then you don't need me."

"I didn't. I checked county title records to see who owns the land."

"Where is it?"

"Behind the parking lot on Broad Street in Sugar Springs."

No!

Why?

A mere ten minutes my senior, but born the day before me, my brother has always held high his "rank" as first-born, thinking he can run my life. It's crazy. Growing up, he always found out what I wanted, somehow managing to steal it for himself. But I haven't even voiced my dream to anyone, except the mayor.

Striving for a casual tone, I ask, "Have you met the owners?"

"No. You present the deal. They're local yokels. They'll jump at a chance of some good money."

The property could belong to someone else. Please, let it be someone else's. There are other properties bordering Broad Street. "So, who owns the property?"

"Sugar Springs' mayor, and get this—her name is Boo."

Chapter 7

MARLEIGH

Elijah needs to keep his arm elevated. The sofa presents an easy place where I can pile cushions beside him. I set up the kiddos with TV trays to watch a Disney movie. I gave him his first dose of medicine thirty minutes ago. He seems like he's not feeling any pain.

"You both be careful now. Aysha, will you help Elijah?"

"Yep!" She looks over his plate. "But you already cut up his 'chilada."

"You can hand him his milk when he wants it."

She moves his glass closer to her, satisfied with her job.

Back in the kitchen, Willow and Nola are already eating. Sweet spicy aroma of mole sauce entices me to eat. Nola pushes the chips within reach. "How's Elijah feeling?"

"Good, right now." I drag a chip through spicy salsa. "Willow, how was your day?" I stuff the chip in my mouth before salsa drips.

"Super. I programmed a new light plot and sound effects for *Noises Off*. We go into tech week on Monday." She pours a spoonful of mole sauce over her enchilada. "The construction crew finished repairing our revolving stage in time for a demonstration to some visiting bigwigs."

I don't remember hearing about any repairs. "What needed repairing?"

"The guy responsible for buying the casters didn't account for the actors' weight." Willow rolls her eyes. "The wheels were too small and several collapsed."

I can't believe they don't have a built-in turntable.

"The things y'all deal with never fail to confound me." Nola slides a spatula under two enchiladas, transferring them to her plate. "I had a great day. I installed software for a new ticketing system at one theatre. Y'all know how much I love to play around with new software—especially when it involves numbers."

She's the CPA for three theatres, plus a software consultant for a fourth. She amazes me. "You and Willow have excellent technical savvy. I fall far short of y'all." I take another bite, then glance at them. It's now or never. I take a deep breath. "However, I have an opportunity to learn new skills from you both."

With a forkful of enchilada midway to her mouth, Nola stops, narrows her eyes, staring at me. "What are you saying?"

I hate to have to cause any worry, since I can keep up my part of the rent for a while. Not too long, if I don't want to drain Elijah's college fund, but it's not a disaster. "Cruella fired me when I left to go to the hospital."

Willow chokes. I slap her on the back, but she holds up her hand to stop me while she takes a drink of water. "Cruella's pathetic. I swanny, she would skinny dip with snapping turtles. What did she say when you told her Elijah had an accident?"

"She thought I meant he wet his pants." I can't help rolling my eyes.

"I'd expect no less from someone who doesn't have enough brains to give herself a headache," Nola says. "For one, I'm glad she fired you. Now, y'all can start thinking about your own theatre." She pours more sauce over her enchilada. "You know I'm onboard."

"Me too." Willow reaches toward the enchiladas, then switches to the chip bowl. "Salsa, please."

I hadn't thought past Elijah's accident, but now unemployment hovers over my checkbook, I wonder if Ridge Academy still has the artistic director position. I don't have secretarial skills to take a temporary job. I suppose I could audition for a role at a professional theatre. I wonder what's coming up at the Fox? I shake my head at the crazy thoughts rolling around in there. For a moment, I stare at them.

Then, their remarks drop into an empty slot. My dream. "Do you think we can do it?"

Nola's nod is decisive. "I already told you we have two investors lined up. Then, there are grants. Besides, between us, we could take out a construction loan. I've looked into it."

Manny. I snap my fingers. "Manny Dupont said he knows a couple of people who might want to invest in us too." Cautious excitement grows in me. God has given me everything I need in best friends—Nola's business mind and Willow's can-do attitude. *Thank you.*

"So ... what do we need to do first for *our* theatre?

Nola swirls ice in her glass but shakes her head when I offer her a refill. "No, thanks. First, we need to decide if we are going to be a nonprofit or a for-profit theatre. Then, we'll need a plan for renovating. I know an architect."

"I hadn't thought about for-profit." I reach behind me, grabbing a pen and pad from the kitchen junk drawer to start a list. "Aren't most community theaters nonprofit?"

Nola shovels in her last bite, pushing her plate to the middle of the table. "They are—also there are grants available for nonprofits, especially if we have an education plan in place."

I write "grants" on the page along with a few other notes. In my mind, my dream expands to its full potential. This is what I was born to do. *Thank you, Lord!*

"You have to decide what you want to do. If we go nonprofit, you can be on our board and draw a salary as Artistic Director, but you'd have to recuse yourself from voting on budgets and your salary."

I stare at Nola. "I'm not sure. This is my dream. If I have to recuse myself, I lose all control. I wouldn't have any say in anything."

Nola shakes her head. "Not true. As AD, you'd have a voting seat on the board. Along with me as your Managing Director, we'd both be there. The only time we'd have to recuse ourselves is for budget votes."

"Who else would we ask to be on our board?"

Willow snaps her fingers. "My folks, of course. They know how good you both are at what you do. Besides, Dad is a company executive, so he has business sense." She glances at Nola. "What about your mom and her fiancé? Isn't he an investment banker or something like that?"

"Financial planner. He'd be a great addition. So, we'd ask my mom and Walter, plus Willow's parents." Nola taps my list. "Write those names down. Now we need someone who knows theatre well plus what producing a show encompasses."

"There's a host of people we know. I think we need to start another list of their names." I add a second column to my list. A tiny seed of doubt takes root—is this the time? I gaze at my best friends. "I think our *first* order of business is to pray about this. Then, when we are *all* sure this is what we're supposed to do, we'll apply for our nonprofit status."

And tell Elijah his big sister is at last taking steps to fulfill her dreams.

In Elijah's bedroom, I pick up his toys and help him get into his pajamas.

"What happened to my jams?" One handed, he holds up the top by its single sleeve.

"Your cast wouldn't fit through the sleeve. Since I didn't have time to buy you a short-sleeved pair, I cut off one sleeve."

"These can be summer jams, then. We'll just cut off its other sleeve." He giggles.

"You're thinking smart now, buddy." I settle him under the covers. "Sugar, I'm not going back to work for the theatre where I've been." I peer at him to catch his reaction.

His eyes open wide, he sits up. "Yeah? Did you tell ole Cruella de Vil to take a hike?"

I'm gobsmacked. "Why do you say that?"

"'Cause she's not nice. She makes you tired."

Wow. This kid has more intuition than most adults. "Well, you're right."

He squints, leveling his gaze on me. "I'll bet she's mad 'cause you left to come to the hospital, huh?"

I don't want him to feel any guilt. "Well ... yes, but it's not your fault."

"I know. It's Timmy's fault."

Well, there ya go. I lay him back down. After we say prayers, he doesn't release my hand right away.

"What are you going to do, Marma?"

"You know what I want to do?"

"Yes!" he shouts. "Open a cum-ah ... a cahmooney theatre!"

His head must not hurt, because he didn't wince. "Yes, we are, but don't say anything to Miss Boo, yet. I haven't asked her about the barn. There are a lot of things we need to do before we ask."

"Like what?"

I explain a few. "But most important of all, we have to pray to be sure this is what God wants us to do. So, until then, this is our little secret."

"Okay. I can tell Jesus, though, then he can tell his daddy we need a barn." He lays his left hand over his encased right one and shuts his eyes tight. Then, they pop open. "Hey, I jus' 'membered. Mr. Bud wants a helper at his store. Maybe you can work there till God says 'okay' on your theatre."

"Good idea. I'd still be close in case you need me. I'll go talk to him on Monday."

My little helper and prayer warrior. I kiss him goodnight. Now, the hard part begins. Waiting for an answer.

I glance up. *Grant us favor, Lord, if this is your will.*

We've prayed. We've waited. It's been three days. How long before we get an answer? In the meantime, I'll go see Mr. Bud. I can handle running a cash register. I hope he hasn't hired anyone yet. Besides, while I'm at Favorite Pastime, I want to get Elijah a new puzzle.

"Sugar? I'm going to go talk to Mr. Bud about working for him. Mr. Herb is here to sit with you."

"Okay, Marma. Hey. Mr. Herb! Wanna play Candyland?"

I close the door on his answer. Frankie James spies me, waving as I cross the parking lot between the farm and apartments.

"I heard about Elijah. Tell him 'hey' for me. I promise not to get hair in his cast when he comes in for his next haircut."

"Sure will, Frankie." I step into the walkway beneath the apartments, emerging on Main Street. A minute later, I arrive at Favorite Pastime. Part toy store, part hobby shop, there's something for everyone. I find several puzzles, choosing two for Elijah, one with Buzz Lightyear. The other has transformer dinosaurs he'll love.

"Hey, Marleigh." Mr. Bud appears in the aisle. "How's Elijah? I heard about his accident."

Everyone seems to know. "He's doing fine. Kids heal so much quicker than us. It's been three days, and already he's begging to go back to school."

"I'm glad. I miss seeing him. He often brings Aysha and Nola by here to say 'hey' on their way home."

"I know. He also mentioned you're looking for some part time help. Did you hire anyone yet?" I hand him the puzzles. "I'll take these."

"Haven't found the right person."

We walk to his check out register. "How about me?"

His eyes pop wide. "You? Yes, but aren't—"

I explain what happened. "Before I settle into something full-time again, I want to be close at hand for Elijah."

"Now, that dawg will hunt. You can work here for as long as you want, Marleigh. Shucks, I've known you since y'all were born. Ain't no need to look further. You can start tomorrow, if you want." He rings up the puzzles. "It's just part time and minimum wage. I wish I could do more, but—"

"It's fine, Mr. Bud. This will help me. Besides, Elijah will love to have me working for you. You're one of his favorite 'peeps,' as he says."

Puzzles in hand, I walk home. At least I won't have to drive to work. Wow, if God grants the theatre, I won't have to then, either. Elijah can come there after school too.

Pray and wait. Pray and wait.

Tapping on my phone's map app, I enter the Midtown address of the restaurant where Willow asked us to meet. I've never eaten at Wild Azalea. Cool name. With Herb watching Elijah, I head out. First stop, pick up Nola.

Twenty minutes later, I pull up in front of the theatre where she's working on audits today. She walks out the door before I can turn off my engine.

"Good timing. I was just fixing to come in to get you." We head to the restaurant. "Have you eaten at this place before?"

Nola turns my radio to a country station, and strains of Merle Haggard's "Today I Started Loving You Again" fill the car. "No. I'm curious why Willow wants us to come to this particular one, although ..." she chuckles. "I have an inkling."

I glance at her. "You think it's a new boyfriend? I'll bet you're right. She held out longer than I expected."

"She's taking her own advice now."

"Oh? What advice?"

"All drama remains on the stage." Nola snorts. "She had a sign made for their actors' call board."

"Cute. I keep hoping our Willow will find a great guy. She deserves one." I change lanes to avoid a car turning left.

Nola bumps my shoulder. "Hey, there's not a pot too crooked that a lid won't fit."

"I know you're right. Maybe this will be the right one."

A few minutes later, my GPS comes alive. "You've reached your destination."

"Thank you." I turn in and park my car.

Nola shakes her head. "Marleigh, you're the only person I know who thanks her apps."

"I can't help it. It's natural."

"Bless your heart." Nola opens the restaurant door, and slipping in ahead of her, I give her the stink-eye.

Willow waves so we'll find her.

"Hey." Sliding into the booth, I glance around. "Nice place. A little above my pay grade at the moment, though." Dark mahogany woodwork and burgundy leather, along with art deco sconces give the restaurant an elegant appearance. Low lighting creates an intimate dining experience. Perfect for romance.

Willow waves me off. "This is my treat."

Nola and I exchange a knowing glance. "Well, thank you. So, what's good here?"

"I always go with the chef's special."

Nola looks over her menu. "I want a backup, just in case."

Willow bats Nola's menu to the table. "I know the chef. He's exceptional. You'll love whatever his special is."

"Hey! Don't get your panties in a wad." Nola slides her menu out of Willow's reach. "I want to look."

"I'm sorry. I really like this guy. I want y'all to as well."

I tap Nola's ankle with my foot, giving her a "told ya so" smirk. "We'll try the special."

"Good." Willow cranes her neck, then waves.

A young, pony-tailed server approaches. Her black vest over a white shirt and black pants add to the 1920s feel of the place. "Hey, ladies. What can I get for you?"

Willow takes over. "What's the special?"

"April's gourmet salad."

"Who's April?"

The server giggles. "It's the month—not a person."

Willow grins. "Oh. Yeah. What's in it?"

"Lots of neat things like pine nuts, golden raisins, and raspberry jam in the dressing."

Not a great description, but I'm game. "Sounds good. I'll have April's salad with sweet tea."

"Make it three." Nola hands back her menu.

"I picked up a part-time gig with Mr. Bud at Favorite Pastime." I spread my napkin in my lap. "Working there will help keep me from dipping too far into Elijah's college fund."

The server brings our sweet tea.

"What about auditioning for some commercials?" Willow tests the tea, then adds another packet of sugar. "The residuals are good."

"I know. I received one the other day. Residual, not a commercial. I let my agent know I was available for auditions right after Cruella fired me."

Willow slides out of the booth. "I'll be right back." She heads toward the rear of the restaurant where there's a restroom sign hanging over the hallway.

Nola and I chat while she's gone. A few minutes later, Willow returns wearing an air of innocence. Straight away, I'm suspicious. Taking a slow sip of tea, I study my friend. A knowing quirk of her lips affirms suspicions.

"Okay, Willow, spill it. What have you done?"

Chapter 8

MARLEIGH

"I want you to meet somebody." Willow folds her hands on the table.

The new boyfriend. Can't be anything else. Nothing else causes her to act coy. I glance at Nola, who winks.

I smooth my napkin in my lap. "I'm game. Who are we meeting?"

"You'll see." Willow glances up. "Ahh, here he comes." She waves.

My gaze follows her wave to the most handsome man I've ever seen. I'm talking movie star handsome. Brown hair cut short, strong jaw, but it's his dark amber eyes I can't pull my gaze from. He crosses the room with confidence, and my stomach makes a strange flip, followed by my heart. This is crazy.

He approaches our table. "Ladies." He looks right at me, not Willow.

I'm in trouble if this is her new boyfriend. I want him to be mine. *Whoa, where did that come from?*

Willow's grin is wide. "Gabe, these are my roommates, Nola ... Marleigh."

Why did she pause before she said my name? To warn me off? Can she tell I'm ... Just what am I?

Gobsmacked.

He acknowledges both of us, but his eyes never leave mine. This is so awkward. I blink, forcing my eyes away.

This is Willow's boyfriend. *Keep reminding yourself.*

"What did you ladies order?" Then, I notice he's wearing a chef's coat. He's not an actor? Score one for Willow. Why am I not pleased? I should be happy for my friend.

"The special. You know I always order whatever your special is, Gabe." She turns to us. "He's head chef—I don't know the proper term for it, but he's great."

He turns an indulgent smile on Willow. "You'd love a flip flop if I served it to you."

What? What kind of romance is this?

Willow giggles. "He's right. Y'all, Gabe is a good guy-friend of mine. We've been buddies for a while." She scoots over and pats the bench beside her.

Gabe slides in. "I can visit for a moment, then I'll need to get back to the kitchen." He folds his hands on the table, smiling at me.

His hands are strong. Clean. I glance at Willow. She doesn't act like she does when she's infatuated. I'm so confused.

"Willow tells me you're an artistic director, Marleigh."

I love how my name sounds on his lips. How would they feel—

"What does an artistic director do?"

"Uhm, actually, I'm not at the moment. An AD, I mean. I'm ... exploring my options." *That's brilliant, Evans.*

"Interesting. I'm doing the same thing, exploring options I mean."

Am I an option?

I wish he'd ask Nola a question. My brain is filled with mashed potatoes. My heart is obsessing over his eyes, his lips. I'm thankful when our server approaches, carrying our salads.

Gabe rises. "I enjoyed meeting you ... both." He shakes Nola's hand, then mine. He lingers over mine a little longer. Heat rises in my neck and cheeks. After what seems like forever, he turns away.

I watch his back disappear into the kitchen. There is something familiar about his back—him walking away. Strange, but I can't pinpoint it.

"What do you think of him?" Willow asks, staring at me, hope in her eyes.

How can I answer? *I've fallen for your new boyfriend?* She may call him a guy-friend, but I think it's a cover to put Nola and me at ease. She wants us to see his potential before we try to dissuade her.

But oh, how I wish it were true.

"Marleigh, he asked me to introduce him to you."

"He did?" I peer into Willow's eyes. There's no duplicity in her gaze. She meets mine with open honesty. "Why? I mean why would he ask you to introduce him to someone he's never seen?"

"He *has* seen you. At a Chamber of Commerce meeting."

I don't remember seeing him. What I do remember is a headache, so I went home.

"He wanted to meet you. He asked Bud Pugh to introduce you, but you left before he had a chance."

"Oh. Then, how did he connect us?"

She shifts her eyes. In an instant, I tune in to a little Willow-skullduggery. "Well ... I ... it's like this ...." She takes a big bite of her salad, chewing slowly.

"Spit it out, Willow—what you did, not the salad."

She swallows, pursing her lips. "You haven't dated anyone for months. All you do is work and take care of Elijah. It's not natural. Well, taking care of Elijah is, but," she frowns, "you should be having fun."

"And ...?"

Willow glances at Nola.

She smirks. "Don't look to me for help."

Shoulders slumping, Willow sighs. "I asked him to meet a friend. As we talked, well, I guess he put two and two together, since Mr. Bud told him who you are."

Now, I'm more confused than ever. "Why did Mr. Bud tell him who I am?"

"I just told you, silly. Gabe watched you and liked what he saw. When I called and mentioned your name, he realized yours isn't a common one. He guessed you were the same person. I happened to call at the right time."

I'm inside a verbal-fun-house. I hear one thing, but my mind twists things, making the words sound different. Questions swirl, dive, racing around me, further confusing me. My old stand-by-date, Michael, was like a Broadway hit. Reliable. Steady. This chef is a new script by an unknown playwright. Risky. Dangerous. None of this makes sense. Least of all the effect he had on me. I've never believed in love at first sight, but my heart is screaming, "Yes, we do!"

GABE

Back in the kitchen, I want to kick myself. Marleigh must think I'm a total idiot. I was so discombobulated. I'm drawn to her like opposing poles of a magnet. My eyes even refused to obey. I dubbed her "Beauty" when I saw her at the chamber of commerce meeting. The nickname fits her so well. Yet her outward appearance isn't what draws me. I feel almost as if I can see her soul.

I want to know more.

"Lenore, is table eleven yours?"

"Yes, Chef."

"Their bill is on me." I pull out my wallet and hand her a twenty-dollar bill. "Tip."

She stares at the twenty, then at me, ponytail bouncing. She snaps her eyes open wide. "Thanks, Chef."

I hide out in my office, berating myself for sounding like such a halfwit with Marleigh. I ignored her other roommate—what was her name? Nola-not-Nora. All I could think was I'm meeting Beauty.

I'll call Willow later and ask if I messed up my chance. Then again, I could bypass her. Call Marleigh for a date. My stomach pitches.

Holdernewt! I'm as nervous as a middle school boy asking a girl to dance. What is wrong with me?

I pick up a pen to attack my food order. I write sugar, flour, baking soda, Beauty. I drop the pen. This is crazy. I've dated lots of girls. Never have I dealt with this kind of distraction.

I've never met anyone like Marleigh, either.

With my heart pounding in my ears, I pick up my cell phone to tap in her number. *You dunce.* I lay down my phone. She's still here in the restaurant. I can't call her now. What a Neanderthal. A total numbskull—and in complete infatuation.

I send a text to Mateo: *going to Restaurant Supply*, then head out the back door, grabbing a jacket on my way. The supply house is meat-locker cold. Being in there will help cool me off.

I keep one eye on my watch and one on the quality of dishes going out to diners. "Ramon, show Josh how to wipe a plate edge." The kid's a decent cook, but he doesn't pay attention to presentation. Our dinner rush will be over in ninety minutes. Then, I'll call Marleigh.

At eight o'clock, the kitchen is quiet. Ramon checks tomorrow's midday menu, while our line cooks clean their stations. If this were Friday, we would be hopping until eleven with after-events clientele. Tonight, the last couple of tables have business occupants. They'll move to the bar soon. I give a nod to my crew and head home.

After a shower, I sit on the couch. I take a deep breath to calm my nerves before tapping in Marleigh's number. She answers on the second ring.

"Hello?"

"Hi. This is Gabe Sadler."

"Who?"

Oh, great. I must have made a terrific impression—she's already forgotten me. "Uh, I'm the chef at Wild Azalea. We met at noon today."

"Oh, Gabe, I'm sorry. Willow neglected to tell me your last name."

"Oh, good. I mean, I'm glad her lapse is why you didn't know who I am." *Dork!*

Her soft laughter is music to my ears. "I enjoyed your April Salad. The ingredients surprised me."

This may be easier than I thought. "How so?"

"I've never put some of those in a salad."

"What was new to you?"

"Okay, using sun-dried tomatoes, for one. I always use fresh, but yours added an unexpected robust flavor."

"You could be a food critic."

"Oh, no. I'm not criticizing anything."

"They call someone who does restaurant or food reviews a critic. What do they call people who review theatrical shows?"

"A critic." Her laugh sends a shiver across my shoulders. "Funny, I haven't ever associated 'critic' with food or restaurant reviews."

Ask her now. "So, what's the best show playing around here?"

"Oh my. Let's see. I love *Noises Off*, which opens a week from Friday at a theatre Nola works for."

"Would you like to go see it with me?"

She's silent—doesn't say a word. Am I rushing things?

"To be honest, I have two tickets for opening night already. Nola gave them to me. Would ... would *you* like to go with *me*?"

"Are you sure you don't have someone else lined up?" I hold my breath.

"No. She always gives me two, but I never use the other one."

Relief whooshes out of me. This is my lucky day. I'm surprised she doesn't use her other tickets, though. There has to be a lineup of guys trying to date her. "Then, I'd love to. How about I take you to dinner first?"

"It's Nola's night to cook, so dinner's great."

"Okay, I'll bite. Is Nola a bad cook? Does she need lessons?"

A giggle tickles my ear. "Nola isn't a cook at all. When it's her night, our menu has two items—pizza or Mickey D's, which the kids love. She's not interested in cooking, but she's the best CPA a person could have."

Kids? Willow didn't mention kids. But she wouldn't have asked me to meet Marleigh if she were married. Would she? "Whose kids?"

"Gabe, I'm raising my five-year-old brother. The other is Nola's little girl." Marleigh's voice is soft. Not quiet, but tender.

I hadn't bargained on kids in a relationship. But I like Beauty. I'll have to go slow, though. "I like kids, Marleigh. I think what you're doing is admirable. I take it, your parents aren't ... uh ..."

"My father died when I was young. My aunt came to live with us. They took in foster children. The day Elijah arrived, we all fell in love with him. After a few months, Mama adopted him. Biracial children are a little harder to place. Besides, since we'd had him since he was four days old, we were approved right away. Now, I'm looking into adopting him if I can. I've raised him alone since he was two. Mama and Aunt Susan died in a car accident."

"Amazing. I mean, I'm not raising a child, but I mentored two boys through the Big Brother program a couple years ago. Then, their mom remarried." I'm too busy now to take another one—not even sure I want to. I don't have the background to help a messed up kid.

"I'm impressed, Gabe. I don't think I've known a man who is in a Big Brother program."

"Growing up, I didn't have a good relationship with my brother. I had the crazy idea I could redeem the loss or at least keep another boy from what I went through."

"Do you and your brother get along now?"

I wish. "I'm sorry to say we don't." I don't want to ruin this relationship before it starts. I'll leave Dylan out of it.

"I'm sorry."

"Yeah, me too. However, I went into the Big Brother program because of him, and I like to think I've made a good impression on those kids. So, what's this *Noises Off* about?"

I hope it's a comedy, so I can hear her laugh again. What could be better than a theatre date with Beauty?

Chapter 9

MARLEIGH

The door bursts open at Favorite Pastime, making its bell jangle. From the register where I'm checking out a customer, I glance up. Willow, Nola, and the kiddos stroll in—well my friends stroll. Nola holds back the kids until my customer leaves.

"Hey, Marma!"

Elijah throws one arm around my waist, but before I can bend to kiss him, he runs off to the storeroom. Aysha follows him, hollering, "Can we help ya, Mr. Bud?"

Beside me, Nola pulls out her phone, tapping its screen. "What time are you off?"

"At one. Do you have this week's menu and grocery list?"

"Yes. I'm sending it to you, but first, Willow is taking you to get a new outfit for your date. Have you forgotten you need something special for opening night?"

Forget my date with Gabe is in—I glance at my watch—one-hundred-forty-six hours-thirty-two minutes? "No, but I have plenty of dresses. One of those will be fine."

Willow shakes her head. "It's black-tie. You need to have something to dazzle Gabe."

I take a mental stroll through my closet. She's right. Most of my evening wear is business dressy. "Does Gabe know it's black tie?"

"Yes. I told him." Willow wanders toward the front of the store, while my gaze strays to the storeroom, then returns to Nola.

"Does Willow think those two will stand still for dress shopping?"

"Not even." Nola slides her phone into her pocket. "I'm taking them to the Splash Pad while you and Willow find a dress. Once you're done, we'll all meet up at Three's."

Willow's phone chirps. Her gaze goes to her cell, then to the front window. "I'll be right back." She hurries out.

"What do you think that's about?"

Nola crosses to the door, peers out, craning her neck, then gestures for me to join her. "Looks like a new boyfriend."

Out on the sidewalk, Willow is talking to a handsome man. "Why do you think he's a boyfriend?"

Nola turns away. "She's in 'the mode.'"

I move to get a better view. "He doesn't look like an actor. He's rather Ivy League."

"Maybe you can find out while you two are shopping. Aysha? Elijah? Are you ready to go to the Splash Pad?"

The kids race out of the storeroom, give me a quick hug, then zip out the door.

"Keep your cast dry," I call after Elijah.

From her tote, Nola pulls a plastic bag and a roll of duct tape, lifting them high.

When my morning shift is over, I meet Willow outside the upscale consignment store, Play It Again. Inside, soft strains of Moon River drift from the store's audio system.

"I've already scouted out their dresses." She beckons me to a dressing room. "I found four. They're in dressing room 'B.' Come on." She disappears into the cubical.

"Remember, I don't have a lot of money to spend." I follow her with a sigh. Willow has wonderful taste but no money-sense.

She sticks her head out the curtain. "Of course, I do. We're *here* aren't we, instead of at the mall?"

The dressing area is large enough to accommodate us both. Cool silk of outfit number one glides over my head. It's gorgeous but not the right shade of teal for me.

I try the second one—siren orange, a color I love. I slip on the dress and turn around. Facing the mirror, I press my hand to my chest—my *bare* chest. Heat rises in my neck. Willow laughs, trying to adjust the shoulders. The neckline still plunges almost to my navel.

"Nope, *too* revealing, but I love the color."

The third one is a light-weight georgette with a multicolored geometric pattern. Its top has a single long sleeve, leaving one bare shoulder. I try it on. The skirt hugs my hips, then flares out. I love it.

I peer at Willow through the mirror. "What do you think?"

"I think Gabe will be a goner." She picks up the price tag. "This is more than affordable. Since we're the same size, I'll split the cost with you. I can wear it to something."

I high-five her. "Works for me."

I reject the fourth item as not quite elegant enough, being a jumpsuit, but I see why Willow chose it. Its pattern is Van Gogh-esque—a perfect fit for Willow's unique style. "Why don't you get this?"

She holds it up in front of herself, twisting to see in the mirror. "You're right. I'll keep this for Jessica's wedding."

"Perfect. All her colors are in it." I hand Willow thirty dollars. While she pays, I text Nola.

MARLEIGH: "We're ready."
NOLA: "What did you find out?"
MARLEIGH: "Didn't come up. we'll ask at Three's"

Three Marketeers is next to Morrow's Furniture, so we walk. Both Elijah and Aysha love Three's. They have lots of samples, so our kiddos graze their way through the store— we all do.

Nola forwards our week's grocery list. While Willow and I shop, she finds a couple of frozen veggie pizzas with enough pepperoni to render the kids delirious.

After checking out, we head home. The children skip ahead of us, so I nudge Willow.

"Is there something you should be telling us?"

"Who me?"

Her wide-eyed innocence isn't going to work.

"Don't play airhead with me, Willow Raines. Who's the dude?"

We reach home. With the kids in the barn seeing the goats, we three schlep groceries to the kitchen. "Okay, spill. Who is he?"

"I met him a couple of months ago." Willow places a gallon of milk in the fridge.

My mind computes dates. "*Before* the drug dealer?"

"Yeah. Crazy, huh? I met him at the bank. His name is Sergio Landi. I was making a deposit for my managing director." She slides bread into its drawer. "Sergio was there checking on a client he placed at the bank. He's a financial services recruiter. Anyway, he followed me out of the bank and asked me to have coffee."

"And you did?" Nola plants her fists on her hips. "Without knowing him?"

"The bank is next to a Starbucks, so I figured I was safe."

Our Willow would trust a masked bank robber if he was polite. "Sugar, you need to be more careful."

"I *am*. I've learned my lesson after jerk-face-James. But even though this was before him, I wouldn't give Sergio my phone number or anything. We met a couple of times for coffee. Then, I met James and became temporarily insane."

Nola pours sweet tea for all of us, setting the pitcher on the table, then sits. "So, have you been on actual dates with him? More than just coffee?"

"You betcha. He loves theatre," Willow joins us, "but he isn't involved like any of us. He's taken me to a couple of shows." She nods at me. "Like Michael did with you."

When Nola and Aysha moved in, we made an unspoken rule about not questioning each other when we went out. Maybe it's time we change it.

"And I had him meet Gabe."

My ears perk at Gabe's name. "Why?"

"Because Gabe told me to after the druggie. He even ran a background check on Sergio. You'll be happy to know he's one of the good guys." Her sigh tells us everything. Willow is falling in love.

There's a pothole in her account of this, though. "How did you reconnect with him?"

"Yeah, he didn't have your phone number." Nola crunches an ice cube.

Willow giggles. "I made the theatre's bank deposits, until I saw him again. He placed another client there a few days later."

"I'm so happy for you, Willow." I can't help adding a prayer, though. *Please, God, don't let him break her heart.*

"And now, I'm off to meet him for supper." She waves over her shoulder.

I set our glasses in the sink, then face Nola. "What are you doing this evening?"

"Well ..." Her lips twist. "We need to talk."

Uh-oh. This can't be good. I lean against the sink. "About what?"

"About the theatre. Come on. Let's go chat on the couch. You look like a cornered rat standing there."

Her smile relieves some of the tension in my shoulders, but not all. I follow her into the living room, where she flops onto the sofa.

"I've been doing some research about board members being employees." She scoots over, so I can sit by her side.

"What did you find?"

"We already know you can be a paid employee of a nonprofit. From those we want on the board, you won't have any trouble. I want you to take time—think about not being chairman. Let someone else chair the board."

Popping up, I pace, questions and scenarios vying for my attention. If someone gets on the board who has a different philosophy, they could cause a lot of headaches—or persuade the rest to go a different direction.

Worst case scenario—they could vote me out.

I stop. "If we didn't become a nonprofit, could I own the business?"

"Yes, however we'd have to pay taxes on any profits" She rests her chin in her hand. "We won't be able to survive if we don't have enough money."

I don't know many profitable community theatres. They don't charge enough for tickets, making just enough to cover the next show. I bite my lip. "If we're not a nonprofit, we'd have to pay more to license a show, as well."

She nods. I drop into a chair. What will I do? If we incorporate, I lose total control. I've spent the past several years dreaming over every detail of this venture.

"I need to think."

I walk outside and stare at the barn. In my mind's eye, I see a complete theatre. Young people and adults on the stage, gaining confidence. A business providing livelihoods for my best friends. A legacy for my soon-to-be-son.

I hope.

I wrap my arms around my middle. "God, why did you give me this dream if I can't keep control over it?"

GABE

I tug at my cuffs, then ring Marleigh's doorbell. This tux is a little tight across my shoulders, the result of working out with a personal trainer. I'm going to have to buy a new tuxedo.

Willow opens the door. She's beautiful in a blue gown. "Come on in."

Is she going to this shindig?

In the living room, Sergio steps forward, his hand extended. "Hey, Gabe. I didn't realize you were coming tonight."

I guess she is. "Good to see you, man. I'm in the dark too."

"Nola's suggestion. Since the tickets are next to each other, we may as well go in one car." Willow turns toward the stairs. "Come on, Marleigh. If we're going to eat first, we'd better get moving."

My gaze darts to the stairway. A moment later, Beauty appears. She's gorgeous, snatching away my breath in a long dress leaving one shoulder bare. I step forward and hold out my hand. Her fingers entwine with mine.

"You look fantastic."

"So do you. Better than the chef pajamas." She winks.

Heat flares low in my gut.

While the ladies gather their bags and wraps, I look around for the kids Marleigh mentioned, but don't see them.

Beauty smiles. "We're ready."

Sergio opens the door. "We'll take my car."

I didn't even see his Mercedes when I arrived—my mind wasn't on cars.

Marleigh and I settle into the back seat. Without driving, I don't have anything to do with my hands. *Stop rubbing them on your pants.* I clasp them between my knees.

"Where are we going?" Sergio catches my eye through his rearview mirror.

Oh, yeah. "I made reservations at Canoe—for two, but I'm sure I can pull a few strings."

"I haven't been there, but with your recommendation, I'm game. I know how to get there."

I send a text to the restaurant changing our numbers. I get a thumbs up reply, so I settle back.

"I was kind of hoping to meet Elijah." Kids weren't in my plans yet, beyond the Big Brother gig, so I'm a little tense about Marleigh's little brother. The sooner I meet him, the sooner I'll know if this thing with Beauty is going to work. Or not.

"He's staying with Nola's mom." Her soft hands lay in her lap. "I try to protect him. He opens his heart to people. I won't have him hurt."

Makes sense. "I understand. I'm sure I'd feel the same if I were in your place."

Her smile is warm. "Thank you."

I could get lost in her smile. Even more in her eyes. I've never met anyone like her. She's authentic. She hasn't grilled me about my past, present, future—or my bank account.

Unlike Elaine. Dylan set me up with her. She was like dating a barracuda bent on catching the fisherman. I learned my lesson. No more letting other people arrange blind dates for me.

"What?" She blinks, her smile turning saucy.

"What?"

"You were staring at me. Is there something on my face?"

How does a guy tell a woman she's so beautiful he lacks the ability for intelligent conversation?

"Hey, Gabe, are there any particular menu items you recommend at Canoe?"

Bless, you, Willow. Rescued from sounding like a total dork. "I'm partial to the Georgia shrimp for an appetizer. For entrees, either scallops or beef tenderloin. Truth be told, everything is great." I glance at Marleigh. Now she's staring at me. "What?"

"What?"

We both crack up, dissolving the tension. I take her hand in mine. It feels so right. "I think we're on to something here." I keep my voice low. My thoughts are for her alone.

"Yeah," she whispers. "I think we are."

Be careful, man. Slow down.

Sergio turns into Canoe's parking lot. "And here we are."

Our table overlooks the Chattahoochee River. The girls ooh and ahh over the view.

A young waiter hands me a menu. "Thank you." I wait until he leaves. "Canoe is in the Fine Dining Hall of Fame. I worked here for a summer right after culinary school."

Sergio closes his menu. "Everything looks so good. Why don't you choose for us?" He glances at Willow. "Is everyone all right with Gabe choosing?"

"Sure." Willow hands her menu to Sergio.

"Me too," Marleigh says.

I order something different for each. "We can all sample some of everything."

Conversation flows easily. Sergio entertains us with some of the more unusual people he has placed in the financial world. He's a good man and an interesting new friend. I want to ask if he knows my dad or brother, but not tonight.

After a wonderful meal, we head to the theatre. The tickets Nola gave us are perfect—fifth row center. The best part is Marleigh keeps her hand in mine.

The play is hilarious, but my gaze wanders too often to Marleigh's lips. My heart beats faster as I fantasize about kissing her. When she laughs and glances at me, I force my attention to the play, but rub my thumb over her hand. I don't want this night to end.

During intermission in the lobby, our conversation turns to music. I ask Marleigh, "Are you a fan of Bluegrass?"

Willow giggles. "Is she ever. She wields a wicked mandolin."

"No way. I play at the banjo." I wink at Beauty.

"I love Bluegrass." She tilts her head. "But what do you mean by '*play at?*'"

"I'm not very good. I just started to learn a few months ago. Would you like to go to the Music Barn with me next Saturday night? I have a friend who's performing there."

"I'd love to. I've heard about it but haven't been."

Sergio nudges Willow. "Are you a Bluegrass fan too?"

"Aren't most Southern girls?"

"The ones who are in good standing." Sergio glances at the dimming chandeliers, the audience's cue intermission is about over. "Time to get back." He holds me back as the ladies slide into our seats. "Hope you don't mind us tagging along next weekend."

I'd rather have gone alone with Marleigh, but after his rescue, I owe him. "Not at all."

But soon, I'll need to ask Beauty out somewhere we can get to know each other—away from music, theatre, and distractions. Maybe even include her kid. See what he's like. She says he's open to everyone, but what if he decides I'm moving in on his territory? That happened to Mateo. And the kid ruined what might have been a great relationship.

Chapter 10

MARLEIGH

Sitting at the kitchen table, I nibble my pen. I've added several wedding tasks on my to-do list—table favors, a caterer—but something else escapes me. I need to check online to see what I'm forgetting. My plan for this afternoon is to visit the bakery, then the florist, finally coming back here to have Jessica and Walter choose several other items from a catalogue.

I lay down my pen. The day hasn't begun, but I'm already exhausted. If the barn is going to double as a wedding venue, I need to hire someone to be our wedding planner. I can't keep this up, not while concentrating on theatrical productions.

My heart thrills just thinking about the theatre. The more I pray, I feel like God is holding the door open for me. Yet ... I hesitate, chewing on my fingernail. Oh foot, if this thing fails, Nola and the other investors will lose their investment. It would be my fault.

Trust Me.

"Marma?" Sleep still clings to Elijah's eyes. He yawns, rubbing them and climbs onto my lap for snuggles. "Can I have pancakes?"

I wrap my arms around him, drawing in his sweet little-boy-scent. I hug him—and my secret—for a little while longer. "The batter's all ready. Let's eat, then we're going to Jaemor Farms. Just the two of us."

Wide awake now, he hops off my lap. "Yes!" He pumps his left fist. "Can we pick blueberries?"

"They're in season."

He gets dressed while the pancakes cook, coming back for me to button his shirt. Then, after we eat, we say goodbye to Nola and Aysha, who are leaving for their own special day.

When we arrive at Jaemor Farms, we pick up a basket. Elijah slips its handle over his cast.

"Hey, this works great. Can I get another cast for next time?"

"No, silly." We pick berries until our basket is full. Inside the building, I select a few oranges too. "How about an ice cream?"

"For real? I don't have to wait until after supper?"

Oh, how I love this boy. "Not this time, sugar. Today is special."

He tilts his head, staring up at me. "Why?"

"Let's get our ice cream first, then I'll tell you."

I select cherry with chocolate chunks, Elijah chooses strawberry. We head outside to a picnic table to enjoy the treat.

He takes a few licks, then stops. "Can you tell me now?"

I nod. "What do you think about me adopting you— making you *my* son? I'd be your mama—not just your sister."

His beautiful brown eyes widen as he looks up at me. "A for-real forever mama?"

"Yep."

He stands on the bench and throws his arms—cast and ice cream—around my neck. "I've wanted that my whole life."

I run my napkin over the back of my hair, making sure it's free of strawberry. "I called my lawyer yesterday. He's started our paperwork. There's nobody to ask, so there's nothing to prevent it."

"Why's there nobody to ask?"

"Remember you were left at the fire station? I told you we never knew who your mama or daddy were. But I know God meant you to be *my* boy."

"Yeah." He licks his ice cream a couple of times.

I wait for him to process what he's thinking. After a moment, he lays a cafe-au-lait arm next to mine on the table.

"Mrs. Davis says I'm part African-'merican an' to be proud of my ancessories."

"Ancestry. You should be proud. We don't know if your mama was African-American or if it was your daddy. What I do know is you're a very special boy."

"Yeah." He licks his cone again. A glob of ice cream sticks to his nose. He tries to get the confection with his tongue but fails. I wipe it off with a napkin.

He grins. "What are you?"

"I'm what they call Heinz 57."

"You're ketchup?"

"Kind of. My ancestry is made up of French, some Scotch-Irish, with a few other tiny bits thrown in."

He crunches on his cone. I can almost see the wheels turning in his little head. "Can I still call you 'Marma'? 'Cause my first *mama* didn't want me, an' my second *mama* died."

I'm the only "mama" he knows. He doesn't remember our mother or Aunt Susan. His memories are "foggy," as he says.

I gather him, along with his ice cream cone, into my arms. "You sure can. Do you know how much I love you?"

"To the moon an' back?"

"Even more." I cup his little face between my hands. "Nobody can promise they won't ever die, but I can promise I will take good care of myself, so I will be here for you until we are both very, very old. What do you think?"

He grins, offering me a lick of his cone. I oblige him and offer him mine. He chomps on it with a giggle.

"One more thing, sweetie. This is important." I wait for him to give me his full attention. "Your first mama wasn't able to care of you, but I know in my heart she *wanted* you."

"How can you know for sure?"

"Because she chose to give birth to you."

His brows draw together. "You mean she didn't wanna get a 'bortion?"

I blink back tears stinging my eyes. I hate he even knows what the word means.

"Every night, I thank God she chose to give birth to you, Elijah." I hold his chin in my hand. "I couldn't love you any more if I had given birth to you. I can't wait to call you 'Son.'"

I am the recipient of his biggest grin ever. Then, a slight frown mars his brow. "You couldn't give birth to me. You aren't married." Content, he finishes off his ice cream. "I'm glad you're gonna 'dopt me an' be my for-real forever mama."

There are so many more things I could tell him, but he's no longer thinking about it—as a five-year-old should. He knows he's loved. It's all he needs.

Like an exploding water balloon, a deluge of aromas engulfs us when I usher the bridal couple into Sugar 'n' Spice. I can pick out cinnamon, maybe vanilla, but the others blend so well, I can't name any individual one. Ah, my taste buds tingle in anticipation.

Walter licks his lips as he rubs his hands together. "Let the tasting begin."

"I hear you, Walter North." Prichelle's sultry voice—as smooth as her icing—precedes her as she enters through the kitchen door. In contrast to her voice, Prichelle is short and round, proof she samples all her baked goods before selling a new confection, which is why I recommend her.

In her hands is a tray filled with small slices of several cakes, which she places on a table. Over the next half hour, we taste, rate, discarding a few.

Walter is the persnickety one. "Why can't we have raspberry filling with red velvet cake? The colors match."

Jessica lays a hand on his arm. "Let's take Prichelle's advice, darling. After all, she's the expert."

He nods with some reluctance.

"Tell you what, Walter, we'll add a small groom's cake." Prichelle jots a note on her pad, then points to a small slice of chocolate cake. "Chocolate with raspberry filling. Happy?"

He takes a bite, closing his eyes while he chews. Jessica leans close to me. "He's in gastronomic ecstasy."

"I heard you." Walter doesn't open his eyes. "This is perfect for my cake."

For the wedding cake, they finalize on a white cake. Sliced strawberries will be arranged between the layers, finished with whipped cream frosting. We place the order, leave a deposit, then head to the florist.

Peonies are Jessica's favorite flower, so she chooses a small bouquet of blush pink. "I want my dress in this color."

By the time we finish, my head swims with so many details, it's giving me a headache. I love Jessica but wish I hadn't agreed to this. To top it all off, because I'd silenced my phone, I missed a call from Gabe.

GABE

I can't believe Marleigh's kid. He sure isn't what I expected. For the past hour, he's been silent, concentrating on his fishing line in the water. He hasn't even moved. If I didn't know better, I'd say he was willing the fish to bite. He's a pretty cool kid. I have to congratulate myself on my idea of inviting him along—although Beauty is reading, not fishing. Elijah's having fun, so maybe I've won him over. The fact Marleigh let me meet him is a good sign. She trusts I won't hurt him.

"I catched one!" Elijah jerks on his rod like I showed him.

I move to his side. "Okay, reel him in a little. Good. Now, let him run and tire out. That's right." He's a bright kid, too. "Pull up on the rod a bit. Good. Reel him in some more."

Soon, a small-but-keeper-sized bluegill appears. I grab my net, bring his fish onboard, then high-five Elijah. "Way to go!"

"Can we keep him, Marma?"

Marma?

She glances at me. "I guess so."

"Sure. He'll make a good dinner."

Elijah's happy face turns to wide-eyed horror. "I don't want to *eat* him. I wanna *keep* him."

Marleigh shakes her head. "Sugar, lake fish aren't like goldfish. They're wild. He either needs to be used for food or tossed back so he can go home."

Go home? Huh. Must be how kids think.

Elijah turns a pleading face to me. "Will you help me?"

"Sure."

Though I assure him I won't hurt his fish, Elijah cringes when I remove his hook with a pair of pliers. Then, together, we put the fish in the water. I hold on until the bluegill begins to wiggle. I let go when it gives a hearty flap.

As it swims away, Elijah waves. "'Bye, fish."

Curiosity gets the best of me. "Do you ever eat fish?" Does Marleigh?

"Yeah. I like fish sticks." He turns wide eyes to Marleigh. "Are they from here?"

"No, sweetheart. They're from the ocean."

There's a lot to learn about kids. I've never dated anyone who has one, but I get it. These two are a package deal if I want a relationship with Beauty. And I do.

"Can we fish some more?"

"Sure, buddy." I retrieve a worm from the cooler and thread the wiggler on his hook.

"I don't think I'd like to eat a worm." Elijah wrinkles his nose. "Are you sure fish like 'em?"

"They do, but sometimes, I've fished with cheese. You get a better quality fish with cheese."

Marleigh looks up from her book. "For real, or are you making it up?"

From her frown, I guess she's implying she's always truthful with him. "You can relax. It's true. You can also use corn." I hand Elijah his rod, then help him cast. "When I was in Hawaii, I went snorkeling. Someone told me to take along a bag of frozen mixed vegetables. You should have seen the school of fish swimming around me. They were the kind you see in saltwater aquariums. They loved the veg—ate right out of my hand."

Marleigh shades her eyes against the sun. "How fun. Were you in Hawaii for a vacation?"

"Work. My dad wanted a restaurant on the big island—in Hilo. I went over to see if they were in financial trouble. They were. Dad bought them out, turned the place around, then sold it."

"Why did your dad—don't lean over the side, Elijah—sell the restaurant if he wanted it?"

I shrug. "It's what he does. He buys struggling restaurants and turns them into gastronomic gold mines."

"Why not help the owner turn it around? Like what's-his-name, the chef on TV."

"Gordon Ramsey? He's good at what he does, but my dad isn't a chef, just a businessman." *Who doesn't care a twig for the people he forces out.* "He buys low, brings in a great chef consultant to rethink the space, then sells for a high profit."

Marleigh's attention is on Elijah not me. I snap my head around to see him disappear over the side.

My heart slams against my ribs. Marleigh leaps to her feet, but before she moves, I dive into the water.

He's already bobbing on the surface, laughing and sputtering. I'm grateful he has on his life jacket.

"That was fun! Can I dive in again?"

My pulse returns to its normal rhythm as I float beside him. "What happened?"

"I saw a big fish swim under the boat an' kinda fell, watchin' him."

On her knees, Marleigh frowns, but her shoulders sag with relief. "This is the reason I insisted you wear a life jacket."

"But I can swim."

"Yes, you're a good swimmer, but if you hit your head, you could be knocked out—like you did when you fell from the monkey bars at school—and if you didn't have a life jacket on, we might not have reached you in time. You could drown."

He doesn't look like he believes her. Then, again, kids think they're immortal. I know I did at his age. Dylan and I thought we could fly if we had capes like Batman. My brother jumped out our second-floor bedroom window—ended up with a broken leg.

"But I had the jacket on. Can we go swimming?"

Marleigh shakes her head. "No. You weren't supposed to get your cast wet. We're going to have to go by the doctor's office to have another one put on. Besides, it's time we get home. I'm on the evening shift at Favorite Pastime."

We lift Elijah back into the boat. He wraps up in a towel, resting in Beauty's lap. Water drips from my hair, my shirt, my shorts, puddling beneath me.

"I'd love to do this again—all three of us, I mean."

Marleigh nods. "We've had fun, haven't we, buddy?"

Elijah nods and closes his eyes, worn out, I guess. He's nothing like the kid Mateo told me about. Then, again, being Beauty's brother, I can't imagine him any other way. Maybe I'll get him his own rod to use next time. Bud Pugh has a small selection at the hobby shop.

Although, I don't have a lot of history to judge by. I need to keep a close watch on him. Any relationship I want with his sister depends on him.

Chapter 11

MARLEIGH

At the kitchen table, I login to my bank and stare at the screen. My heart takes a nosedive viewing my checking account balance, which teeters on the brink of zero. What I earn working for Bud is barely enough for my part of our rent, let alone food. The dollars won't stretch any further. I click on my savings account. The balance there is healthy thanks to Mom. My resolve wavers. I set aside those funds for Elijah's college education. I hate to withdraw anything.

Nola wanders in seeking coffee. "Why such a glum expression?"

I hold out my cup to her. "I need your help, Ms. Financial Advisor."

"Coffee first, advice second." She selects a French roast, makes her coffee, then sets my mug on the Keurig's platform.

"French vanilla, please."

She pops in a pod. "So, what do you need help with?"

"Have you checked my bank account this month?"

"No." She places my coffee on the table. "Is there a problem?"

I sigh. "Not if we don't need anything beyond food for the next couple of weeks."

"I've told you this before." Nola leans against the counter, taking a sip of java. "You're not robbing Elijah's college fund if you borrow some to, one"—she lifts a single finger—"provide him with food, clothing, et cetera, and two"—she lifts a second one—"you can borrow from him to help start the theatre, because his legacy is tied to your dream." She joins me at the table. "When you start drawing a salary as Artistic Director, you can replace what you borrowed long before he graduates from high school."

"I hear you, but it's hard for my heart to be convinced."

"Well, this is one time you'd better let your head rule your heart." She lays a hand over mine. "Marleigh, you're embarking on your life's dream—our dream. I remember as little girls, we played theatre all the time. We even talked about owning one someday."

Nola turns my computer to face her, taps a few keys, then smiles. "There, I've transferred it for you. I moved a couple thousand to checking. No argument. I know without a doubt your mom and aunt would want you to use part of their money to provide for Elijah *now*. They would also be your biggest cheerleaders to launch your dream." She sits back, folds her arms, daring me to reverse the transfer.

"I'm so glad we're besties. I'd hate to have you as an enemy. You're too smart."

Her grin is impudent. "I'm Normally Normal Nola applying logic."

"Which I appreciate."

"I know. What if we set up a recurring transfer for now? I have firm commitments from two investors. Once we incorporate, we'll set up bank accounts. Then, we can start paying you. You won't have to borrow too much."

I rinse my now empty cup in the sink. "This is real. We're doing it? I guess I'd better approach Miss Boo. If we can't buy the farm, I'll ask if we can lease the barn."

Nola hands me her cup to wash. "Tell her I have all the numbers in a proposal, if she wants them."

I walk across the yard to her cottage. At the mayor's back door, I take a deep breath to settle my nerves. This is the turning point. Everything depends on her answer. *Please, Lord?*

"Morning, Marleigh. Come on in." Mr. Herb tucks his newspaper under one arm and holds the screen door open for me. "What can we do for you?"

"Is Miss Boo here? I'd like to talk with both of you."

He raises one eyebrow. "Oh? Well, she is. Come on in." He hollers over his shoulder, "Boo? Marleigh wants to talk with us."

We step into their front room. The antique furniture suits them—right down to Tiffany lamps and hand-crocheted antimacassars on the back of their sofa.

"Morning, sugar." Miss Boo joins us. "How's Elijah's arm?"

"He had to get a new cast yesterday afternoon."

In his chair, Mr. Herb stuffs his newspaper beneath his thigh. "Why?"

I settle on the settee. "He fell overboard when we were fishing."

Miss Boo sits next to me, chuckling. "He's a curious little rascal. He always wants to know how and why everything works."

"He keeps me hopping." I draw a large breath. "I wanted to talk to you both about a dream I have."

She turns sideways to face me. "We're all ears."

I hope I can say this succinctly. Then, again, there's isn't a lot to say. "It's my dream to open a community theatre here in Sugar Springs. I'd like to buy this farm, or at least the barn, and convert it. If you aren't ready to sell, then could I lease the barn?"

Miss Boo stares at me for a second as if she can't believe what I said, then glances at her husband. What's that about?

Mr. Herb's grin is cheeky. "I've never heard you say anything so fast or without a single breath, Marleigh."

Heat rises in my neck. "I know it's a bold request."

Once again, Miss Boo exchanges glances with her husband. When he nods, she turns back to me. "We have thought about selling."

My heart leaps with joy.

"We've reached an age where we want less maintenance. We've talked about renting one of those new apartments in town."

I'm on the edge of the settee, yet strive for a little composure. "If you decide to, when are you thinking of moving?"

Mr. Herb barks a laugh. "Yesterday, if I had my way."

"But, Marleigh, there's something I need to tell you."

I walk back to the farmhouse in a state of shock. As soon as I open the door, I find Nola in the laundry room folding clothes.

I hop up onto the washer. "You are *not* going to believe this."

She hands me a pair of Elijah's jeans. "Oh?"

"Someone else has asked to buy the farm."

"What?" She bends to pick up a towel she dropped. "Who? Better—why?"

"They didn't say, and I didn't ask. I was too surprised."

"Now what? Are we out of consideration?"

"No. She said they're going to think through how they want to move forward."

Nola leans against the wall. "Well, I suppose we'd better get busy incorporating. We may as well."

"What if we don't get to buy the property?"

Like her mother, Nola considers for a moment. "We'll try to get the new owners to lease the barn to us."

"I suppose so, but what if they have different plans?"

Her grin turns wicked. "We'll use all our wiles on the new owners."

I can't help cracking up. I need to laugh. My stomach is still churning. "I guess we ought to settle on a name. Call Willow."

Nola raises her right eyebrow in question. "Willow? Why?"

"She's best at coming up with names for things."

Reception is bad in the laundry room for some reason. In the kitchen, I tap in Willow's speed dial number.

"Hey. What's up?"

"How soon are you coming home? We have a huge task ahead of us." I give her the short version.

"I'll be there in twenty minutes." She clicks off.

I don't know what she's telling her boss, but while we wait for her, Nola and I put away laundry. She helps me by putting a pot of water on to boil, while I start my spaghetti sauce.

"I'll be right back. I want to pull out all my paperwork on the theatre."

I chop onions while Nola fetches her paperwork. After I finish, I blot my eyes with my sleeve, add oil to a hot skillet, then drop in the onions. "Nola," I holler. "Bring your laptop too."

She returns with a fat folder, but her iPad instead of her computer. "The kids are using my laptop to play games. I've turned on parental control."

With the meat browning, I add chopped tomatoes from our garden, along with a pinch of sugar.

"Why are you adding sugar?" Nola's nose wrinkles.

"Gabe told me it cuts the tomatoes' acidity, delivering a more balanced flavor." I pull out two teaspoons, handing one to Nola.

We each taste the sauce. Nola's eyes widen in surprise. "Well, whatta ya know. He's right. This is better than any you've ever made before."

While my sauce simmers, I add the pasta to boiling water. "Willow should be home any minute. Will you slide the bread in the oven?"

When everything is on the table, we call Elijah and Aysha just as Willow walks in the door. After the blessing and plates are filled, we commence eating. For a few minutes, no one speaks. Finally, I tell everyone what the Higginses told me.

"We aren't one-hundred-percent sure we will be able to buy this farm. So, in the meantime, we're going to incorporate."

"Why do you have to cooperate?" Aysha asks.

Nola sounds out the word for her. "It's when we become a legitimate company." She wipes a blob of sauce off her daughter's chin.

Elijah grins around a mouthful of spaghetti. Aysha thinks it's "gucci." She parrots slang like a teenager. Thankfully, none are bad words.

Willow reaches for a piece of garlic bread. "So, where does this leave us?"

Nola lays her iPad, plus a folder of papers, beside her plate. "In need of some names, which is why we asked you to come home."

Elijah frowns. "I came up with Lic'rish's name."

"Yes, you did, and it's a wonderful name. How about you kiddos go watch TV for an hour. Then, if we need help, we'll call you. I'll put on *Hocus Pocus Two*."

They both holler, "Yay!"

"Don't forget bath time after your movie."

After they're settled, Willow and I clean up the kitchen, while Nola begins our paperwork.

"I'll enter our information online later. This saves time if we change our minds about anything." She poises her pencil above her pad. "First, what are we calling the corporation?"

Willow hands me a plate to put in the sink. "I think since our wedding venue and drama troupe will have different names, we need a parent company name with pizazz— something like ..." She scrunches her face, thinking.

Nola and I share an excited glance, waiting in anticipation. After a suspenseful moment, Willow gasps. Her eyes light up. "MaNWEA Arts Corporation!"

What? "Did I hear you right? Man-wee-uh?"

"What does it mean?" Nola asks.

"It's an acronym. Ma is for Marleigh. N is you, Nola."

Now Nola gasps. "Willow, Elijah. Aysha. MaNWEA. It's brilliant, Willow!"

Chuffed, she wiggles with pleasure at the compliment.

I think it's perfect. "I love it. The kids will too. It couldn't fit better."

Nola writes it down. "So, the main corporation is nonprofit. We will do business as what?"

As I dry my hands, I peek over her shoulder, eyeing what she has written thus far. "I've thought of nothing else for a long time. I think Sugar Springs Players is best for the acting troupe. It answers the who, what, and where we are." I hang the dishtowel to dry. "But we need to name the theatre too."

Nola ticks off names on her fingers. "Sugar Springs Theatre. The Barn House Theatre. Curtain Call Theatre."

"Act One." Willow adds." Upstage Theatre. Sugar Springs Spotlight Theatre."

Bullseye! "Spotlight! 'The SS Spotlight.' I love it."

"Me too." Nola writes down our new name. "You nailed it again, Willow. Now, since we're on a roll, what about our wedding venue?" Nola's gaze bounces between Willow and me. "I checked the law. As a nonprofit, we can own a for-profit. The wedding venue should be for profit—we just have to pay taxes on it. So, what should its name be?"

"Hmm ... it has to have a theatre theme." Miming, Willow dons her "thinking cap" again. "Something like onstage weddings or weddings in the spotlight."

I settle next to Nola. "The name should inspire a happy-ever-after or bring to mind an epic love story. I'd suggest *Beauty and the Beast*, but who wants to marry a beast?" Although, that would be a fantastic first musical for us to produce.

Amid chuckles, Willow brings cookies and sweet tea to the table. "What about other fairy tales or heroines from one?"

Not a bad idea. Every bride wants to think of her life as happy-ever-after. I certainly do. My heart skips a beat as I think of Gabe.

"Maybe something about a prince-slash-princess would be better," Willow says as she paces.

An image of Gabe on a white horse pops into my mind. I follow it. He swoops down, lifting me into the saddle in front of him. I sigh as we ride away into a sunset.

"Marleigh? Where are you?" Nola taps my arm.

"Daydreaming. Uh ... about the theatre."

"Sure, you were." She nudges Willow. "Ya think a certain chef was in her daydream?"

My friends know me too well.

Willow, our romantic, stops pacing. She raises her hands, fingers splayed. "I've got it. 'Once Upon a Forever—Wedding Venue.'"

I stare at her, then Nola. She squeals first. "Perfect!"

"The name combines two songs from ..." Willow pauses to see if I'm tracking her.

I can't believe how her mind works so fast to come up with names like this. "*Into the Woods* is so popular, everyone will catch the reference."

Nola makes a note on her iPad. "We did it. Everything is named—our parent company, troupe, theatre, and wedding venue. On Monday, I'll fill out our paperwork to incorporate online." She takes a deep breath. "We've taken our first steps in making our dream come true."

They've made my dream theirs. I don't think anyone in this entire world has better friends. Nola and I get our kids into their beds, then settle on the couch for some TV time.

Willow has a date with Sergio. Things are going so well in their relationship. Maybe she'll choose to get married in the barn too—like Nola's mom. It's going to be a dramatic setting with the ceremony onstage.

"I know what I've forgotten—the cyclorama. What do you think your mom will want for a backdrop for her wedding? I'm sure they don't want the typical baby-through-college-years pics."

Nola laughs. "Yeah—no. I have a perfect photograph. After their ceremony, we'll project something different for the reception. This theatre is going to be a magical place for weddings." Her eyes twinkle. "Maybe even yours."

Chapter 12

MARLEIGH

"Marleigh, can you walk the kids to school?" From the kitchen table, Nola checks her planner app. "I'm taking Mom to shop for her wedding dress. She says she wants a cocktail dress the color of the peonies she chose. I'm taking her to a few of her favorite boutiques. We could be all day."

"No problem. I'm meeting Gabe at Mo' Joe Java for coffee anyway, so I can take them before I meet him."

"Thanks. I owe you one."

The kiddos run into the kitchen, slide into their spots in the banquet, and dive into their breakfast.

"As soon as you finish, we need to move to a groove." I lay a damp cloth on Elijah's head for a couple of minutes while he eats, then remove it, tousling his hair. His curls bounce into obedience.

Aysha watches wide-eyed. "A washcloth makes his hair curl?" Her hair is fire-poker-straight.

"Yes, its dampness helps revive his curls."

"Mama?" Aysha's holler could wake the dead. "Can we put a wet washcloth on my head, so my hair will curl?" Her eyes plead.

"Aysha Hope Winthrop, use your inside voice. I'm right here, for pity sake."

"I'm sorry, Mama. But can we?"

Nola peers at me over her laptop screen. "You started this."

"A washcloth won't, but there are some things we can do to give you curls. We'll go to the beauty supply later, but right now, y'all need to eat. Then, we'll head to school."

As soon as they're ready, we walk past the barn—I send up a quick prayer for favor—to Peachtree Springs Road, then turn right. I love how close their school is—a mere half-block away. I take them to their classroom, offering a quick hello to their teacher, Mrs. Davis.

"You two have a good day. Remember—be careful." I kiss Elijah's cheek, knowing all too soon he won't allow public displays of affection. Aysha is already playing with a doll.

I stroll back to Mo' Joe's. A Ferrari is parked outside. I look up and down the street. Could its owner be the same beast who knocked me over? I'd like to tell him what happened. Remind him, in an agreeable manner of course, to be more careful when he exits a shop.

I step inside, glancing around for Gabe and the beast. I don't see the offender, but Gabe's in a back corner, waving.

"Good morning." He rises pulling out a chair for me. Mr. Rich-and-Rude could learn a lesson from Gabe.

"Thanks." I point to the full cup in front of me. "This mine?"

"I hope I remembered how you take it, but if not, we'll get you another."

I take a sip. French vanilla coffee with heavy cream glides over my tongue. How does he always know what I like? "It's perfect." *Like you.* "What brings you to Sugar Springs at this hour in the morning?"

He cocks his head and frowns. "Didn't I tell you I live here?"

"No. Where?"

"Closer to Lake Lanier, but still within city limits."

"Living on the lake must be a dream come true." Not as gucci—as Aysha would say—as a barn theatre, but close. I take another sip of coffee.

"It's great. Relaxing, although I'm not there enough to enjoy it. But," he pauses and takes a sip of coffee, "if I can accomplish it, I plan to open my own restaurant."

"Wow, me too! Not a restaurant, but a community theatre. I don't know if you saw the barn the night we went to the theatre, but I want to buy and renovate it. I already have a couple of investors."

Gabe doesn't seem to appreciate my dream. He doesn't smile. In fact, he looks like his face is made of stone—void of expression. Did I cut him off? "I'm sorry. I was so excited wanting to share my dream with you."

"It's a nice one, Marleigh. Uh, I have to run." He heads to the door. I blink, confused. What just happened? He didn't even finish his coffee.

I stare at his retreating back. Outside, he stops by the driver's door of the Ferrari. He pulls keys out of his pocket.

He unlocks its door.

Without a backwards glance, he climbs in and zooms off, leaving me gaping.

Gabe is the beast who knocked me over without so much as a backward glance?

"Why didn't you tell me the Ferrari was his car, Willow?"

"First of all, you never saw the guy's face, so how could we know it was Gabe's? There are a lot more Ferraris in Atlanta besides his. You have to understand Gabe's background. His dad is a powerful entrepreneur, who doesn't care who he hurts." Willow opens the kitchen utensil drawer, digging through it.

"What are you looking for?"

"The potato masher."

I open another drawer and remove the desired object. "I moved it. What does Gabe's background have to do with his rudeness?"

She takes the masher from me and attacks her broccoli with zeal. "His dad's MO is to force people out of struggling businesses. He believes results justify the means. Gabe doesn't." She sweeps aside fallen bits of vegetable. "I've seen him change in the years I've known him. The day he almost ran you over, I'll bet he'd had an argument with his dad."

"An argument is no excuse for his behavior."

She looks in her bowl, nods, then drops the masher in the sink. "I'm not excusing him. I'm just asking you to understand and extend some grace." Her challenging stare cuts straight to my heart.

Grace.

She's right. His behavior was not nice, but it wasn't personal. He didn't know me. It's not like he planned to knock me over. Plus, he hasn't exhibited anything since. "I know you're right. Please, tell me more about him."

"Mr. Sadler pushed Gabe into culinary school, but Gabe found he had a real talent for cooking. He excelled." She adds cheese to the broccoli. "His father wanted him to be on the inside of the business. You know how we hear scuttlebutt about any theatres in trouble? Well, he hears about restaurants. Then, his dad swoops in, forces out the owner or buys him out for pennies on the dollar."

"He told me a little about them buying out restaurants, but nothing about forcing people out of business. This sounds like a different family altogether."

Willow turns on the burner beneath a skillet. "I know. He's balked at following his dad's practices. They butt heads all the time."

"I'm glad you talked me off the ledge. There's still one thing left unanswered. Why Gabe left so fast after I told him about our dream of turning the barn into a theatre."

"What do you mean?"

"He told me he had a dream of starting his own restaurant. When I jumped in, telling him about my dream, he clammed up. His expression turned Mount Rushmore hard. He said he had to leave. I wanted to follow him, but all other thoughts fled when he climbed into the Ferrari."

Willow scoops up some fritter mixture and drops the batter in hot oil. "You know how guys are. They want the spotlight all the time."

"You mean I hurt his feelings? Is Gabe that sensitive?"

Willow gives me a look that says I'm an airhead. "*All* men get their feelings hurt, but are too macho to admit it."

"I guess I owe him an apology. I swanny, I feel like such a dweeb."

"You'll both get over it. Once he stews for a while, he'll realize you didn't mean to steal his thunder."

"I guess." I sniff a wonderful aroma wafting from her frying pan. "Those smell delish."

"They are. Just wait."

I set the table while she finishes cooking. I waffle from wanting to call Gabe right now to tell him how sorry I am to not wanting to relive the moment.

My phone rings, startling me. I drop a fork on the floor. Grabbing up my phone, I'm disappointed to see it isn't Gabe, but Miss Boo.

"Hey. What can I do for you?"

"Can you come to City Hall around seven o'clock? After the council meeting, I'm going to announce a competition for the purchase of our farm. This will be an opportunity for you to meet the other interested parties."

"Of course." *Meet our competitors?* "We'll be there."

I tap the off button and turn to the girls. "Miss Boo just asked the oddest thing. She wants us to come to the city council meeting tonight after supper. She's launching some kind of contest to see who buys their property. Under normal circumstances, competitors bid, but never meet. This is so strange. Can you both come?"

Willow shakes her head. "I have a date with Sergio tonight, so I can't go with you." She disappears up the stairs.

"What about you?"

Nola shakes her head. "I want to, but I have two clients whose fiscal year-end is this month. I need to work on their financial statements. I'm working here, so I'll be with the kids at least. When you get home, you can tell me what happened. Did she say other parties—as in plural?"

"She did. I thought there was only one other."

"I've been under the same impression. My curiosity is piqued. If I can have two hours uninterrupted, then I can go with you. We'll call my mom to sit with the kids."

Willow returns to the kitchen. "I heard you talking. Why don't I take the kids with me tonight? Sergio adores them. Since we hadn't decided on where we'd go anyway, we can take them someplace fun."

"Thank you. I'll take them to work with me this afternoon. Mr. Bud loves their help. They love to sweep his storeroom."

"Perfect. This way, I can get my work done *and* go with you tonight, Marleigh. Thanks, Willow."

Halfway up the stairs again, her voice floats down. "Anytime."

I call the hobby shop and tell Mr. Bud I'm bringing the littles, so he'll have something more than sweeping for them to do. I call the kids in from the barn, and when I tell them they're going to work with me, they both let out a whoop. A few minutes later, we leave for my last afternoon working at Favorite Pastime. After this, I'm unemployed. We have to get the barn. Somehow, we just have to.

Once the kids are settled in the storeroom, Mr. Bud takes my elbow, moving me to the front of the store.

"After Elijah fell overboard, did you decide he can't go fishing anymore?"

What? "No, why?" I glance over my shoulder toward the storeroom. I don't want Elijah hearing anything he shouldn't.

Mr. Bud scrubs his chin whiskers with two fingers. "Huh. Gabe was in this afternoon to return the child's fishing rod he bought. I assumed the purchase was for Elijah, so I asked him why he was returning it."

How odd. Gabe knew Elijah had a great time.

"What did he say?"

"He said he didn't think they'd be fishing together anymore."

This gets more bizarre by the minute. "Did you ask him anything else?"

"No. I had the distinct feeling he wasn't in the mood to talk."

Chapter 13

MARLEIGH

Nola rolls a pizza cutter over a cheese pie. "Are you as nervous about tonight as I am?"

"I'm not sure I can even eat. So much rests on the outcome." I take a tentative bite of pizza.

"What do you suppose Miss Boo has up her sleeve?"

I swallow. So far, my stomach doesn't hate it. "I've run a lot of different possibilities through my mind, but I reject each of them."

"Same here." Nola lifts another slice onto her plate. "I can't believe she'd hold a bidding war in person and at the council meeting. It's not like her at all."

"Do you suppose Walter might have some insight on this? He has to have run across situations like this in his career."

"Great idea! I'll call right now. We don't have much time." Nola taps his number into her iPhone. "Hey, Walter."

While she explains, I finish my slice of pizza. I debate another, but decide I can't manage it. Then, Nola puts Walter on the speaker phone. "Go ahead. Tell us what you think."

"Okay. You have to understand Boo and Herb Higgins are no country bumpkins, in spite of farming. They are both savvy business people. Keep in mind they love Sugar Springs. Boo's grandparents were the ones who campaigned to have Sugar Springs incorporate back in 1926."

Nola glances at me. "So, you're saying this is personal somehow?"

"No. Well, yes, but they have a vested interest in the town. With Boo being mayor, she wants to leave an impactful legacy when she retires, honoring her ancestors."

I lean closer to Nola's phone. "Does this give you any idea what she might have in mind?"

Walter sighs. "One—you can bet whatever she does will benefit Sugar Springs. I wish I knew more for you girls."

"Thanks, Walter. At least you have us thinking a little more clearly." Nola taps off. "So, we can't do anything except go to the meeting and wait to hear what she has to say."

"It's almost time to walk over there. Are you going in those?" I point at Nola's fashionable ripped jeans. They're cute, but not the right image for tonight.

"No, I'm going to wear a suit. You need your flowered skirt. The outfit speaks to your artistic nature."

Flowing midi-skirts are my favorite summer attire. They're cooler than jeans. I change, freshen my makeup, then we walk to City Hall.

The moment we open the front door, voices swell and recede from the council chambers. When we enter, the mayor acknowledges us with a wink, then nods toward the front row on one side of the room.

I take Nola's elbow, steering her toward the right side. "I think she wants us to sit over here."

In an attempt to see if I can figure out who our competition is, I slip the scarf off my neck, twisting to drape it on the back of my chair. I don't see a single person I don't know. Maybe they'll enter later.

"Do you spot our competition?"

Keeping one eye on Miss Boo, I settle myself. "No."

A moment later, she opens the meeting. The council goes through a few mundane business items. Discussion is short. Voting is quick. A proposal for a few amphitheater renovations is brought by a council member. The city manager argues against it. They table it until next month.

Like she did to us, the mayor winks at someone, nods, then she raises an eyebrow to Nola and me. Without turning my head, I peek sidelong.

My blood turns cold.

I don't believe my eyes. I can't breathe. Nola clutches my hand as Gabe takes a seat in our row. Stone-faced, he aims a sharp nod in our direction.

I snap my gaze straight forward, crossing my arms over my stomach. I try to take modulated breaths. I'd rather flee, but I'm frozen, my legs refusing to move.

He used me. All his attention has been for this—to steal my dream.

Worse, he used Elijah. Hot angry tears threaten, but I refuse them.

Miss Boo rises. "Tonight, I have a proposal, which goes along with Marc's request to renovate the amphitheater." She glances at Gabe, then us. "Herb and I have decided it's time to retire from our farm. We're selling the property, but we have three interested parties."

Nola whispers, "I never saw a third person sit in our row."

I shake my head, opening my mouth, but nothing comes out.

She squeezes my hand.

"To that end, we talked all night. We want to do something to benefit Sugar Springs, and this is what we came up with—a contest. Each interested party will propose a campaign to bring business back to downtown." She nods to Councilman Cohen. "This is where the contest benefits your amphitheater proposal. It can also help pay for it. Since Highway 20 expanded to four lanes, people drive past us instead of through town. This council will vote on your proposals. The winner will be the one to buy our farm. You will turn in your proposals to the council at our work session in three weeks. We will announce the winner at next month's Council meeting."

The city clerk moves to end the proceedings. It's seconded and approved.

It's over.

I leap to my feet fleeing the chamber as fast as possible without drawing attention. I don't look back to see what the betrayer did.

Beside me, Nola's strides eat up the sidewalk. Her face is dark red, her lips a thin line. I've never seen her so angry. Neither of us speak until we are inside the farmhouse.

Tossing her handbag in her mudroom cubby as she stomps through to the kitchen, she rants. "I can't believe it. Wait until we tell Willow about her *buddy*." Nola fills the tea kettle. "Are you okay?"

Am I? No. A longs sigh drags out of me. "I'll survive this, I suppose, but it's going to be a fight to the death." *Death of a dream*. I pound my fist on the counter. "I hate him. How could he do this to me? To Elijah? He used my sweet boy." I drop into a chair and bury my head in my arms, struggling not to give in to tears.

"I can't believe how unfeeling he is." Her hand massages my neck. "He's not worth crying over."

"Tell my broken heart." But she's right. Crying can wait until later. The heat of my anger dries my eyes in a heartbeat. "He was everything I ever wanted in a guy. Except he was a fake. Everything was a lie. He's worse than Willow's former drug dealer boyfriend."

Nola brings our tea to the table. "When Willow gets home, we'll plan the best campaign this town has ever seen. We *will* win."

I may have let him steal my heart and spit on it, but I won't allow him to steal my dream or Elijah's future. "I have an idea."

Nola snatches her laptop from the desk. "I'm all ears."

I jump up from the table. "What do you think of an arts festival?"

"Go on, tell me more." Nola hooks one arm around her chair's ladder back, watching me pace.

Fueled by anger, I can't sit still, so I pick up my tea. "Besides paintings, what about photography? Plus, we could include a battle-of-the-bands and a theatrical production."

"I like it. What about the restaurants having tasting booths?" Nola adds. She types in our ideas.

"Books. We'll invite local authors to have tables to sell their books."

Willow, Sergio, and the kids burst in the back door. "Hey! How did the Council meeting go?" she asks.

I shake my head. "Let us get the kids to bed first. Sergio, please stay. You need to hear this."

Willow gapes. "Whoa. What happened?"

"In a minute." Nola takes Aysha's hand, then mouths "little ears" to Willow. I grab Elijah's, ushering him to his room.

A few minutes later, we're back around the table. I'm not sure where to begin. "The first thing you need to know is Gabe is our competition for the farm."

"He used Marleigh." Nola's spoon clinks against her cup, tea splashing onto the table. "And he used all of us."

Willow exchanges a glance with Sergio. "I have a hard time believing this. I never would have thought Gabe capable of this."

"Well, it's true. He did." I take a deep breath. "And now we are in a fight for our dream. The mayor announced it's a contest. We have to come up with the best idea to bring business back to downtown. Nola and I have the idea of an arts festival. What do you think?"

Willow's enthusiastic nature takes over. "I love it. It's brilliant. What do you have down already?"

Nola reads back what we have listed. Willow fingers her necklace. "What about craft artisans? We can charge for the booths too."

"Good idea."

"Clothing." Nola taps her keyboard. "Boutiques can sell their wares."

"Don't forget hobbies." I point at Nola's screen. "Mr. Bud will want a booth."

"Hey, what if we add a farm-to-table restaurant on the farm?" Willow interjects. "Then, we could do dinner theatres. I know the perfect chef who … who … oh." She winces. "I forgot."

"No, I could never trust him. Ever again."

She wilts. "I'd like to strangle him."

Sergio puts his arm around her. "Someday, maybe. But what do you ladies think about asking service organizations? Kids' clubs, scouting, soccer, etc.?"

He has a good mind. "Those are wonderful ideas."

"Everything you have mentioned works." He jots a note on his phone. "However, to have full impact on downtown and bring business back, the festival can't be one weekend alone. To maximize our efforts, we need to propose every weekend all summer long."

Our? "Are you in this with us, Sergio?"

"You bet I am." He takes Willow's hand. "Not only am I with you, but Willow and I will do some reconnaissance to find out what Gabe has planned. Who is the third party? Do we know anything about them?"

I shake my head. "The mayor didn't say." I glance at Nola. "Did you see anyone new at the meeting?"

"No. So, maybe you two can discover who is this alleged third party. I'll get this all laid out in a workable spreadsheet. I need names and their art category. Then, we will start an invitation list."

"And marketing ideas." Sergio moves his gaze to Willow. "Social media, postcards, the stuff you're good at. And, if the city will go for it, a billboard at the closest major crossroads."

She nods. "Okay, we'll do the spying plus marketing."

My anger has been put aside by my friends, but as the evening ends, sorrow for what could have been takes its place. Once I'm alone in bed, my tears flow. My heart is broken.

"Father, am I losing my dream as well as the man I love?"

GABE

Following the mayor's gestured request, I slip into the front row. I stumble when I see Marleigh and Nola. I don't think I even entertained the thought they would be here. Why I didn't think they would, I don't know. Owning the property is Beauty's dream too. I nod at them as I find my seat.

By the time it's over, I'm so low I'd have to look up to see the sole of my shoe. People begin to mingle. I reach out as Marleigh speeds past me, but all I catch is air. Nola glares at me as she follows Beauty. I hope they don't think I orchestrated this.

A crowd surrounds Miss Boo, so even if I want to ask her a question, I can't get to her. I've never felt so alone. With leaden feet, I leave.

How could something as wonderful as two people with a dream of starting their own business turn into this? I suppose Miss Boo had no idea Marleigh and I have been dating. If she had, I'm sure she never would have pitted us against each other—at least not in public.

I was upset when Marleigh first told me about wanting the farm for her theatre. Now, I feel like a louse for my knee-jerk reaction. I should have taken time to talk it out. Maybe we could have reached a solution. Something workable for both of us.

If I could, I'd kick myself. Instead, I punch the elevator's parking level button a little too hard. Great—it sticks. I wiggle it in hopes of its release. No luck. The call light doesn't turn on, either. I lean my forehead against the wall. Frustration gets me nowhere. Sighing, I take two flights of stairs down to my car.

And then, there's that third party. I hadn't heard anything about another being interested—let alone a name. Does Beauty know? Talk about irony. I can't call to ask her. She'll tell Willow for sure. I doubt she'll speak to me ever again, either. Or Sergio. Why is a dream I never sought—but embraced—causing so much grief? *Way to go, Sadler.*

I step off the final stair tread. What about this campaign? What am I going to propose? I climb into my car and start the engine. What would bring me to a downtown area?

Restaurants.

Not a bad idea. Maybe we can hold a street tasting to show what type restaurants are available in downtown. I can enlist other chefs. We all know competition is good for business.

Except when I'm competing with Marleigh.

With the engine purring, I drive home, but once in my driveway, I don't click the remote to open my garage. Instead, I sit looking at the lake, which is beautiful even with a mere crescent moon reflecting on the water. But to me, a cottage looking over a healthy farm is far better.

I need to sell this showplace. Dad's the one who talked me into buying this house to project an image like the Ferrari does—which Dylan bought.

Always project an image of success.

Somehow, his idea of success isn't mine. I gaze at the Ferrari's instrument panel. It's fine for someone else, but to me it's pretentious. An SUV would suit me—*Chef Gabe*—a lot better.

I go inside, turn on my PC, and check the value of my house. Wow. Dad was right about the investment, anyway. It's tripled since I bought it. This would buy the mayor's land without a loan.

So why am I not excited?

I feel like my heart is being ripped in two.

How could God have let us both have a dream tied to the mayor's property?

What a debacle. Marleigh's dream or mine—only one of us can win.

What if neither of us do?

Chapter 14

GABE

Chirping pops my eyes open. Still dark out, so why are the birds awake? They quiet, so I close my eyes. Then, their incessant chirps start again. A groan rumbles in my throat. Not birds.

Who calls at four-thirty-five in the morning? I roll over and peer at my phone. Dylan. Just what I need after a night of no sleep. He won't leave me alone until I answer.

"Talk."

He ignores the gravel in my voice. Doesn't even stop to think he woke me.

"What were you doing at the meeting last night?" Dylan's voice is rife with animosity.

He was there? "The city council meeting? Why shouldn't I be there? Why were *you* there?"

"I wasn't. I sent Tinley. But you didn't answer my question. Are you interested in the mayor's land?"

The hairs on the back of my neck rise in high alert. *Keep your cards close to your vest*—one philosophy of my dad's I use. So, I parry with a question of my own. "Why would I be interested in her land?"

"I don't know, but if you are, forget it. I want their property. I'm planning to build a strip mall, anchored by a specialty market. The grocery in this town is a sorry excuse."

He thinks any deal is done because he wants it. His idea doesn't meet the mayor's specifications. Besides, other than apartment residents, a strip mall won't draw in new customers. What is he thinking?

To put Three Marketeers out of business.

Of course. He's so focused on his forest that he doesn't see the trees' needs.

"Look *little brother*, I'm telling you, if you're thinking you can win this, think again." His harangue marches on. "I want their land. Don't forget, I can outspend you."

Ignoring his emphasis on "little brother," I rub my tired eyes, downright annoyed. "What does Dad have to say about it?"

"He and Mom are leaving on a cruise next week. He's grown soft in his old age. I've talked him into retiring."

Talked? Forced is more Dylan's MO. Maybe I should give our old man a call.

Dylan plows on not expecting an answer. "Anyway, do as I say. Back away from this contest. Find something else to play with and let me handle this. I'll squash the girl, then bring you in with me. We can go on like before but move beyond restaurants. Grow our empire. I'll see you in the office next week." He clicked off.

As usual, my brother expects everyone to acquiesce to his way without question.

When he says, "Jump," everyone else says, "How high?"

Not this time. Not anymore.

Sleep is impossible now. Hoping a hot shower will revive me, I pad into the bathroom, catching sight of my sorry self in the mirror. I stop and study Dylan's "little brother."

I don't like what I see. I hate who I'm becoming. *Never look back. The end justifies the means.* My brother learned from the best—Dad.

The problem is I adopted their methodology too, displaying it without conscious realization the day I first saw Marleigh. Okay, I didn't know it was her, but I was a first-class jerk so focused on my agenda that I didn't realize I'd knocked over someone—let alone a woman.

I lean forward, my hands on the sink for support. *Lord, I hate the me I've become.* At least I have one thing for which I can thank my brother. He's taken Dad's philosophy too far, opening my eyes. I'm done. My decision also confirms another one I made last night after wrestling with God. *Thank you, Father.*

Liberated, I rub my hands together. I'm ravenous. A hearty breakfast is in order after a shower.

Twenty minutes later, I plate my breakfast, and take it outside, snatching my iPad from the desk on my way.

On the deck, a light breeze cools the air. I take a bite of my omelet, which would have been better with bacon or ham, but I didn't have any. My view is sparkling water. A skier races behind a boat, jumping its wake.

The day promises to be a hot one. I'll take advantage of the dock and go for a swim later. There won't be many more days to swim here.

How many times have I gone swimming here since I've owned this place? A half dozen at most. I could dive in from any access point. People here have an open beach policy with neighbors—even past ones.

After I finish my breakfast, I set the plate beside my chair, then open my iPad. I search for a familiar realty website, then research properties in downtown Sugar Springs to be sure I'm up to speed on rents.

Ready to pull this trigger, I check my phone's contacts for Jody Davis's number. He's a good realtor, who I trust to be discreet.

"Hey, Jody. Gabe Sadler. It's time to sell this lake house. When can you get it listed?"

"I can have my photographer come today. Will you be there?"

The quicker the better. "Yeah, I'm off today."

After we agree on a selling price, he asks, "Do I need to find you something closer to Wild Azalea?"

"No." A vision of the farm cottage occupies my mind's eye. "I'm thinking of a townhouse or apartment in downtown Sugar Springs. But there's another option I want to explore. You have to promise me it's between us, okay? My name stays out of it."

"I'm intrigued. Tell me more."

MARLEIGH

After crying half the night, I fell asleep somewhere around four this morning. It's now six-thirty.

"Are you sick, Marma?" Elijah kneels on my bed.

If a broken heart is an ailment, then, yes. "No, sugar. I just couldn't sleep." I don't open my eyes.

Little fingers pry gently at one eyelid. "Have you been crying? 'Cause my eyes look like yours when I cry. Are you sad?"

I move his hand and open both eyes. "Kind of, but I'll be all right." I hug him, then sit up. "Hand me my robe. I'll get your breakfast."

With swollen, bloodshot eyes, I stumble into the kitchen for coffee.

Nola glances up. "Good grief. Let me get you some eyedrops." She opens a cupboard. "Why don't you go back to bed? I can get the kids off to school."

The Keurig gurgles to life. "I'll be fine. I have to keep my mind occupied."

"Yeah, I get it. After Steve died, if I wasn't busy, I'd fixate on his last moments and be a basket case. I think women whose marriages die or have their heart broken grieve too."

She's right, but we don't have the closure of a funeral.

As soon as my cup is full, I add cream, blowing on the surface so I won't scald my throat. When it's cool enough, I down the entire cup, then pop in another pod for a second one—this one medium roast. I need lots of caffeine this morning.

"I want to get started on our proposal. If we can convince everyone in town to get excited about our ideas, we'll have a leg up on our competition." I sip on my second cup, eyeing my laptop on the counter. "Like you, I need to see details down in a workable document, so I can gain perspective of what needs to be done."

"I'll email you what I worked on last night."

By the time I finish my second cup, Nola's email dings in my laptop. While she pours cereal for the kids, I enter our ideas into yet another spreadsheet.

Across its top, I key in categories, then beneath those, I insert shops and artists' names. My next column will be for notes on what enthuses each artist.

Like Willow. She's the poster image of a blonde airhead, fooling people with her artistic ways. But if I want to grab her attention, I show her a spreadsheet. Willow is all about order. Her closet is even organized by season and color.

I need help if I want to apply similar logic to each person we approach. Fortunately, I know where to get it. Bud Pugh. He knows everyone, even newcomers. He's the most non-threatening, endearing man whose ability to disarm people at their first meeting is legendary.

"Nola, while you take the kids to school, I'm going to Mr. Bud's. I have a lot of brain-picking to do."

"Bye, Marma." Elijah stands by my side, ready for a kiss. "I'm glad you're happy now."

I pull him into my arms. "I love you. Have a great day at school."

"Love you more. You have a great day too." He points to my notes. "Whatcha workin' on?"

"My strategy to win this contest so I can buy Miss Boo's farm."

His grin spreads from ear to ear. "I believe in you."

What would I do without my little man? My hero and his sidekick run out the door, as Nola follows with a holler, "Wait up, you two."

Before I shower, I call Favorite Pastime to be sure Mr. Bud is okay with me coming over to chat. After I end the call, I step into a nice, hot shower.

With water cascading over me, a vision rises of Gabe and Elijah dripping from my boy's tumble into Lake Lanier. Tears for what might have been mingle with the drops from my shower.

Focus, Marleigh, focus.

I shake my head to clear the image. In my room, I pull on my favorite jeans, a nod to the seventies with embroidered flowers down the outside of one leg. I add a top in deep rose, a pair of navy espadrilles, topping off my outfit with my favorite gold hoop earrings.

Five minutes later, I'm pushing open the door at Favorite Pastime. "Good morning, Mr. Bud."

"Ah, the sun begins to shine." He motions me to his office.

I wave at Ed who's waiting on a woman. He acknowledges me without taking his attention from his customer.

"My grandson is working out so well, I can leave him alone. He's taken possession of the store. It's what I'd hoped for."

I pray we all get what we hope for. "How gratifying."

"You're not here to jaw about Eddie. What can I do for you?"

"Your expertise on all the people in Sugar Springs."

"All?"

"Well, mainly merchants and artisans." I explain my strategy for our proposal, then open my laptop to show him the spreadsheet. "I need your discretion on this, Mr. Bud."

He winks. "One hundred percent. I won't breathe a word."

"Thank you. So, let's start with Albano's. What would cause Vince to want to partner with us?"

He scratches the back of his ear, then scrubs his chin whiskers. After a moment, his eyes light up. "Free marketing. He loves promotion but hates to pay for it. Vince Albano is tighter than Willie Nelson's head band."

I type 'free marketing' in the comment column next to Vince Albano's name. "The town has a marketing budget we should be able to use. Selling tables to outside vendors will also go to the ad fund."

"Right, but we don't need to tell Vince." Mr. Bud chuckles. "Let him think he's receiving a bonus."

He draws his chair a little closer, squinting at my screen. "So, who's next?"

"Let's go down Main Street from Albano's, then back up the other side. Next is Play It Again."

"Right. Owned by sweet Zully Grayson. She and Rina Tanaka from the art gallery are fast friends."

I add this tidbit of information in both ladies' columns. "So, what would bring them to our side?"

"They'll be onboard if you can convince them that it will benefit Sugar Springs. The more money our merchants earn, the more those ladies can give away."

"How do you mean?"

"You should see them in action." He slaps his knee. "After Snowmageddon, those two formed Helping Hands Ministry. They managed to finagle every plow in the area to deliver the groceries they'd convinced the stores to donate."

"I remember Snowmageddon, but I never heard about their ministry." I was all of sixteen. I thought the storm was a lark. No school. Cardboard sledding. Guilt pricks my soul. "I had no idea people needed help."

"Don't feel bad, Marleigh. Most of us didn't. But those gals have God's ear. He tells them who needs their assistance."

"We skipped over the ice cream store. What about Izzy Foster?"

Mr. Bud sucks in his lower lip and shakes his head. "Izzy's a piece of work. Ya never know what side she'll fall on in any given situation. She's as inclined to vote down something beneficial to them as she is to champion it. Cantankerous woman."

I put a question mark beside her store. Then, Bud points to the apartment leasing office. "If Yolonda Gates thinks anything might keep a potential renter from her office, she'll nix it. She's also a glass-half-empty kind. So, she might take a negative view of the festival."

"Instead of seeing the benefits of drawing people into downtown? Once they see the apartments, they might want to live here."

"True, but she could view the extra traffic as inconvenient."

I sigh. There are a few apparent naysayers. However, if the others see the potential in our ideas, we have a good chance. "Where do you think Frankie James stands?"

"The more hair he can cut the better. He'll buy in."

"Great." As we continue through the town shops, I realize more than ever what an asset Mr. Bud is to me and Sugar Springs. I shop downtown, but I've neglected to get to know people better—to hear their stories. I'll use the time we spend canvasing to learn more about them.

I type in all the information Mr. Bud passes on to me. This will take some critical thinking on a few people, but I'm beginning to feel like this is possible. After all, what could go wrong?

Chapter 15

GABE

I thump a last throw pillow in its middle like my mom showed me when I would help her straighten up the living room. Good timing too. The doorbell rings.

A ginger-haired woman stands on my porch with her back to me, her camera whirring and clicking. The photographer. Strands of gray hair mingle with red. Must be middle-aged. Her curls bounce against her shoulders as she faces me. A smooth, unlined face negates my guess. Huh.

"Hello, you must be Gabe Sadler." She glances at a small note in her hand. "Jody Davis sent me to photograph your home. I'm Ginger Wells. I must say this setting is spectacular. Your yard is well-maintained. You'd be surprised what I see in my line of work. Some houses don't have an iota of curb appeal, but yours? Jody won't have any trouble selling this place."

Wow. I'm guessing she's not Southern by birth. She speaks faster than the speed of light. I have trouble following her. "Please come in."

She snaps a couple more shots of my front yard and one of the porch, then follows me into the foyer. She gasps. "Your view," she takes several photos, "must grab everyone's attention when they first come in."

"Yes, it does."

She stares at me like I'm from outer space. "I can't imagine leaving this place."

"I'm not here enough to enjoy it. Let me show you around, so you can see what you want to photograph."

"Thanks. Let's start on your deck." She follows me outside, her camera capturing everything as she walks. "This is amazing. Is the dock yours?" Her camera whirs and clicks.

"Yes, it comes with the property."

"What about the deck furniture?" She lowers her camera.

I debate a moment, while I survey the modern decor I inherited when I bought this place. If I rent, I won't need it. If I end up on the farm, I'll buy new things better suited to a farmhouse. "Sure."

We go inside after she has several shots from different angles. Each room gets photographed from several vantage points. "To show the spaces off to their best advantage."

No wonder Jody uses her. She's thorough. After several minutes, she offers her hand.

"I have enough inside for Jody to pick through. I'll take more outside, but I don't need you for those. I enjoyed meeting you. This is a great place."

I've seen her work in Jody's office, so my decision is easy as I shake her hand. "Thank you. Do you have a card? I may need to hire you in the near future. I'm planning to start a business."

She digs one out of her pocket. "Wonderful. Here you go."

After we finish our conversation, Ginger moves to finish her work. Standing by the French doors, I catch a glimpse of her walking around the side of the house. She hikes to the lake, turns, photographing the back of the house. With her photos, Jody will have the house sold before I have a new place to live. I'd better get to work.

When Ginger leaves, I enter my home office. I want to get my proposal ready. This morning, I had a revelation for a new twist on my original idea. I work through lunch. By four o'clock, I have my financials on paper. Now to gather some graphics and photos. I pull out Ginger's card. Would she have any photos I could use?

I give her a call. "This is Gabe Sadler. You photographed my house this afternoon for Jody Davis."

"Yes, Mr. Sadler. What can I do for you?"

"Please, call me Gabe. I'm planning to open a restaurant. I've created a proposal to present to investors." I'm not about to tell who. She's a nice lady, but I don't know her well. "This may be a little presumptuous, but do you have any photos I could buy?"

"I sure do."

I give her the details of the look I want.

"I can visualize it. I've photographed a couple of places you might like. They aren't here in Georgia, but the interiors should work. I'll send a few watermarked samples. Once you choose what you want, I'll send you prices, an invoice, and a release form, along with the actual files."

"Thank you, Ginger."

Several minutes later, my email dings. I open her photos. Perfect. I reply with which shots I want to use. Her invoice is a bit pricey, but the images are worth it. I click on the link and pay.

Within a few minutes, I have everything. I insert the photos into my proposal, take a deep breath, as I tap 'print.'

My dream appears before my eyes. I pray for God's favor for this to become a reality.

I print a few more copies before I fix my supper. The next item on my agenda is to keep a close eye on my brother. I need to find out how he plans to solicit support for his campaign.

MARLEIGH

Over the past two days, we told the kiddos about our festival idea to win the contest. Aysha said it's gucci. Elijah declared we'll win "hands up." I made appointments for Nola and me to see each merchant, eating up half our time, but it's worth it. We've chosen the least busy part of the day, and with the kids in school, it's time to go.

"Nola?" I call upstairs. "Let's get going. I have our list of people to visit."

She hops onto the banister, sliding down, landing on her feet, laughing. "Don't tell Aysha I broke a rule."

"I won't. Are you as excited as I am about today?"

"Do monkeys like bananas?" She digs into the tote on her shoulder, pulling out a rubber banded stash of what look like brochures. "I made these last night. They contain proposed financial benefits, including remedies for any possible problems—like parking and traffic. We'll show as well as talk about our campaign. Hit two of the senses."

I look one over, admiring the colors and graphics she's added. "These are perfect. We need to get them printed to give out to more than just the merchants. They should go to hotels. Hey, what about real estate brokers?"

"Already working on it. Once we win this campaign, I'll add every business included in the festival."

I love her confidence. I link arms with my enthusiastic bestie. "You know, I believe we're going to see this happen."

In a few minutes, we arrive at the Italian restaurant, Albano's. The door is locked. I knock on the glass.

"I called Vince, and he told me ten o'clock. Where do you suppose he is?" I cup my hands around my eyes, peering through the window. "Oh, here he comes."

He unlocks his door, ushering us inside, where we're plunged into old world Venice. Wall murals painted with arched openings, depicting canals complete with gondoliers. All the tables are covered with the requisite crisp red-and-white checkered tablecloths. I don't detect the aroma of cooking food, though. Too early, I guess.

He locks the door again. "I don' wanna no customers in this early. Let's go inna my office."

Customers love Vince's thick accent. I doubt he's ever tried to lose it even though he's been here twenty-two years. Once we settle in the space he uses for an office, Nola hands him a brochure.

"I'm sure you've noticed a reduction in new customers since the highway expanded."

His mouth puckers like he sucked a lemon. "The city told us thousands of cars will passa by each day. But do they come to my ristorante? No. They *passa by*."

Nola's smile grows. "We have a plan to bring them to your place." Pointing out the various items listed in her brochure, she explains the festival will draw people to downtown.

"What about parking? I no see enough parking."

"There's plenty. Statistics show we can expect around ten percent of those passersby. Besides the parking we have within downtown, we've arranged for shuttles from the church lot across the highway, and since it's weekends, the school grounds are available."

"Hmm." He narrows his eyes. "I likka you ideas, but how you going to advertise? I no wanna pay."

Like a well-practiced tennis doubles team, Nola picks up the ball. "And you don't have to. Since this will benefit all of Sugar Springs, the city has a marketing budget we will be able to tap into. Plus, we will get a lot of free promotion through people talking on social media."

A big grin splits Vince's face. "Then, counta me in."

Our first "yes." I want to jump for joy. I restrain myself, while Nola discusses a few ideas.

"Didn't I hear when you first arrived in America, you had a food cart in New York?"

He startles, but looks impressed. "How you hear?"

Nola gestures to me.

"Bud Pugh told me. We thought you might have fun replicating the cart to use outside for the festival. Street food is big with people who don't want to miss any activities but need to eat. Once they sample your food, they'll want to come back for a full meal inside."

He rubs his hands together. "I likka you plan. I know what I'ma gonna sell. Thanka you, ladies."

As soon as the front door closes, Nola high-fives me. Next on the list is Play It Again. Buoyed by Vince's response, I start toward Zully's store, when Nola pulls me back.

"If we split up, we'd get through this faster."

I shake my head. "You are much better than I am at explaining what we're doing—how the festival will benefit them. Everyone knows you're a CPA. I'm just artistic."

"Don't sell yourself short, Marleigh. You have good business sense."

"You and I know, but people think of theatre types as airheads. I can bring fun to a festival, but when people think of you, they think of money."

She sighs. "Okay, but one of these days, you'll get some confidence in your other abilities—like parenting. You've taught me a thing or two."

Huh. I thought Nola had parenting down pat. I guess we all have warped images of ourselves.

Inside Play It Again, Zully is with a customer, so we browse—Nola for her wardrobe, me for costume ideas.

Five minutes later, Zully approaches us. "Can I help you with anything before we go to my office?"

I return a caftan to the rack. "We can look later." We follow her to the rear of the store, where we settle into a small space, nothing more than a desk with a pile of boxes for privacy. Clothing racks line one side. Our chairs are side by side with little room between us.

Nola pulls out one of the brochures, handing it to her. "We believe this festival will bring folks from around north Georgia to downtown again."

Zully's eyebrows dip. "I was against the highway expansion from the start. I knew a wider road would bring trouble."

She catches me by surprise. I thought all the merchants had been for it. "A summer of festival weekends offers a destination for families. We've planned activities and interests for all ages to bring them back into Sugar Springs."

She sits back, crossing her arms. "At least fifty-thousand vehicles pass us every single day on the highway. If even ten percent of those drive through town, can you see the ensuing traffic jam?"

Nola turns the brochure toward Zully. "We propose to divert traffic around Main Street to the school and other town parking lots." Nola points out the shuttle service we propose.

Zully peers at each of us for a moment. "Why are you doing this?"

The question takes me aback. "Were you at last Monday's City Council meeting?"

Her dangling earrings dance when she shakes her head. "I wasn't."

"The mayor is going to sell their property," Nola explains. "We want to buy the farm, turning the barn into a community theatre."

Zully's eyes light up. "Ooh, I love to go to plays."

"But there are others who want the land." I lean forward. "So, the mayor came up with this contest to benefit the town."

"I'm confused," Zully points at the brochure. "This is a contest?"

"Yes." Nola nods. "To see who will create the best proposal to bring traffic back through Sugar Springs, thus profiting everyone."

"Who else wants their land?" Zully's frown is still in place. I'm not sure she understands.

"There are two others, but our theatre will serve the community through entertainment or participation. The other plans serve themselves more."

"Well," Zully folds her hands on her desk. "To be honest, I'm not sure where I stand on this." She picks up Nola's brochure. "I love community theatre, but ... may I keep this? I see you have some financial projections listed."

"Yes." Nola nudges me. "Thank you for your time, Zully. Call us with any questions you might have."

Back out on the street, Nola twists her mouth. "Zully didn't go quite as planned, but don't lose hope yet. Let's try Foster's. Izzy and Buzz have a lot of influence in town."

A sigh works its way out. "Okay."

"Don't be such an Eeyore." Nola opens the ice cream shop's door, where Izzy and her brother, Buzz, are in a heated discussion.

I glance at Nola. "Are you—"

Their argument stops faster than a fleeing rabbit changes direction. "Marleigh! Nola!" They rush toward us.

"What's your pleasure?" Buzz has his ice cream scoop poised to plunge into the preferred flavor.

I don't know about Nola, but ice cream always boosts my creativity. "I'll take a small cone with chocolate cherry jubilee."

"You read my mind," Nola says. "I'll have the pistachio, then we have something I think you'll both love."

Taking advantage of the shop being clear of customers, other than us, we plunge ahead, but when we finish, their response is divided. Buzz is all for the festival, but Izzy can't see the fixes for the problems.

She points her finger in her brother's face. "The last time I let you talk me into something was the garlic parmesan ice cream." She turns to us. "You can imagine how popular that flavor was."

Buzz shakes his head. "Izzy, this will bring us more customers. Don't you want business to increase?"

"More business means more work for me."

Nola steps into the fray. "How about you two discuss it. I promise you'll see the benefits."

As we leave, they take up the same positions we found them in twenty minutes ago.

Outside, I toss my napkin in the trash. "Have you ever met funnier siblings?"

"I have. Once—" she gasps, pointing across the street.

As I turn, my wounded heart shatters.

Gabe and a dark-haired woman walk hand-in-hand into Valentina's Mexican Restaurant.

Chapter 16

MARLEIGH

"Are your hands washed?" I ask over my shoulder, then flip another pancake. "And your faces?"

"Yes, ma'am." Elijah presents himself for inspection.

I bend and kiss his cherub cheek. "Then, sit down. Your breakfast is almost ready."

"Aysha." Nola points to her daughter's hands. "Your fingers are not what I call clean. What were you doing out there? Rolling in the muck?" She tickles Aysha's neck, making her giggle.

"No, ma'am. You're silly. We were helping Miss Boo feed the goats." Aysha looks at her hands. "But Scrappy tried to eat me."

She marches to the sink, holds her hands up high for Nola to wash them.

I set their breakfasts on the table. "Willow? Nola? What do y'all want?"

"I'll take pancakes," Willow winks at Elijah. "If y'all leave me any syrup."

"There's a whole 'nother bottle," he thumbs over his shoulder, "in the pantry." He squeezes another squirt over his pancakes with an evil grin.

Nola dries her daughter's hands, then reaches into the bowl of fresh eggs. She hands me two. "Scrambled, please. Willow, how are you and Sergio coming on the ..." she glances at the kiddos, "the *project* you two are working on?"

I gesture to the egg bowl, "Two more, please."

"We don't know anything yet." Willow takes a bite of her pancakes. Her eyes widen. "What did you add to these? They're great."

"Just a little cinnamon."

"What a great idea. Did Gabe giv—" Her shoulders slump. "Bad question. Sorry."

While I whisk the eggs, an image of Gabe with a dark-haired woman pierces my heart again. I bite my cheek in an attempt to banish it.

"Sergio said we might want to ask Mr. Bud if he's seen anyone else talking to the shop owners. Are you two going to canvas again today?" Willow spoons sugar into her coffee. "Maybe you can use a little subterfuge—ask Mr. Bud for help. We'll be in serious trouble if we don't get more onboard."

"We are. We will." Nola takes her plate from me and sits beside Willow. "We didn't get to as many as we wanted yesterday." Nola sighs.

"What's the reaction from those you talked to?"

Nola's nose wrinkles. "Vince is with us, but Zully hasn't made up her mind yet. We received mixed opinions from the owners of Foster's. But," she smiles, "today's another day, as the saying goes."

Elijah, who has been watching with great interest, stares at us. "Doesn't everyone want the fez-ival?"

"No, sugar. Not everyone." I need to be careful with what I say.

"Why not?" He frowns and takes his empty plate to the sink.

What should I say? "A few see problems instead of opportunity." I pray my answer satisfies him.

He narrows his eyes, purses his lips, then turns his attention to Aysha. "Are you done?" He points at half an uneaten pancake.

"Uh-huh." She removes the piece of pancake, laying it on a paper towel. "For Bambi." Then, she sets her plate next to the sink.

They head for the door, but I stop Elijah. "Before you go play, remember Mr. Herb is watching you today, so don't go anywhere without telling him."

"Okay," they both shout. The screen door bangs shut behind them where they collide with Sergio. He steadies them with a hand on their shoulders, making sure they won't fall, then lets them go. He waves at us through the screen before entering.

"I was almost swept away by mini tornadoes." He bends, kissing Willow. "Hmm, you taste like maple and cinnamon." He slides into the banquette next to her. "I've been doing some research on our competition.

All our attention focuses on him. As if one voice, we all say, "And?"

"Gabe hasn't been around at all. If he expects to win without merchant support, he must have one humdinger of a proposal. His absence concerns me a little."

It's not Gabe who worries me. I know why he wants the land, but I believe our goals offer more to the community than his. The unknown entity is what I want to know about. "Do we know who the other person is, yet?"

Sergio shakes his head. "My intent for us today is to discover who while keeping an eye on Gabe. Just because he hasn't been in town doesn't mean he won't come today. As for the third person, I have a feeling it might be an investment group of some sort. Land here is valuable which attracts investors."

I gather up everyone's plates, then set them in the sink. "Let's get started. Then, since we're leaving the kids for part of the day, how about a barbecue this evening?"

Sergio, who has fast become part of our family, pulls Willow from her seat. "I'll pick up the dogs and hamburger while we're out."

"I'll start a list," Willow taps her phone, bringing up her reminders app, "of anything else we need."

We set out on our mission, spirits high.

GABE

I click off my phone, glad I followed my instinct to call our broker. Dylan is moving money around within the family trust. If we didn't have the trust, I'm not sure what my brother would do. I'm pretty sure Dad doesn't know what my brother is up to.

What a lousy thought to have about one's brother. Then, again, I'm sure Abel trusted Cain at some point.

Pushing my brother from my mind, I lay a file folder in my briefcase. Since I don't have to be at Wild Azalea until three this afternoon, I made an appointment to see more of Ginger's photography at her studio.

I park the Ferrari on Peachtree Springs Road where there's less traffic, then walk to Ginger's studio, which is inside the museum. Parking would be easier on main street or in the lot, but I don't want the car to get any dings. It's time to sell this albatross. A Ferrari wasn't something I had to own—or even wanted. Dylan, trying to tie me to him, bought it to add to his arsenal. "Don't forget *I* bought the Ferrari for you."

Making a reminder in my phone to call Wade Williams, my mechanic, I arrive at the museum. As I head to the back, I wave at Kathryn Baskin—the town's and county's historian. She's also the museum's curator. Today, she's adding a new display.

"Morning, Gabe. What brings you in?"

"An appointment with Ginger." I don't go into why.

"Well, have a good one." She hands a nail to her husband, who's on the ladder. "Slightly higher to the left."

I wave over my shoulder. "Thanks."

Ginger glances over the top of her computer monitor as I enter. "Morning. Grab a seat." She turns the monitor for me to see it, then rolls her chair, joining me. "Here are a few shots I gathered from what you sent me. However, we can take a field trip to get others if you'd like."

"Let me see what you have." We spend several minutes scrolling through photos. After a couple of minutes, I find a couple I love. "I'll take those two, but I like the idea of a field trip. Do you have time today? The place I'm thinking of is twenty minutes away."

Ginger shuts down her computer and grabs her camera bag. "Let's do this."

MARLEIGH

"But how does this festival benefit me?" Frankie waves his scissors before taking another pass at his customer's hair. "People don't stop for a haircut during a festival."

"Hang on there, Frankie." His customer raises one finger. "I found you when I parked for a concert at the amphitheater. Knowing parking was going to be at a premium, I came an hour beforehand, so I walked in for a haircut."

The barber leans back, considering the man. "Yeah? Well, whattya know." He shakes his head. "Okay, then. George convinced me. It's worth a shot." Frankie gestures toward three empty chairs. "As you can see, I'm not overbooked."

Nola hands him a brochure. "You will be, if you follow some of these tips, Frankie.

After looking them over, the barber grins. "I'll start looking for a helper."

Two hours and four shops later, I wonder why I ever thought this would work. "I can't understand Joe's attitude. Or LaLa Jackson's."

Nola hikes her tote higher on her shoulder. "Whoever heard of a coffee shop or a lunch counter not wanting more business."

"Something's not right." We cross the street, heading to Morrow's Furniture, then Three Marketeers.

We lay out our proposal but, as expected, Pete Morrow's response is negative. "I'll have people using my parking lot for the festival. My customers won't be able to shop."

Nola points to a section in the brochure. "Taken care of. We ordered special signs."

Pete plants his fists on his hips. "You think them signs'll work, do ya?"

His sarcasm annoys Nola. "Pete, we have people who will be directing traffic. Your spots will be safe."

"Yeah? Well, there ain't enough of them."

He's delusional. Morrow's has been in a decline for years. There's never more than two cars in his lot—one of which is his. He refuses to stock modern furniture.

"Okay. Here's the deal." Nola jots a note for him to see. "We'll give you two more spaces for the first weekend. If they don't fill up, we take them back the following weekend."

"Nope. I don't like this festival idea one bit. No way. No how."

We give up on Pete. In Three Marketeers, Hannah Bass signals us from the office. Her siblings are helping customers.

"I'm glad you're here. I was at the council meeting, so I'm looking forward to hearing your proposal."

"Thanks, Hannah." Nola pulls out another brochure pointing out the main features.

"I figured you'd come up with something good. I can see how your plan might help us too, if we manage to stay open."

What? They're the main grocery supplier for people who live downtown. Most don't go anywhere else, preferring the convenience. "Why wouldn't you?"

"People are wary. Last week, someone came in and was eyeing our floors. When I asked what was wrong, thinking they lost something, I learned someone is spreading rumors about us. Even called the county to give us a safety inspection, lying about what they saw. I've noticed a decline in revenue this past week."

My gaze locks on Nola's. "I can't believe he'd sink to such a low level."

In the kitchen, Willow fills glasses with ice. "Who wants sweet tea?"

"I do. Nola?"

"Please."

Willow hands glasses all around. Sergio drains his glass and hands it back to her. "Thanks, babe." He glances at me. "I need to be hydrated to tell you what we learned."

"What did you find out?" I set my glass on a napkin.

Willow sits next to Sergio. "Gabe has a brother."

"I remember him mentioning one, but they don't get along. So, what about him?"

Sergio and Willow exchange a glance. "He's the third party."

What? Could he ... would he ... how can he? I quit trying to force sense into it. "What does this mean?" I shake my head. "I mean, I know what you're saying, but how does his brother affect us? Are they working together?"

Sergio once again drains his glass of tea. Funny, I've never seen him take just one sip. He sets his glass back on the table, laying his hand over the top, shaking his head when Willow asks, "More?"

"I don't know for sure. I think they might be from what I've learned, though. His brother—name's Dylan—wants the land for a strip mall, anchored with a grocery store. I'm assuming Gabe would operate the grocery. I know he wants his farm-to-market thing. I saw snippets of a lunch counter in the market's blueprints."

Willow leans her elbows on the table, resting her chin on her clasped hands. "I've seen those on Triple D." She frowns. "I have to say I'm disappointed in Gabe, though. I don't like their tactics. They're underhanded."

"How did you find this out?" Nola asks.

"One of my clients works for the Sadlers. I knew he was employed by a restaurant investor, so I asked for a little advice on a project." He shrugs. "I told him I had a client, since I was fishing for information. While he talked, he pulled out plans for something he was working on for his boss. I almost gave myself away when I saw 'Dylan Sadler' printed in the corner of the blueprints."

"Were they his proposal for the Higgins' land?" I don't want to know, but I do. I have to find out what I'm up against.

"Yeah. The whole strip mall." Sergio rubs the back of his neck. "The odd part is it's not thought through, in my opinion. Why build a strip mall behind the apartments? Something doesn't add up. Business wise, his idea is lame. Ripe for failure, given all the shops downtown."

Nola narrows her eyes. "Unless one has an axe to grind with someone."

"Okay, let's say you're right." My gaze takes in my friends. "But if Gabe's working with him, who would they be out to get?"

Sergio points at me. "You."

"Me? Why? His brother doesn't even know me. Besides, Gabe said they don't get along. Unless he lied to me. No, I don't think it's me. My guess is it's the Bass family."

"Who are they?" Sergio asks.

"They own Three Marketeers. Someone—you can guess who—is spreading rumors about them, trying to put them out of business."

Willow raises one corner of her lip on a sneer. "The Sadlers' favorite method—threaten and intimidate." Her lips flatten. "What doesn't make sense in this is Gabe. He isn't like his brother. At least I didn't think he was. Could his friendship with me have been a lie too?"

The back door opens. The kiddos rush in, their cheeks red. Elijah pulls bottles of cold water from the fridge. I give Nola a conspiratorial wink, knowing they've been up to something.

"What have you been doing? And don't tell me nothing."

They grin at each other.

Elijah thrusts out his little chest. "We told Mr. Herb. We been workin' on a project—like you." He grabs Aysha's hand. "Come on. We gots more to do." They race out the back door toward the barn.

"I'll holler for you when it's time for supper. We're having barbecue." Nola chuckles. "I guess they can't get into too much trouble there, but what project could they mean?"

Chapter 17

MARLEIGH

"What's happening with your adoption?" Nola picks up the remote, silencing the TV.

With the kiddos in bed, it's time to catch up on our week and relax, at least for us. Willow is out with Sergio.

I slip a bookmark into my novel. "My lawyer checked the Putative Parent Search database. Nobody ever put in a 'change of mind' search for Elijah." I pull up my feet, tucking them beneath me. "Now, all we need to do is wait ninety days, then go to court. Our case is an easy one, he says."

"Wonderful. I know the two of you must be happy about it, although a legal piece of paperwork won't change your relationship. You already have a loving one."

"For me, you're right. But for Elijah, formalization will. He'll feel more secure. Sometimes, he prays for God to let me be his mommy, so nobody can ever take him away from me." A shiver goes down my arms. "That's why I was so upset when Willow—albeit unknown—dated James-the-drug-dealer."

"Well," she holds up her glass of sweet tea in a toast. "Here's to a blessed adoption, a fantastic festival, a brilliant first show in the SS Spotlight, and mom's wedding in Once Upon a Forever."

"From your lips to God's ear." I clink my glass to hers, then an image on TV catches my eye. "Hey, the show's starting."

Nola turns up the volume as we settle back to watch an episode of *When Calls the Heart*. As we watch, I keep a notepad on my lap for show ideas and people I need to hire. I add an asterisk next to the word "hire."

When our program is over, Nola turns off the television, then picks up her laptop from the coffee table as if she'd read my mind. "I thought I'd give you a report on fundraising."

"Good, I need to know if I'm going to be able to hire the stage crew we'll need. I can get by with two for now—if I can steal Mitch and Angel away from Cruella. We'll have to meet their level of pay, though."

Nola taps on her keyboard. "I think we will. I'm sure Mitch will come for less just to get away from her."

I shake my head. "I don't want him to. If we can raise what we need for the first couple of years, we can afford to pay what he's worth. Besides, one of Mitch is worth two regular grips. He saves us money, and he'll train volunteers. I think we can become self-sufficient within two years."

She crunches numbers for the next hour, while I check over the list, laying it out in bullet points. It's a daunting one. Sets, props, and costumes are a given, along with royalties to license a show. Add in salaries, office supplies, hospitality—it's overwhelming.

"Wow." Nola stares at my list. "I don't think I realized there was so much to producing a show."

"There's more, but we don't need to go into everything right now. I think this," I circle my bottom-line number, "is what we will need for our first year. Instead of paying for fancy ads, we'll use social media for marketing. It's almost as good as word-of-mouth."

Nola types numbers into her spreadsheet. "We have seating projected at two-hundred-fifty." She calculates the number of seats we need to sell for each show and remain in the black. When she's done, she gives a sharp nod. "I think we'll be okay."

She pushes the now-empty bowl of popcorn out of her way. "Our children's program will pay for itself with its camps the first year. Once we're on our feet, we can look at grants for an education arm."

And to think, this all started with me wanting a community theatre in a barn. "Hey, do you think the wedding venue will help fund the mortgage?"

"That's the plan."

She's thought of everything. "So, where are we in funding?"

"Well on our way. Your referral from Manny Dupont at Ridge Academy resulted in one man asking to be the executive producer for our first show. He believes in what we're doing. Oh, he also hinted at a longer relationship."

Mama always said anything if seems too good to be true, it isn't. "What does he want?"

Nola chuckles. "Nothing. He loves the arts and as a businessman, he understands the difficulty in raising funds."

"For real? If so, great." I hate being such a skeptic. "Here's hoping he finds a donor with deep pockets."

Nola snorts. "You forget, funding the arts for a nonprofit is tax deductible for businesses—for anyone. Successful enterprises need tax deductions. Then, when people find out they fund the arts, they get more business,"

"And need more tax deductions. Brilliant. We'll have to list all our sponsors in the playbills."

After making another note, Nola raises her head, blinking. "You know what else we need? A lawyer on our board. We need to be sure everything we do is without question, so we don't lose our nonprofit status."

The doorbell interrupts Elijah blessing our supper. I can't believe it. "Who can that be? Their timing is awful."

"Or good, depending." Willow rises. "I'll go. If it's Sergio, do y'all mind if he joins us?"

"Not at all." I've come to love him, mainly because he loves Willow, but he helps us out more than he realizes. I'm sorry the next voice I hear doesn't belong to Sergio.

"Marleigh? Nola?" Willow's voice trembles. "I think y'all had better come out here."

Nola and I stare at each other. What now?

We hurry to the front room. A woman with Willow clutches a clipboard and pen. For some reason, her clipboard gives me chills. If she held a small notepad, I'd think her a reporter inquiring about the contest. I try to offer a smile, but I'm afraid my mouth grimaces.

"I'm Marleigh Evans."

"And I'm Nola Winthrop. How can we help you?"

Dressed in a plain, cheap suit judging by its cut, her appearance plays down a pleasant face. "Could we sit? This may take a bit of time."

If she's trying to intimidate me, she's succeeded. I want to throw up. "Sure." I gesture to the front room.

Once seated, she poises her pen over the clipboard. "I'm from the Department of Family and Child Services."

DEFACS! A chill goes down my spine.

"A charge has been made accusing you of employing children under the age of fourteen, which is against Georgia state law."

"No, we're not." I take a breath, trying not to sound panicked. "We don't have any employees. We aren't a company yet." I turn to Nola. "Are we?"

Nola takes a deep breath. "Yes, we are. I filed the papers last Wednesday." She turns her gaze on the woman. "I'm sorry, did you tell us your name?"

"No. It's Mary Elizabeth Andrews."

Are we supposed call her by both names? I settle on formal. "Ms. Andrews, we have not employed any children. Who told you we were?"

Her shoulders straighten as she sits taller. "I'm afraid I can't reveal that information."

Nola dons her best professional personae, pulling out her own notepad. "When and where was this supposed to have occurred?"

"This past Monday afternoon. Downtown. Children were going into businesses querying the owners about a contest."

Nola and I shout at the same time. "Elijah! Aysha! Get out here!"

"Ms. Andrews, Nola and I each have a five-year-old. I believe they may have taken things upon themselves. Let's see."

Her countenance softens a little. Our children stampede into the room, skidding to a stop. Elijah offers his heartrending grin to the visitor, then sidles up to me.

"Whassup, Marma?"

"Sweetheart, tell me what you two did yesterday."

His lips purse into a pout as tears pool in his eyes. "We wanted to surprise you."

"It's all right, sugar. Just tell us."

His gaze cuts to Ms. Andrews, then back to me. "We saw how sad you were 'cause not everybody wants the fez-ival. So, we asked some of our friends an' went to each store an' asked 'em to join in the fun. That's all, Marma. Honest."

Aysha nods in agreement, her eyes wide with fear.

Ms. Andrews smiles at the children. "A noble thought." Her attention switches back to us. "But why were they allowed to go downtown without supervision?"

"They aren't." I take hold of Elijah's shoulders, turning him to face me. "You were supposed to be helping Miss Boo feed the goats. What did you do?"

He looks away.

"Elijah?"

Unable to lie to me, he breaks into sobs. "I told Miss Boo I was goin' to play with my friends at the school playground. Robbie's mama was watching us."

I tip his chin up with my finger. "And was she?"

"K—k—kind of." He sniffles. "She stayed on the playground, but we waved when we came out of each store, so she knew we were okay. She wanted to help you, Marma."

"Elijah?" Ms. Andrews waits until he turns to her. "Will Robbie's mama verify what you've told us?"

"What's veri-vie?"

"Verify." I put a protective arm on his shoulders. "It means will she tell us the same thing you have?"

He nods vigorously, as does Aysha, who says, "She lives right next to the playground."

"And who is Miss Boo?" Ms. Andrews notes her name on her clipboard.

"Boo Higgins is mayor of Sugar Springs and owns this house. She lives in the cottage out back."

"Will she confirm this?"

"Yes." I nod. "Elijah, go ask Miss Boo to come over. Tell her it's very important. You two stay with Mr. Herb until we send for you." I glance over my boy's shoulder at the social worker. "I don't think we need them any longer. I'd prefer to keep them away from any discussions we have."

"I agree." She lays her pen down. "From what you've told me, as long as it's confirmed by the mayor and Robbie's mother, I'll close this file. However, I must caution you to keep a close eye on your children. Once you are in our system, whether the accusation was false or true, you remain in the database."

I'm going to throw up. "Ms. Andrews—" should I say anything about Elijah's adoption or not? How much does she already know about us?

The social worker holds up a hand to stop me. "I think I know what you're going to ask. As long as it's confirmed the children acted on their own, this will not affect your adoption of Elijah." She lays her clipboard beside her. "However, you will want to be very careful in the future. If anyone calls about you, or if the school reports any unexplained bruises, there could be trouble, since you're already in our system."

Nola puts her own note pad down. "We both grew up here. Everyone knows us and the kids. They are quite safe in town. Everyone watches out for all the residents' children."

Ms. Andrews' expression appears somewhat skeptical. "Be that as it may, I must warn you again. Be sure they are supervised at all times."

Miss Boo rushes in the door. "What's wrong?"

I hurry to her side. "This is Ms. Andrews from the Department of Family and Child Services. Will you tell her what the kids asked you on Monday afternoon?"

Her brows knit together. "Let's see, you and Nola had a meeting. The kids were staying with us. Elijah asked if they could go play on the school playground, with Robbie Nesbitt's mama, Cecilia, watching them. I know CeCe, so I allowed it." She turns her gaze to me? "Shouldn't I have? With the school right across the street, I thought you wouldn't mind."

"I don't. You're fine, Miss Boo. I always trust your judgment."

"Thank you, Mrs. Higgins." Ms. Andrews notes her confirmation. "Do you have contact information for Mrs. Nesbitt?"

Miss Boo fires off CeCe's phone number and address from memory, then leaves. On her way out, she winks over her shoulder—her way of telling us to "hang in there."

Ms. Andrews rises. "Ladies, I'll go see Ms. Nesbitt. Please don't contact her before my visit. If her version of what happened matches, then I will let you know by mail when it's been collaborated and proven to be a false report. However, I must remind you to remember you are in our database, false report or not. Be more careful in the future."

After the door closes behind her, Nola calls the kids home. We sit them down and let them know the seriousness of what they did.

"You told Miss Boo a lie." I shudder, thinking of potential consequences this could have had.

"No, we didn't. Ow!" With Aysha's vehement denial, her pigtails smack her in the eyes. "We *went* to the playground ... for a little while." She looks at the floor. "Then, we asked Robbie's mama if we could go to stores an' help you win th' contest."

"It's cross-my-heart-truth." Elijah always defends Aysha. I hope she realizes what a good friend she has.

We decide to drop the matter after a stern admonition to never do anything without telling us first. They promise, then go back into the kitchen to finish supper.

Nola raises an eyebrow at me. "You aren't going to tell Elijah why it's so important?"

"I won't put any fear in him. If his adoption doesn't go through, he'd think it was his fault. Do you remember how I grew up always being the one blamed if anything went wrong?"

She links a reassuring arm through mine. "I do. I know how it affected you. You made the right decision."

We join the others at the table, but I push my plate aside. My appetite's gone. "One thing won't leave me. How could anyone, let alone Gabe, have done this?"

Sergio, who arrived as Ms. Andrews left, shakes his head. "I don't believe this was Gabe. His brother, yes, but not Gabe."

They may be able to extend grace to him, but I'm not. All I can think of is Ms. Andrews' parting warning.

Chapter 18

MARLEIGH

"I'm as nervous as a long-tailed cat in a roomful of rocking chairs." Standing behind Elijah, I straighten his bowtie in the foyer mirror. He looks so cute in his light blue pants and vest.

He giggles. "You're funny." He scrunches his mouth sideways—his thinking mode. "I'm as nervous as a kitty at a dog show."

"Good one. How about nervous as a mouse in a cat hotel?"

"Cats don' have hotels. You're silly."

"They don't?" I help him into his suit jacket. As frightening as last week was with Child Services, tonight is exciting, but still nerve wracking. If we don't win this contest, we are back to the proverbial square one—and me without a job.

"Nope." His attention moves to Aysha, who fidgets with her dress all the way down the stairs. Poor baby. She's not a frilly little girl. She's her daddy's mini-me. She loves her camo. My guess is because Nola does such a good job of keeping Steve's memory alive for her.

"You look ... nice, Aysha."

Nola sends him a thankful glance, but Aysha sticks out her tongue. "This stuff itches. Do I *haaaave* to wear it, Mama?"

A familiar memory surfaces. "I hated petticoats too Aysha. I don't know why they put them in little girl's dresses."

Nola throws her hands in the air. "I give up." She helps Aysha step out of the undergarment. "But will you leave on the dress without the itchy stuff?"

I have to bite my lip to keep from laughing at Aysha's expression. She'll play the martyr, suffering for us. I'm sure Nola will hear about it for days and pay penance for making Aysha wear a dress. Nola's daughter is a true drama queen in training.

"It's time to go." Nola ushers us all out.

Sergio arrives as we lock the door. He and the kiddos make a merry troupe walking ahead of us to City Hall. We three gals are quiet, each lost in thought.

Inside the council chambers, we sit where Miss Boo requested, the front row again. A few seats down, Gabe is in conversation with a man, whom I assume is his brother. He doesn't look anything like Gabe, though, except maybe in their coloring.

His brother nods at me. When Gabe turns his head, I look away.

"Marma," Elijah whispers. "Do you feel bad seeing Gabe?"

I take a deep breath. I've always been honest with Elijah. I won't lie to him now. "A little. I cared a lot for him."

"Me too." My little guy says no more, but I hear the sorrow in his voice. I add another tick in the Beast's negative column.

When the council meeting is called to order, my heartbeat kicks into high gear. Nola reaches over, squeezing my hand.

Thank goodness, the meeting is short tonight, only taking forty-two minutes. At its end, Miss Boo and Herb stand together. Our mayor steps forward.

"The merchants have voted, and this council has reached a decision on the contest. One proposal will bring a much needed infusion of business to downtown."

Gabe's brother puffs out his chest. Does he know something? I swallow, clenching my folded hands.

"The winning proposal is from—" Miss Boo pauses.

My trembling palms turn clammy.

"MaNWEA Arts Corporation. Congratulations, Marleigh, Nola, and Willow!"

We won! We can buy the farm. *Thank you, Lord.*

The applause is loud. A photographer steps in front of us, snapping photos. Willow, Nola, and I meet in a three-way hug, while the kiddos cheer inside our circle.

"Marleigh, will you say something?" Miss Boo extends a microphone to me.

I'd prefer Nola to speak, but she pushes me forward. I turn to face the audience. Gabe looks happy. For us? I don't see his brother. I suppose I can't blame him for leaving. Nola nudges me with her elbow.

"Oh, right. The festival idea came to us," I indicate to my cohorts, "because people all over north Georgia look for entertainment on weekends. I know we three always search for something with activities for adults and children. Since Sugar Springs has so much to offer, we thought why not have a festival. But instead of one weekend, we figure if we do one each weekend throughout the summer, we can draw visitors from all over the region for food tasting, crafts booths, live music, battles of the bands, live theatre, and more. Sugar Springs will become *the* place to go for great entertainment."

Out of the corner of my eye, Gabe applauds with enthusiasm. After the way he lied to me, I'm not sure this isn't a phony display. I lose sight of him as people surround me.

A few minutes later, I search for him again, but to no avail. I reach for Elijah's hand, but he pulls away, pleading to go to the refreshment table with Miss Boo. She takes both kids in hand, helping them as we answer questions.

While Nola is busy with a councilmen, Mr. Bud and Herb approach us.

"We'd like to volunteer to head up the festival committees," Mr. Bud says. "Take the organization off your shoulders. Besides, Herb and I work great together."

"Always have." Herb scratches his neck. "We're cousins, y'know."

"I didn't." I should have seen it. They don't resemble each other a lot, but they are so much alike in personality.

Bud's grin is cheeky. "Y'all aren't old enough to remember us as rabble-rousers." Both men cackle.

Willow wags a finger at the duo. "We'd love to have you, as long as your shenanigans don't cause trouble." Her grin belies her warning. "I've attended some of your other events in the past. They're always well-planned."

"Goes to show ya," Herb thrusts out his chest, "never discount the savvy of old men." They grin at each other when Willow giggles. Those two are a hoot.

"I'll contact you for a steering committee meeting next week." She hands them one of Nola's brochures. "You can start pulling together your committees."

Bud studies the paper for a moment, then his eyes pop wide. He slaps the brochure against his palm. "Let's add an antique car show to one of those weekends."

"Great idea." Herb eyes Willow. "Y'know, people will flock to see car shows. I can almost guarantee you they'll attend multiple events."

"If you hadn't volunteered, I was going to ask you to chair it." I hug each of them. "What do you think of having a contest to name it?"

"The festival?" Bud cradles his chin between his thumb and index finger as he considers.

I nod. "Yeah, we can't keep calling it 'the festival.'"

"I like your idea," Herb says. "It'll involve more people. After all, perceived possession always guarantees good results. We'll get to work and announce the contest right away. Hey, what will we give to the winner?"

"How about season tickets to the SS Spotlight?"

The cousins exchange a mystified look. "The *what*?" Herb asks.

"The SS Spotlight is the name we chose for our barn theatre. The SS is for Sugar Springs."

Miss Boo, Aysha, and Elijah join us. "Best name ever," the mayor exclaims. "Congratulations, Marleigh. Come over in the morning to sign the papers."

I'm pleased over winning the rights to buy the property, but the deep joy I once felt is no longer there—it lost its buoyancy with Gabe's betrayal. Still, I put on a smile. I have to move on for the sake of our venture—for Nola, Willow, Aysha, and Elijah.

If only—

GABE

"And the winning proposal is—" Miss Boo pauses for drama. *Don't let Dylan win, please God.* "MaNWEA

Arts Corporation. Congratulations, Marleigh, Nola, and Willow!"

I like the name they chose for their parent company. I caught the acronym right away. As I applaud, I realize how thrilled I am for Beauty, which surprises me—not because I'm happy for her but how much. Maybe more than if I'd won.

And so much more than if Dylan had. I turn, only to see Zach Tinley's back disappearing through the door. A fleeting concern over my brother's temper when Tinley tells him the results crosses my mind, but Marleigh's win is fair. Her proposal was best.

I admire the effort she put into achieving her dream. I'd love to go congratulate her, but I know she doesn't want to see me. She made it quite clear I ruined my chances with her. However, maybe with my new proposal, we can at least be friends—help one another. I slip out of City Hall.

Once outside, I turn on my phone. There's a message from Jody Davis. I call him back.

"Congrats, dude. We've had a bidding war. Your house sold for fifty-K over asking. All you have to do is accept."

"I accept." One more tie to Dylan is severed. He's gonna be so ticked. Funny, the idea of making him mad used to tickle me. Now, I no longer care.

"You don't sound thrilled, man."

"Sorry, Jody. I am. I'm just at odds right now."

"Yeah, I understand. A beloved home, filled with memories—I get it."

I let him think he gets it. He's one of those good guys, all about family. "Thanks. Email me the offer. I'll sign it tonight. Don't forget the apartment. I'll take the second one we toured, if it's still available."

"Sounds good. I'll alert the leasing office to hold it. Drop by in the morning to sign your lease. Your buyers want a thirty-day closing. I told them we'd agree."

"Works for me. See you in the morning."

I follow the leasing agent as we walk around the corner apartment. I love its windows with all the natural light coming in. "You're right. I prefer this over the other one you showed me." There is one downside—its view. Instead of downtown, its windows overlook the farm.

And Marleigh.

"I thought you would. Let's go back to my office to sign your lease. The apartment will be ready for you next week."

In her office, I give her two checks—for first and last month's rent and a security deposit. She hands me my keys.

"We will clean and paint everything. If you need to come in to measure, just let me know." She hands me her card.

Next, I meet Jody in his office to get details on the sale of my house. "Hey, can you arrange for new drapes in my apartment?"

"Sure. I'll have my wife do it. Lindsay has great decorating sense. Any color you don't like?"

"No, but why don't you take Lindsay by the house before closing. She can see my furniture, using it to choose colors for me."

After I leave, I pull out my phone, praying this will go as well. A moment later, Sergio picks up. His hello is cautious.

I can't blame him. "Thanks for taking my call, man. I wasn't sure you would."

"What's up, Gabe?"

"Can I take you to lunch today? I'd like to run something by you."

The momentary silence is loud, then he says, "Sure. Where?"

I suggest Valentina's in Sugar Springs. I check my watch. It's ten-thirty. "See you in an hour."

When I arrive, Sergio is already seated. He rises, extending his hand. His firm handshake and welcoming smile bode well.

I take a deep breath. "Let's chase this gorilla out of the room. I messed up bad with Marleigh. I don't know if I will ever win her back, but this isn't about our past relationship."

"I'm glad. I missed your friendship, but I'm also *her* friend." Sergio sits back, relaxing against the banquette's cushioned back. "So, what's this about?"

I open an envelope containing what I'd like to propose to the ladies. I hand them to Sergio. He reads the papers, glancing up at me, and then raises a brow in what I hope is approval.

When he finishes, he slides the proposal back to me. "I like it. I think they will too. I'll do everything I can to help convince them."

MARLEIGH

The architect spreads his plans over our kitchen table. As he walks me through what he's drawn, I tick off our needs in my mind. The way he has different levels shown on his blueprints confuse me, though.

"Let me pull up my list, then show me where you have each item. We may need to tweak a little."

Finn nods. "I took what you sent me, then borrowed plans from another barn-to-theatre renovation our firm did in Arkansas. I moved things around where you indicated over the phone."

Willow joins us.

"Finn, this is Willow Raines. She's Atlanta's best stage manager. She knows backstage, lighting, and sound as well as any twenty-year veteran. She'll be your contact for all things technical."

"Willow." He nods at her. His expression is one we've seen before. He turns a page. "What do you think of this? Have we missed anything?"

Willow glances at his plans for the span of a single heartbeat. "Finn, I may look like a dumb blonde, but if you try to pass off HVAC plans for theatrical electronics to me again, you'll be fired on the spot."

The man grins. "I'm sorry, but I had to. Barry put me up to it."

"Barry Larson?" She giggles. "I should have known. How is the old skunk?"

"He's fine, still as big a prankster as ever. When he heard we won this project, he told me about you. I'm impressed with your experience." He snickers. "And reputation."

"Barry used to work for me." Willow turns on the overhead light to help illuminate the plans. "Glad you can put his experience to use. He's a good guy."

Finn turns over another sheet. "Here are your rigging specs. We will bring in a consultant for sound and lights. I imagine you already know what you want."

She nods. "We do, but cost will be our deciding factor. At least, at this point."

We spend another hour on the plans, moving around a few things. I give him the go ahead when I'm confident we have everything where we want. Next week, we will interview building contractors Finn is recommending. Willow's phone rings, and she excuses herself to take the call.

I close the door behind Finn, then lean against it. It's been quite a morning. We signed papers at the bank for the property and building loan. Now, we have our plans for the theatre.

My besties come into the foyer. Willow scans the space. "Finn gone?"

"Yes. Did you need to ask him something?"

"No." She glances at Nola, who nods. "We need to ask *you* about something."

"Sure. What's up?"

The doorbell rings. Willow pulls the door open to Sergio. What's going on? "Are you in on whatever this is?"

He nods. "Let's go into the front room."

Uh-oh. "Is there a problem with our loan?"

"No, not at all. I—well," he escorts us into the front room. He gestures to the couch, where I sit next to Willow. "I met with Gabe earlier. He has a proposal for you about the farm."

"No. I don't want to hear anything he has to say. Conversation over."

Willow lays her hand on my arm, stopping me from rising. "Hear us out, Marleigh. This could be good for MaNWEA."

I sit back, folding my arms. "I can't imagine how anything *he* has to say would be good for us."

Sergio hands an envelope to Nola. "Please, just hear us out."

I don't want to. I don't trust Gabe. But a still, small voice in my heart says, "*Do you trust me?*"

"All right. I'll listen. But I'm not making any promises."

Sergio taps the envelope Nola holds. "This contains all the projections and financials. Gabe would like to purchase or lease the cottage, turning it into a farm-to-table restaurant. He'd also buy or lease five acres to grow what he needs."

Nola exchanges a glance with me, then studies the papers. She nods when she finishes. "This is good. It's well thought out, not overpromised. It could be a boon for us. Dinner and theatre."

"What about his brother? Is he in on this?" From what I know of Dylan, I don't want anything to do with him.

"No," Sergio says. "Gabe has broken ties with him. He told me watching you strive for your dream impressed him. What you want isn't self-serving like his family. He didn't like who he'd become. Gabe's changed, Marleigh."

I'm not sure I believe him. "Yet he's betraying *them*, now."

Willow shakes her head. "No, he isn't. We already won the contest."

"Wasn't he working *with* his brother?"

Sergio shakes his head. "Gabe told him no, but his brother only hears what he wants."

"Maybe he has changed, but I still don't trust him." I get another internal nudge to give him a chance to achieve his dream too.

I study my friends. "If I say yes, you three will be the ones to deal with him. I don't want to be involved. I loved him, and he threw my love back at me. I won't allow him to break my heart again."

Ever.

Chapter 19

GABE

So much to do in a short amount of time. I scrub a hand through my hair. Yikes, I need to see my barber too, but a haircut will have to wait. The movers are on their way.

I strip the sheets off my bed, tossing them into a waiting laundry basket. They can go to the apartment as is. I turn around, taking in every corner of my room including the open closet. I'm ready.

The high-pitched beeping of a truck backing into my driveway alerts me. Has to be the moving company. When I emerge from the hallway, two men stand in my foyer looking around. One of them is as big as an NFL linebacker. His coworker is half his size. They amuse me for some reason.

"Ah, Mr. Sadler. Good morning. Thanks for leaving the door open for us. We're ready to start."

"Great. I'll show you around."

Room by room, I walk them through the house. "Not everything is going. The new owners purchased a lot of my furniture and artwork. I've marked what goes with orange sticky notes."

I've lived here over three years, yet never added any personal touches. A few photos and office files are already in my new Yukon. Wade found a buyer for the Ferrari. I paid cash for the new SUV yesterday and can live off the rest until the restaurant's profitable.

The last room I take the movers to is the kitchen. "This is the only room you have to pack for me. Everything else is done."

Big-Guy opens cupboards, noting the contents. "Wow, you sure got some fancy pans. You a chef or something?"

"Yeah. I'm opening a new restaurant in Sugar Springs in a few months."

"Oh yeah? Nice. Me an' my wife like to eat out Friday nights. I'll watch for you. What's the name?"

Name? I haven't even—"The SS Garden Table." The name pops out of my mouth without a thought. But I like it. It's perfect. I just hope Beauty doesn't object.

The men get busy emptying the cabinets. They assure me packing won't take long, since I'm leaving a lot more than they're taking. Big-Guy figures they can deliver everything to the apartment, unload, and be gone by four-thirty.

"Thanks, I'll be back before you're done. If you need me before then, you have my cell number."

Next, I meet with Jody for closing. In less than an hour, I'm handed a check for $1.35 mil. It's way more than enough to build out my restaurant and plant my farm. The rest will be a nice nest egg for retirement.

Hey, maybe ... an idea is birthed on an investment as I shake the new owners' hands. "I hope you both enjoy the home."

Vicky smiles while Alex puts his arm around her. "We love it. I don't know how you can leave."

"As a chef, I was never there. I'm using the money to start a new restaurant in Sugar Springs. I hope you'll look for the SS Garden Table in three or four months."

"We sure will. Good luck."

Jody walks me out. "I like your restaurant's name."

"Thanks. I appreciate all you've done, Jody. I hate to cut this short, buddy, but I want to get this," I wave the check envelope, "into the bank right away."

By the time I've opened the first two accounts, it's after one-thirty. I'm starving, so I grab a sandwich at The Lunch Counter, then drive back to the house. I find Big-Guy closing the truck's doors. He's happy to be a little ahead of schedule since it's a Friday afternoon.

We arrive at the apartment at three-thirty. With the only furniture being my bedroom set, they unload fast. They're gone in under an hour.

And here I stand surrounded by boxes. I scratch the back of my head. At least they're labeled. My new furniture doesn't come until tomorrow, but I don't need it tonight.

I put sheets on my bed, throw my laundry into the stackable washer, put my clothes away, and go back to the kitchen. I can at least brew coffee while putting all this away. After finding my Keurig, I pop in a French vanilla pod, triggering the memory of discovering Marleigh's favorite coffee is the same as mine. Will we ever share that again? I shake my head to dispel the longing. Time to get to work.

First, I open every cupboard and drawer. I make a mental layout of the kitchen arrangement, so everything is functional. It's a pretty good design for an apartment.

I munch on crackers and cheese while I work. By nine, I'm done and have the boxes broken down. I'll take them to recycling tomorrow morning.

I turn off the lights, stand at the window, and my heart swells with anticipation. Marleigh agreed—albeit with reluctance—to sell me the cottage and acreage I requested, but Sergio handled yesterday's closing for her.

In a way, we both won. She gets her dream. I get mine. Except, in the midst of everything, I lost her.

I look up to the heavens. The evening star is showing off in the twilight.

Will Beauty see the change in me? Is it enough to win her back?

I know the plans I have for you.

The words of Jeremiah 29:11 resonate in my heart. The rest of the Scripture says they are plans for good—not for disaster, to give me a future. To give me hope.

My hope is Marleigh will be in my future, but what if it isn't God's will? What if someone else is best for her?

Lord, I won't like it, but if it's your will for her, then help me be the kind of friend she needs.

In the farmhouse, lights upstairs blink out. The kids are in bed. Low light filters through their living room curtains. Is Marleigh watching TV, or is she too excited about starting renovations on the barn? How I would love to talk with her.

After a moment, I turn away, closing my drapes. Jody's wife did a nice job choosing those. I like the colors.

The mayor and her husband are moving out tomorrow. Monday, I'm meeting the architect about the cottage's renovation. After a shower, I climb into bed with pad and pen in hand.

With a TV news channel on low, I doodle with some new ideas for the cottage. If I expand its footprint, I can seat about seventy-five guests. I could add a second floor, making an apartment for myself above the restaurant. I think I'd prefer living there to this apartment long term.

My phone blasts the annoying Muppet Swedish Chef ringtone I set for Dylan last week. I sigh, knowing I won't get any sleep until I answer him. "What's up?"

"Are you showing up for work Monday? Since we both lost the mayor's stupid contest, I want to offer the woman a deal. She can have the barn, but I want the rest of the property. I found another anchor store. I need you back on the job."

Ready. Aim. Fire. "Not happening. I bought the cottage plus five acres from Ms. Evans. I'm building *my* dream, Dylan. So, there's no deal."

A string of curses assaults my ear. "You're a chump. What's your dream gonna net you? You realize I can guarantee you millions?"

"Don't want it. There's more to life than money, bro. Can you say you've ever gone to bed at night satisfied the creative work of your hands has made something people enjoyed? Has made life better for someone? Can you?"

"Are you in or not?" There's a harder edge to Dylan's voice.

Doesn't matter.

I'm done. "Not."

"You're going to regret this."

MARLEIGH

After I walk Elijah and Aysha to school, I stroll into the barn. As I've done ever since I moved here, I stand in the center envisioning my dream, turning in a slow circle to see what our audiences will view when they enter—comfortable audience seating, a stage at the opposite end from the door, and a sound booth residing at the rear of the house. A long counter for concessions awaits in the back. Upstairs will be our offices.

"Morning, Marleigh." Finn's voice calls from the open doorway where he's silhouetted against the light.

I motion him to come in.

"I know what we have on paper, but tell me what you see."

Tell me what you see. Those five simple words are the reason I hired him. He wants to help build a dream, not merely a structure. I point out various areas. "The main barn is forty by sixty feet, so we will need to add an addition. Can you get old barn wood, so the walls look like they were always here?"

"Sure can. You mentioned reclaimed wood in our phone call, so I've already adjusted your plans. I contacted someone for the cladding. too. Let's take a look."

We walk to a table I set up for us, where he spreads out blueprints.

"Here," he points to one wall, "is where I've added dressing rooms. A costume shop is here. For your scene shop and properties storage area, I have a couple of ideas. We could put them on the second floor with a freight elevator." He flips to another page. "But why not dig out a daylight basement? Platform dollies can then be used to haul up set pieces." He shows me where the door would be, how it opens to backstage.

"What's the cost difference?"

"Believe it or not, digging out a basement is a lot less than an elevator. I'll get an estimate for you."

"Okay, but could we ..." I flip back to the first page, "add those onto the back of the barn? We can get by with around twenty-five-hundred square feet. I'm thinking if it's there," I point out the spot on the plans, "it can be accessible to the stage through an overhead door."

He sucks in his lips. "I didn't think of another addition. It's a great way to go, even with getting old barn wood cladding, it's a few thousand cheaper." He puts pencil to paper, drawing. "If we move your scene shop to an addition at the rear of the barn, with an overhead door between it and your prop storage, then another overhead door to the stage, you have the perfect work space. Build it, move it to storage, then to the stage."

"That is the best design of all, Finn. Thank you." That keeps everything on one floor.

He high-fives me. "Okay, I'll have your final plans by tomorrow. Now, what about contractors?"

"Do you know any who are experienced in building theatres? I've worked through two with companies who weren't. The outcome wasn't good."

Finn pulls out his phone and scrolls through his contacts. "I know a couple of companies who have." He places a few calls, setting up appointments for interviews. "By the way, I'll be installing a sign board today. 'The future home of the SS Spotlight Theatre.'"

The next night, Willow has a festival steering committee meeting. Nola and I tag along to be sure everyone knows she is our spokesperson. At six-thirty, Jessica arrives to babysit the kiddos.

"Mimi!" Aysha throws her arms around Jessica's hips. "We gots Candyland all set up."

The kids grab her hands, pulling her into the front room. We wave goodbye, then head over to City Hall.

When we arrive, our cochairmen, Bud and Herb, sit with six others around a large conference table. I don't know two of those people. Sugar Springs has grown in the years I've been working.

Willow opens the meeting. "I'd like for everyone to tell us your name, how long you've lived here. If you're new, tell us what brought you to Sugar Springs. Then, tell us what area you're handling, if you already know. I'll start. I'm Willow Raines. I've lived here all my life. I'm stage manager at a professional theatre, but I will be leaving there once the SS Spotlight opens."

Willow nods to the woman on her left, Hannah Bass. She was three years ahead of me in school, but I got to know her in drama classes. She's a classic redhead with the requisite freckles and a legendary sense of humor.

"Hey, y'all, I'm Hannah. I too have always lived in Sugar Springs. My siblings and I own the grocery store, Three Marketeers. We are so glad MaNWEA's festival idea won, since one of the other two," she frowns, "tried to put us out of business. I'm coordinating food vendors."

The next person is Willow's brother, Carson. As a musician, he's perfect to head up the bands/music committee. Bud's grandson Ed will oversee security.

The next man, who I hadn't seen when I came in, is Angel, a rigger from Cruella's theatre. What in the world?

"Hey, I'm Angel Ruiz. I don't live here, but I'm hoping to be working at Marleigh's new theatre in the near future." He pauses, meeting my gaze. He raises one eyebrow in question.

"You sure can be, Angel. Let's talk after the meeting."

He nods. "I've worked with Marleigh for several years." He turns his attention to Bud and Herb. "I have experience with parking." He laughs. "I guess all of us have, but I mean I supervised parking for a downtown lot in Philly. I can handle all things traffic for you."

The next woman is new to me. Short in stature with long black hair, her outfit is funky. She appears to be quite artistic.

"I guess it's my turn. I'm Rina Tanaka. I moved to Sugar Springs five years ago when I bought the art gallery."

Okay, now I understand her fashion flair.

"What drew me to this town was its proximity to Lake Lanier along with the entertainment venues. Once Marleigh's barn theatre gets going, we will have all the arts covered. I'll oversee the art show."

Sara hesitates before speaking. She's mercurial to say the least—shy one minute, exuberant the next. "Hey, everyone. I'm Sara Villamizar. I own the gift store. I can head up the craft vendors. Oh, my parents immigrated when I was five. We ended up here. I don't want to live anywhere else. Everyone is so friendly and welcoming."

I'm thrilled she's bought in to our idea.

Bud stands up. "Thanks to everyone who came tonight. A couple of folks couldn't be here, but Tom Metford will handle the car show." His eyes flicker to mine for an instant. "Gabe Sadler agreed to head up a janitorial crew."

What? Gabe working as a janitor? I shoot a glance at Nola, but she appears as surprised as me.

"Okay, y'all. We've covered all we need to at tonight's meeting. I wanted everyone to get acquainted. We'll meet every week, since we don't have long till summer. So populate your teams and write up a proposal for what you see as your objectives. Be prepared to show us everything next Monday night."

I gather up my notes and motion Angel over. "Nola, do we have enough funding to hire Angel now?"

She nods. "We do. Go ahead. Pay him what he was making. Maybe he can help with construction or something."

"Great." I shake Angel's hand. "I'm so happy to see you here. This is Nola, our managing director. I was going to contact you and Mitch when we were closer to finishing construction. So, what's up at the Apollo?"

"I quit. Couldn't take anymore of Cruella's nasty temper."

"Well, we're about to start working on our renovation. What do you know about construction?"

"A lot. My dad was a contractor. I worked for him for years. When he was hurt, he had to give up his business."

"What made you go into rigging?"

He shrugs one shoulder. "I was in theatre in college. My girlfriend acted, so I took theatre tech but ended up working for my dad. When he retired, I decided to go back into theatre work."

I hadn't known his background. "Well, I'm tickled to have you. You can start tomorrow at what you were making." I give him our address, bidding him goodnight.

Arm in arm, we three roomies stroll home. The evening is balmy and beautiful. I try to keep my voice casual.

"Willow, did you know Gabe was going to volunteer?"

"I didn't. I was as surprised as you were. But after what he told Sergio about changing, I think he's trying to show us he has. We need to give him a chance."

I'll consider what she says, but one word gives me pause. Is Gabe's contribution all show?

Chapter 20

MARLEIGH

"I wanna stay an' watch th' men work, Marma." Elijah pleads with his hands folded beneath his chin. My wee thespian isn't a whiner, so I bite back a grin.

"I know you do, sugar-pie, but you have to go to school. Besides, it's your turn to share today. I thought you wanted to tell your friends about Miss Boo's new baby goat."

His eyes brighten. "Oh, yeah. I forgot. Can I watch after school?"

"Abso-tootin-lutely. When we walk *to* school, we'll stop to take a peek inside." Nola has a teacher conference this morning, so Aysha went with her. I'm beginning to think her daughter will grow up to be a writer. She's always telling stories. It's unfortunate some adults think she's lying.

When we stop in the barn, the contractor, who Finn and I chose, addresses his crew.

"Remember, this is light demo." George pauses until he has everyone's attention. "Some of the materials we will reuse, so be careful with those. Holler for me if you have a question." He signals a foreman. "I want you to select five men to set the new support posts."

I want to see those put up. Those posts and the new crossbeams will replace ones blocking audience sight lines. As the crew scatters for their assigned areas, I let Finn know I'll be back.

I drop off my boy a few minutes later. "I'll be here at two o'clock to get you." Elijah waves, then disappears inside the building.

When I return, Finn and George are bent over blueprints on a table. I join them, studying the plans as Finn turns from the architectural page to a mechanical page, then back again. After a couple of minutes, George nods and joins his crew.

Still staring at the blueprints, I can't make heads or elbows of any of it. "Finn, I feel like I'm trying to read Sanskrit."

"As long as George knows, we're good. His crew has some great guys. We'll get the steel posts in place today." He points to a spot on the architectural drawing. "We'll wait until Monday to set the beams."

"Why wait?"

"To give the concrete time to cure."

"That makes sense. I admit I've had nightmares about the barn collapsing when the old ones come down."

Finn lays a hammer and straight edge on each end of the computer drawings, so they don't roll up. "I knew you were nervous about it. You watch too many of those DIY shows."

My cheeks warm. "Guilty."

"You might want to leave now. You can come back later."

"Why?" I angle my head. "Did I do something wrong?"

"No, but soon we'll have two jackhammers going. Unless you have the right ear protection, you don't want to be here."

"No, thanks. I'll see you later." I head for the house. I want to start putting out flyers for auditions. We need both adults and children for our first show. I'd like to run a couple of children's drama camps this summer. I'll spend some time creating another door hanger after we're open.

The jackhammers start up as I enter the kitchen door. Wow. I can imagine how loud they are in the barn. Grabbing my laptop, I walk into the small office Nola and I share on the far side of the house. The noise level is a distant hum in here.

At our desk, I open my computer. The one name we haven't come up with is for the children's theatre. If I follow our theme, we can call it the SS Spotlight Children's Theatre. I think the girls will like it.

I divide age groups, youngest being five-to-seven-years old. The next group will be eight through twelve. The teen camp will come next year.

I'll create the names for the camps after a quick phone consult with Willow. I tap her speed dial number on my phone.

When she answers, I explain what I have. "But we need names for the camps. Do you have any thoughts?"

"Wee Players comes to mind for the youngest. What about Proscenium Players for the next age group?"

Willow always comes up with good names. "I like it. We could teach stage terminology in their camp, as well as produce a musical. I like those. Let's roll with them. I'll get the flyers created."

"Hey, let's add a technical theater education program for teens to our down-the-road plans. I know they're taught some in high school, but I'd love to mentor a few kids who have an affinity for theatre tech."

A good program to help us with grant funding. "It's a fantastic idea. Write up a proposal for us to present in an application."

I work on camp brochures until it's time to pick up the kids. Walking to school helps stretch out the kinks from sitting so long. I need a decent chair. The one thing Cruella did I liked was having good desk chairs. I tap a note in my phone to order three.

I join a gathering of moms waiting for their kiddos. We chat about the coming festival until the school doors burst open and children stampede outside. Elijah and Aysha run toward me.

"Can we go see the barn now?" asks Aysha. "'Lijah told me 'bout the men starting to work."

I grab both their hands. "Yes, you may, but you have to obey George, okay? You will stand on the side to watch. Do not get in anyone's way. Promise?"

They both let go of my hands, then hold up a pinkie finger. I clasp theirs in mine. "Pinkie promise," we say in unison. I still won't leave them alone but will stay nearby. I want them to remember the barn's conversion, since this will be their legacy.

Inside, George has small hard hats for them, which delights them. He also has child-size hammers and a pile of wood scraps for them to help build "their theatre." My mama-heart warms.

George appears to be in his forties. Too young for grandchildren and a little old for small kids. "George, you have made their day. How many children do you have?"

"Six. All boys but one."

"Did they dog your heels while you worked?"

"All the time—in particular, my daughter." There's evident pride in his voice. He pulls out his wallet, proceeding to show me a couple of photos of a small girl around five, standing beside him, hammering on a stud. "Now she's the only one who works with me." He points to a tall ladder with a worker near its top. "She's up there."

This man is a gem of a contractor. As we chat, Mr. Herb saunters into the barn. They're moving to their apartment today. Why is he here?

"I'd like to watch this old place get reborn." He turns to me. "I'll keep an eye on the littles. Go see Boo."

My brows draw together. "Is something up?"

I'm the sole witness to his almost imperceivable nod. "Okay. Don't let them get in anybody's way, please."

He shoos me out, promising to keep a close eye on them. I cross the yard, curiosity building with each step.

Boo opens the door and ushers me to her living room where Nola sits reading a newspaper. She glances up wide-eyed as I approach.

My gut clenches. Whatever they have to say won't be good. "What's wrong?"

She points to a photo on the front page of the *AJC*, Atlanta's largest newspaper. It's Gabe talking with Miss Andrews, the social worker who came to see us. Then, I read the headline.

CHILDREN'S GROUP LEADERS REPORTED TO DEFACS FOR VIOLATION OF CHILD LABOR LAWS.

GABE

The headline is devastating, but the photo? It's Dylan's best impersonation of me. While we are identical twins, there are subtleties. For one, his profile is different due to his baseball-broken nose. He purposely turned to *face* the camera, so the photo would be mistaken for me. He lied and impersonated me, giving my name.

I've never understood unbridled rage. Until now. I'm not sure if Marleigh knows Dylan and I are twins. I don't often mention our relationship to people. I try not to speak of my brother at all.

I need to tell her, but I know she won't answer my phone call. I've tried before. Instead, I call Willow. When she doesn't answer, I send her a text.

GABE: I have to explain. Please take my call.
WILLOW: ok

The minute she answers, I say, "The photo isn't me. It's my twin brother, Dylan."

"*What?*"

"Yeah. We're identical, except he broke his nose, so his profile is different."

"Why didn't you ever tell us?"

"I ... he's ... we don't get along. At all. Never have. I've always tried to keep my life separate from his." I explain some of the nuances of being his brother.

Willow sighs. "I sympathize with how you feel. Let me tell the others. I'll call you back later."

"Please be sure Marleigh understands. I'm on her side." I don't say any more. I want to tell her I love her, but she won't believe me. Not now. Maybe never. The last thing I want to do is push her.

Dylan has sunk to new levels. To be honest with myself, I'm starting to question his sanity. Money has always been his god, but he never tried to destroy—no. That's wrong. He did. He and dad always enjoyed ruining a restaurateur's life work. They did their dirty work without any remorse. I always felt uncomfortable. But Dylan? He thrived on it. Got a big thrill every time, always pushing for more.

I pace the apartment, waiting for Willow to call back. I jump when my phone rings, but it's my architect.

"Hey, Neil."

"Can you come over to the cottage? I have a couple of questions."

"Sure. I'll be right there." If Willow calls, I'm next door in case they'll let me come see them.

Neil has the plans unrolled on the hood of his car. "The movers are here for the Higgins's stuff. We can make this decision out here." He shows me a couple of problems. "One is the open concept on the main floor. Taking out walls is not insurmountable, but spanning the space with a beam large enough to support a second floor will cost an extra ten grand."

"Not a problem. Do it."

He writes a note. "Done. I've had an idea. Would you like to add a couple of small, intimate dining rooms? One could have two tables for two or three diners each, and the other could provide room for a table of eight. It's something I saw in an old inn-turned-restaurant in upstate New York."

I envision where those rooms would be. "I like the idea." We discuss placement of the new spaces along with the extra cost. I have the money for it, and I feel intimate spaces could be a draw. We shake on it.

Neil rolls up the plans. "I'll call Taffy, give him the changes. He'll send over his new estimate."

The Welshman Neil recommended as a contractor is unique to say the least. First, his name isn't a nickname, as I found out during our first conversation. He doesn't have too strong an accent since he immigrated over thirty years ago.

My phone rings. It's Willow. "Excuse me. I need to take this." I turn away. "Willow?"

"Come on over."

"Be right there." I head to the farmhouse with my heart pounding. *Father, don't let me ruin this chance to reforge these friendships. And while we're at it, help me to forgive my brother, because right now, on my own, I can't.*

MARLEIGH

"Twins?" I stare at Willow in disbelief. "Dylan is Gabe's twin. Why didn't he tell us?"

Willow shrugs. "I think Gabe tries to ignore his brother—keep their lives separate. They never got along. He didn't think their relationship would be important to us, I guess, because Dylan's not part of Gabe's life. Until he interfered with us. Now it matters."

That's an understatement. I don't have time to get used to the idea, either. Gabe's here. Willow answers the door.

When he enters the front room, I can't help feeling sorry for him. His chin is down. His shoulders slump. He stares at the floor. He raises his gaze, but looks down again.

I can tell this isn't an act. "Gabe, I think I understand. Please sit and tell us."

This time, his eyes meet mine. Naked. Vulnerable. He nods. Sergio reaches over, holding out a clenched fist. Gabe bumps his against Sergio's. It's not much of a fist-bump, though.

"I'm so sorry my brother is doing this. He's not used to losing."

That much is obvious. "I understand, but tell us about you being twins. Please?"

Gabe sighs. "Dylan is twenty minutes older than me, but was born the day before. Our parents thought it was funny, so they always celebrated each of our birthdays on the actual dates. From early on, Dylan always emphasized the *firstborn*—the heir. He rejected the twin aspect of us." Gabe shakes his head. "We never had any twin-bond. Dylan would cheat, lie, and do whatever he had to, so he could beat me. Our parents never saw it."

I can't imagine how they couldn't. "Did you ever talk to them about it?"

"They were almost never home. They bought into the old 'twins are best friends' idea and left us, for the most part, in care of a nanny. But from the time we were three, my brother began to shadow Dad—do what he did, like what he liked. As we grew up, Dad's ego was stroked by Dylan's 'mini-me' act. He was as cutthroat as Dad." Gabe closes his eyes for a moment. "But my brother has surpassed Dad. I believe greed has turned his mind."

Willow reaches for my hand and squeezes it. "Gabe, we know our problems have been your brother's doing—not yours."

I nod in agreement. Gabe's lips pull back in a half smile, but I can tell something is still eating at him.

"I appreciate your forgiveness, but I still owe Marleigh an apology along with an explanation."

"About what?" *Please don't let it be about breaking my heart. I don't think I can stand having my wounds torn open.*

"I was shocked when you first told me about your dream. I had discovered the farm a couple of weeks prior to meeting you. Somehow, I thought you knew. Then, I realized you couldn't know. I was mixed up. All I could think of was how it was like Dylan taking what I wanted. I didn't think it out. At all. I was that upset."

No wonder he left like he did. "I can guess. I think we both thought the same thing. We hadn't known each other long enough to understand any of it."

Nola stands. "I think for the sake of our mutual venture, we should put this behind us. Be friends again."

I meet her gaze. Then, following the nudge from her elbow, I cross the room and hold out my hand. "Friends."

Gabe rises. He shakes my hand. "Friends."

His hand feels good in mine.

Nola and Willow hug Gabe, while Sergio claps him on the back.

Willow slips her arm around my shoulders. "Things are so much easier now."

I agree. My thoughts go to the day Nola and I saw who we thought was Gabe with a woman going into the Mexican restaurant. That was his twin.

I still have to guard my heart, though. I can't risk another heartbreak.

Ever.

Chapter 21

GABE

I gaze at the four of them standing in the girls' front room. The relief of renewed friendships nearly buckles my knees. I understand Marleigh's tentative response. I don't blame her. After all the trouble my brother has caused, it will take time for me to prove myself.

I can start by going to the newspaper. "I'm going to the editor to demand a retraction of this story and an apology."

Marleigh's brows knit. "I don't hold out a lot of hope of a public apology, but I appreciate it, Gabe."

"The truth might do it," Sergio lays a hand on Gabe's shoulder, "when you tell them the whole story."

"Yeah, maybe we'll get a little promotion out of it." Willow slips her arm through Sergio's.

I tend to agree with Marleigh. "I have to try, though."

"How about if I go along?" Sergio glances between Willow and Gabe. "For collaboration."

Sergio is well known in Atlanta. More than I am. "I'd appreciate your help."

He kisses Willow's cheek. "See you later."

She gives me a playful punch on my shoulder. "Be persuasive."

"You can count on me trying my best."

We enter the newspaper's huge building, having solidified our strategy on the drive here. Sergio also called ahead, telling them he has more information on the story. He waves at the receptionist as we bypass her for the elevators. She waves back, so I guess it's okay. I'm glad he's with me. Who knows? By myself, I might not have seen the janitor let alone the editor.

We get off the elevator on the fourth floor, stepping into a large, noisy room. Several desks have occupants tapping away on their computers. Sergio gives a sideways jerk of his head, gesturing to a glass office two doors down. I nod, letting him lead the way.

The man inside rises as we approach his door. A thick thatch of nut-brown, wavy hair crowns a face as chiseled as granite. His eyes are a startling blue. His smile reveals perfect teeth, albeit somewhat coffee stained.

Sergio shakes his hand. "Jim."

"Sergio, how are you? It's been a while." He frowns. "Sadler."

I flatten my lips. How does he know me? Oh. The article. Of course.

As he moves to his desk, he motions to two chairs. "Have a seat."

He waits until we settle ourselves. "So, what is this new information?" He pierces me with a stare. "I thought you told me everything the other day—."

Sergio holds up his hand to stop him. "This man told you nothing. The man you interviewed is Gabe's identical twin brother, Dylan."

Jim turns narrowed eyes on me. "Can you prove it?"

"If you have any other photos from the interview, bring them out. I'll show you."

Keeping his eyes on me, he picks up the phone. "Hey, Cliff, do you still have the extra photos from the child labor story we ran yesterday? Good. Bring 'em into my office." He hangs up. Leaning back, his chair squeaks in protest. "What are we looking for?"

"A profile shot of my brother."

Jim nods. "I know we have one. Cliff told me you, or your brother, balked when the photographer took it—told him none but full face photos."

The door opens. A young man I guess to be Cliff tosses a few photos on Jim's desk before leaving. Jim rests his elbows on his desk as he thumbs through the images. "Ahh, here." He holds up an eight-by-ten.

Sergio nods to me. I turn sideways. "Jim, what do you see?"

Out of the corner of my eye, I see Jim hold up the photo. His gaze switches between me, the photo, then back again. His ruddy complexion pales.

"You don't have a hump on your nose."

I turn to face him. "Bingo. My brother's was broken in a ball game."

"Why did he impersonate you?"

I glance at Sergio. The last thing I want is for our mess to be reported.

Sergio leans forward. "Dylan—Gabe's brother—wants the land Marleigh Evans bought. Thus, his involvement. He made a false accusation to DEFACS about her and her business partner. You can check with them. They will verify what we are saying. We want a retraction of this story with an apology."

"Why?" He narrows his eyes.

I can't believe he's asking. "Because the story is false. That photo wasn't of me. The accusation is not true."

Sergio stands, puts his hands on Jim's desk, leaning on them. He's in the editor's face. "This paper has always prided itself on printing truth." He taps the photo. "This isn't. The young women are trying to start a community theatre with a children's program. This could destroy it."

"There's something missing." The newsman's gaze bounces between us. "What is it?"

Sergio explains the competition the mayor ran to determine who bought her land. Then, I tell him what the children did. When we finish, Jim bursts out laughing.

"That beats anything I could have thought up." He stands. "I'll have the reporter draft a retraction and apology. We'll print it."

We shake hands, then take our leave. I don't speak until we're in the car. "Do you think he'll do it?"

"Yeah. Jim's an honest man. Your brother tricked him, and he doesn't like being duped."

My one hope is Marleigh's reputation isn't damaged beyond repair.

MARLEIGH

This shopping trip is the diversion I need. We scour stores at Perimeter Mall since there are more upscale boutiques there. Jessica finds three dresses she likes in one of them.

"Well, go try them on." I shoo her into a dressing room. Nola follows her mom to help.

I snag Willow's elbow. "Let's see if they have something for us."

"I already found mine. Remember?" She slides hangers across the bars, studying each gown before moving on. "Ooh, this one would look nice on you. Nola, too."

"We don't want the same dresses. Let Nola choose first, since she's matron of honor."

Willow finds one in Nola's size. She takes it to a dressing room for her to try. I keep looking, but my mind isn't on this hunt as much as Gabe and Sergio. Have they secured a retraction? A couple of hours have passed.

Willow whoops as she walks toward me, phone to her ear. "We have an apology, and the story will be retracted."

"I'm glad, though I still worry how much damage was done to our reputation."

"Marleigh, anyone who knows us won't believe that story."

"But what about someone who lives in a nearby town who might want to enroll their child in our camps?"

Jessica walks up behind me. "We can pray. Prayer's our best defense."

She's right. "Thank you for reminding me."

She holds up a beautiful pale rose lace dress. Its color is so light, it's almost cream. "I'm taking this one. It's the exact dress I had imagined. Nola looks perfect in the one Willow brought her."

Now for me. "I think I've found one too." I cross to another rack where I remove a beautiful outfit. It has wide-legged, flowing chiffon pants, a sleeveless top, and sequined jacket. The color is a soft, spring green. When I put it on, it appears to be a dress, but affords me the ease of movement pants offer.

Jessica lays her dress over her arm. "This has been a successful excursion. Let's check out and go home. It's about time for school to be out."

"The newspaper should have our story straight by the afternoon issue. Why don't you stay for supper? Invite Walter to join us." Today has buoyed my spirits. Together, we can all celebrate.

We park the car as our mayor-slash-babysitter walks up with the kids from school. When I jump out, Elijah slams into me, crying his heart out. I glance up at Miss Boo as I wrap my arms around my little boy. "What's happened?"

She shakes her head, a sour expression on her face. "A nasty comment about y'all was made within the children's hearing. CeCe told them it wasn't true, but you know some people *want* to believe the worst. Poor Elijah."

I squat in front of him. "Sugar, the newspaper is going to tell everyone their story wasn't true. Everything will be all right. You'll see." I kiss his wet cheeks, then dry them with my sleeve. "Come on, let's go inside. Mimi Jessica is staying for supper."

My explanation helps, but my heart aches over him witnessing how certain people get malignant pleasure out of someone's misfortune without bothering to learn the truth.

We're relaxing with sweet tea when Walter arrives. "I brought the afternoon paper." He kisses Jessica, then hands his newspaper to Nola.

She lays it on the table. Starting on its first page, she scans for the retraction. Her eyes sweep over the various stories, then she turns the page. Again, scan ... turn. Turn another. And again. The apology is on the last page of the third section. Nola's eyes grow large.

"The apology says, 'We were duped on the original story and are sorry if we misled anyone. This is a hotbed of intrigue, pitting brother against brother.'" Nola locks her gaze on mine. "At least Gabe moved the focus off you. Poor dude."

"I don't blame him for any of this. Still, no matter what the paper says, my reputation has taken a hit."

Elijah sidles up to me, then climbs into my lap. He cups my face in his small hands. "Marma, you tol' me to pray an' ask God to help me. You gots to do the same. An' he'll do it. The Bible says so. An' it's God's book."

I forget he hears everything. "You are so right, sugar-pie. I love you for reminding me." I hug him before he hops off my lap, running to play with Aysha. "I'll call Gabe, let him know it's okay."

Before I can call him, Nola's phone rings. She frowns. "It's the bank. Hello? Yes, this is she. What?" Nola jumps up.

Her reaction doesn't bode well. I stand, not knowing why. My heartbeat accelerates. My mouth turns dry.

"Why? I don't think that's legal. You'll be hearing from us through our attorney."

Walter's brow furrows. "What's wrong, Nola?"

Her mouth opens, then closes. Her gaze moves from me, to each one of us and back. She inhales a deep breath, then exhales. "The bank is calling in our loan—immediately. We have to return all money we've drawn."

My heart stops. The room spins. I drop back into the chair before I faint. "Why?"

She takes a sip of tea, swishing the liquid around in her mouth. "The board is demanding it."

I don't understand. "What does the board have to do with it? The loan committee approved it. We've already drawn from it. This is crazy. What are we going to do?"

Walter puts his hands on Nola's shoulders and sits her down. "You're going to relax. I'll fund the loan for you," he winks, "at a family rate of interest."

Nola gapes. "You're willing to fund us?"

He lifts his hands, palms up. "Of course. I believe in what you're doing. I know the theatre will be a success. It's a great investment." He moves behind Jessica, placing his hands on her shoulders. "Besides, I don't want our wedding delayed. You girls need to get busy."

Jessica reaches up and lays her hand over his. "Wise man."

My heart soars. I stand and hug Walter. "Thank you."

Then, a thought hits me. I hope Gabe's loan isn't called in too. I need to thank him for the retraction and warn him. I bite my lip. We've been saved by Walter, but what about Gabe's dream?

GABE

I answer a knock on my door. "Sergio. Come on in. What's up?"

"I'm sorry to say the retraction only made the last page of section three. That reporter made innuendos to intrigue between you and Dylan."

"Are the girls clear?"

He rubs the back of his neck with his hand. "I think they'll come out okay. But Willow called to ask me to find you. Can you come with me?"

I grab my phone off the counter. "Let's go. What do you suppose happened?" I lock the door behind us.

"With the paper? My guess is Jim told Cliff to retract it, but he's young. It appears he wanted to sensationalize it. Get his byline noticed. Some journalists today aren't like the older ones who were all about getting the whole truth."

When we arrive at the farmhouse, Willow grabs our hands, pulling us inside. "Boy, do we have a lot to tell you."

She beckons us with a crook of her finger to follow her into the kitchen. Nola's mom and Walter are there too. Marleigh, leaning against the counter, seems relieved to see me. She crosses the room, her expression shy as she approaches.

"Hey, thanks for going to the paper. I appreciate it."

"I'm sorry the results weren't better."

"Don't worry about it. We have a new problem, though. Well, not a problem anymore, thanks to Walter."

This has been a day of confusion. "What's this about?"

Nola hands Gabe a glass of sweet tea. "I don't mean to be nosy, but do you have your construction loan with the bank here in town?"

He swirls the ice in his glass. "No. Why?"

Marleigh gestures for us to sit. Their kitchen table is a banquette with enough seating to accommodate everyone. I slide into a spot on the bench next to Nola.

Marleigh sits on a chair near me. "Our loan was called in by the bank. Immediate return of funds."

"What?" I can't believe it. "Why?"

"The board demanded it."

I hold up both my hands. "Wait. That doesn't seem right. Banks have loan committees."

"Exact words I said." Marleigh's grin is off kilter—not a lot but enough for me to notice.

My mind whirls. I could help them, but I don't know if she would accept it. "What are you going to do?"

"I'm funding their loan," Walter says with a shrug. "Investing in businesses is what I do."

What a spot of good luck. No. Not luck—a blessing.

God knew.

Thank you for taking care of them.

"Congratulations." I take a swig of tea.

"Is your loan secure, young fella?"

I startle. "Yes, sir." I don't want to tell them I didn't take out a loan, unless I count it as a loan to myself.

He eyes me. "Well, if you need any financial advice, let me know."

"As a matter of fact, I do have something I believe you could help me with. Can we get together next week?"

Walter hands me his card. "Call me."

"What I would still like to know," Marleigh says, "is why the bank's board recalled our loan."

Somehow, Dylan is in the middle of it. I don't know how, but I'm going to find out.

Chapter 22

GABE

I set the oven temperature to four hundred degrees. This apartment oven is good, but not restaurant quality. If these roasted vegetables come out as I hope, I'll add them to my menu. Since I've left Wild Azalea, I can devote my attention to creating recipes for my own restaurant.

My own restaurant. Saying those words feels good—except my brother keeps invading my thoughts. Why is he so determined to get this property? A strip mall off any main road isn't a worthy investment. It wouldn't bring in much money, breaking even at best.

To figure this out, I have to think as devious-Dylan would. So, I set *why* aside for a moment and follow the trail of *how* he's threatened Sugar Springs' merchants. Wait. I stop chopping vegetables. Could he be—? No. Yes. Threats are a way of life for Dylan.

Laying down my knife, I turn on my tablet, and bring up the bank's website. I don't know why I didn't think of this before. I click on the "About Us" tab.

And there he is.

Dylan is an officer on the board of directors. Talk about a polecat in the hen house. But it still doesn't answer my question of *why* he wants it.

I close the tablet and go back to my vegetables. I toss them in a mixture of olive oil, a bit of soy sauce, a balsamic vinegar reduction, along with a few spices. After placing them in a roasting pan, I slide them in the oven, then set its timer.

Pacing the great room, I attempt to deconstruct this dilemma in my mind. Dylan had a hand in cancelling Beauty's loan—that's patently obvious. There's no other explanation. The girls have sufficient investors. Marleigh has her mother's money. The farmland itself is viable equity. Even Nola invested some of her inheritance. The bank has no logical reason to call in their loan.

Unless ... does the paperwork have a morals clause? Some do. Would the newspaper story be enough to cancel their loan? I grab my phone.

"Sergio, can you have the girls check their loan paperwork for a morals clause?"

"I can, but those are antiquated—not used in today's world. Can you tell me why?"

"I think my brother demanded they use the newspaper story to cancel their loan. He's on their board of directors."

Sergio groans. "What a lousy thing to do. Y'know, I have trouble believing you two came from the same parents. Okay, so we know this was him. What we don't know is why."

"Right. That question is driving me nuts." I check the oven, then walk to the French doors overlooking the farm beyond my patio. "The strip mall he had in his proposal was okay, but the mall wouldn't have given him the return he'd expect. I think there's another reason."

"Subdivision? Expensive houses? Those aren't his normal ventures, are they?"

"No. He did mention a new anchor store, but I still don't buy it. A strip mall in Sugar Springs is like an afterthought."

I turn away from the doors. "Stores visited by Sugar Springs residents. There aren't enough apartments to support it. Besides, a strip mall won't draw tourists. Local merchants are too savvy to want one of his stores." I put the phone on speaker to check the vegetables again. They're close to being done. "He leases for exorbitant prices." Using a large spoon, I turn the vegetables.

"What are you doing?"

"Sorry. I'm working on a recipe for the Garden Table."

"Need a taste tester?"

"Sure. Come over when you can. These can be reheated. I'll throw a couple of steaks on the grill when you arrive."

"Sounds good. I'll ponder what you've told me—see if I can get a handle on what and where to begin investigating. To be honest, I think his strip mall is a smoke screen. See you at five-thirty."

A smokescreen? Hmm, I didn't think in terms of diversionary tactics. I set the phone on the counter and slide the roasting pan back into the oven to finish off the veggies. A diversion makes sense, though. My brother isn't stupid. He's sneaky. Underhanded. Ruthless. So, if his mall is a cover-up, what is he after? I'd like to see if Dad knows anything, but Dylan said they were on a cruise.

But on the possibility that they are home by now, I pick up my phone, tapping in Dad's number, but it goes straight to voice mail. What I need to tell him shouldn't be left in a message.

After our meal, Sergio and I linger over coffee on the patio. "Are you coming to the festival committee meeting tonight with Willow?"

"If I can move after eating your great meal, sure. But why do you need me?"

I pick up our plates, carrying them to the kitchen. "As backup. Willow's going to warn them about Dylan, explaining he's my twin."

"Smart move. I'll tell her to meet us here."

While he calls Willow, I wash the dishes. She arrives a few minutes later. We all head over to City Hall.

As soon as I sit, I get the evil-eye from Rina. As soon as Willow calls the meeting to order, Rina raises her hand.

"Yes, Rina?"

"We have a weasel in the henhouse."

Willow frowns. "What do you mean?"

Rina glares at me. "Gabe went to see Zully, telling her to not go along with the festival. If she didn't go along, her business loan would be cancelled."

Extortion. My brother's worse than a weasel.

Hannah gasps. "He told me the same thing."

"That wasn't Gabe, Rina. He has a twin brother."

"He does?" Rina squints and examines me like an exterminator would a cockroach.

"I do. We're identical except for my brother's nose has a pronounced hump from being broken in high school."

Bud runs his fingers over his nose. "I noticed the bump. Wondered why I'd never seen it before."

"He didn't come to me, but some thug tried to intimidate me." Tom Metford drums his fingers on the table. "He promised he'd make it worth my while if I'd pulled out. Why's your brother doing this?"

"Because he wants us to fail. He's still trying to get the land. Dylan is not used to losing."

Rina's frown hasn't relaxed. "How can he threaten to have a business loan cancelled?"

My brother's web is very tangled. "He can't legally. But here's the kicker. He sits on the bank's board of directors."

Herb gapes at me. "At Sugar Springs Bank?" When I nod, his face mottles red. "We'll see about that." He points a finger at me. "You and I are going to have a chat with Neil Porter tomorrow morning. We'll take the gals too if they all can come."

"Sure, but who is this Porter fellow?"

Herb's grin is wicked. "Chief executive officer at the bank ... and another first cousin."

MARLEIGH

Willow is tied up in tech week at work, so it's just Nola with me. We climb in the back seat of Gabe's Yukon. Mr. Herb sits in the front passenger seat. He stretches his arm across the back of the seat, turning as far as his seatbelt will allow while Gabe eases the SUV onto the main road.

"When we get into Neil's office, let me lead this conversation. I want him to understand how many depositors he can lose over this mess." He glances at Gabe. "We can't have Dylan threatening our merchants."

No, we can't. I feel like this is my fault. Gabe has to feel bad too, since his brother is causing all this. I catch Gabe's gaze in the rearview mirror. "I'm sorry about this. It has to be hard having any family member pit himself against you."

Gabe turns onto the highway with a shrug. "It's been this way all my life. I'm just sorry he's dragged y'all into his fight with me."

Nola leans forward, "Gabe, this isn't your fault. If Marleigh and I hadn't had such a great idea, none of this would be happening."

"I appreciate the sentiment, but," his gaze catches mine in the mirror, "I'm trying to understand why it's happening. Why God is allowing this." He lapses into silence.

Funny, I asked God the same thing last night. I don't have an answer yet, but Gabe doesn't need to know. I'm not sure how strong his faith in God is.

A couple of minutes later, we pull into the parking lot. Inside, the bank resembles any other financial institution in any given city in America. Marble and mahogany seem to be the standard—a motif to have us feeling it's safe—a solid place for our money. I used to come here as a little girl with Mom. She banked here for as long as I can remember.

"Good morning, Herb. How can I help you?" The woman's voice pulls me from reminiscing. A beautiful woman with a head-full of long braids.

"Morning, Luella. I, well we, need to see Neil."

"I think he has a meeting in a few minutes, but I'll see if he can spare some time for you."

"Tell him if he knows what's good for him, he will."

Luella's eyebrows almost disappear into her hairline as she pops her eyes wide open. "Yes, sir. I'll tell him." She scurries away.

I swat Mr. Herb's arm. "Shame on you."

"Shame nothin'. I want him wary when we come in."

"Do you think he'll see us?" Gabe asks.

Herb winks. "He'll see us."

Luella crosses the lobby. "He'll see you. Please follow me."

We're shown to a conference room instead of Mr. Porter's office. A mahogany coffered ceiling rises high above mahogany walls. Windows look out onto a small, enclosed garden. On a large oval conference table, glasses, note pads, and pens reside in front of each chair. While we find seats, Luella removes a pitcher of water from a small refrigerator in a sideboard.

A moment later, Mr. Porter enters. "Herb, what's this nonsense about knowing what's good for me?" He sits at the head of the table, hands folded against its polished surface. When his eyes land on Gabe, he startles. "Dylan? What do you know about this?"

Gabe smiles. "I'm Gabriel Sadler. Dylan is my twin brother."

Mr. Porter shakes his head. "I had no idea." His gaze bounces between Herb and Gabe. "What's going on?"

Herb leans back in his chair, leaning to one side. "First, I'm here as mayor pro tem, appointed by the city council, to act in Boo's stead."

Neil tilts his head, narrows his eyes. His attention to his cousin doesn't waver.

"Tell me, Neil, did you know Dylan Sadler—a member of the bank's board of directors—is threatening town merchants with losing their loans?"

"What?" Neil glares. "Who cooked up such a cockamamie story?"

"I'm afraid this isn't a story, Mr. Porter. My brother wants the land Marleigh," Gabe gestures to me, "bought from the Higginses. This past week, her loan, approved and funded by this institution, was cancelled."

Neil frowns, his brows dipping to the bridge of his nose. He picks up a phone. "Bring me the Evans loan file. I don't know. No, it was canceled last week, so I'm told. Just find it." He hangs up, his attention switching to me. "While we wait for their file, will you fill me in on this ... situation?"

"We provided a healthy down payment for the construction loan. That loan was approved, funded, then canceled days later. I'd like to know why."

Luella slips in the door with a woefully thin file. That could be good ... or bad. Neil takes the folder from her, lays it on the table in front of him. He begins reading.

"Mr. Porter, you have your meeting—"

He shoos her out like a pesky fly. "Tell them I'll be late and to wait."

She startles, blinks, then leaves.

He continues through the papers, then stops. He lifts a newspaper clipping. "What's this about? You know we have a morals clause in our loans."

Heat rises in my face even though the story he's referencing isn't true. Gabe frowns.

"Another of my brother's lies. He called in a false report to DEFACS, following that with the newspaper, feeding them a bogus story. What you don't have there is the retraction and apology from the paper."

I can almost see Neil's mind churning as he eyes me. After what seems an eternity, he picks up the few pieces of paper, taps them against the table, jogging them into order. "So, what are you after? Do you want me to reinstate your loan?"

"No, sir. I've procured a loan elsewhere."

He startles. "May I ask where? I'd like to know the competition, since we fund most all the downtown businesses."

I don't want to tell him. Walter and Jessica don't need to be brought into this. Besides, if Dylan finds out—

"May I?" Herb winks at me.

"Please." I relax.

"I'll tell you what we want." Herb rests his elbows on the table, hands folded. "We want Dylan removed from your board effective today. If not, I can promise you will lose the city as a depositor, along with most of the merchants in the downtown area, not to mention how information has a way of filtering down to general depositors. I imagine the financial loss will be significant."

Neil's face drains of color. Is he having a heart attack? I glance at Herb, but he doesn't seem concerned for his cousin.

"Then, we want charges filed against Dylan. What he's doing is extortion."

Neil doesn't speak. His gaze shifts to each of us, resting for a moment before moving on. What is he looking for? Finally, he sighs and sits back against his chair, mimicking Herb earlier.

"I will have him removed from the board effective today, but I hesitate to prosecute. The publicity will destroy us. You don't want our ruin, do you, Herb? Your beef is with Sadler, not the bank. Am I right?"

Herb's mouth flattens to a thin line. "I understand your concern for the bank, Neil, but the mayor and council have to protect Sugar Springs's merchants." He glances at me, then Gabe, raising one eyebrow. "Are you agreeable to Dylan's removal from the board but no prosecution?"

Gabe's expression is grim. I can't begin to imagine what his thoughts are. Even though his relationship with his brother isn't close, it has to be difficult to have his twin put him in this situation.

For his sake, I nod. Then, Gabe nods too.

None of us say anything as we exit the bank. After we leave the parking lot, Herb turns in his seat. "Let's hope this action will put an end to Dylan's shenanigans."

Gabe's grimace doesn't ease my mind any. "Do you think your brother will do something else?"

His sigh is deep and long. "I've never known him to concede defeat once his mind is made up. My fear is this will fuel his anger. I'm sorry I brought this on y'all."

Gabe's eyes don't meet mine in the mirror. I've never seen him so demoralized.

Chapter 23

MARLEIGH

What a kerfuffle. I tap the "off" button on my phone, then drop a French vanilla coffee pod in the Keurig.

Nola shuffles into the kitchen. "What's wrong? Don't try to tell me nothing. Your shoulders are drooping."

"You know you're scary."

She shrugs. "I know you almost as well as God does. Drop in a Donut Shop pod for me, please. Now, answer my question."

I start her coffee. "I just hung up the phone with the contractor. George heard our loan was canceled, so he took on another project."

"Dylan strikes again."

My stomach curdles whenever I hear Dylan's name. "I can accept his grievance with Gabe, but why me—us?"

Nola shakes her head and slides onto the banquette. "We are not the reason, Marleigh. This isn't personal. Dylan Sadler doesn't care *who* stands in his way. He's a bully. He'll threaten anyone to achieve what he wants."

"I guess you're right, but now we have to start interviewing contractors all over again. The festival kicks off in less than two months. We won't be ready."

Nola chews her bottom lip a moment, then brightens. "We'll ask Gabe's contractor if he knows someone who is good. Someone who is trustworthy. I hadn't told you yet, but we picked up an anonymous donor through Walter. A large one. Enough to cover several of our wants."

Sweet relief flows over me. "Any idea who it is?"

"None. I think Walter knows, but he isn't telling."

"Thank God for whoever it is, because with our time crunch, the work may cost more. I guess it wouldn't hurt to ask Gabe. I know he trusts his contractor—the man's doing a fantastic job on the restaurant. I wonder if he knows someone who's built theatres."

Nola jumps out of her chair, snatching up her mug as she does. "Come on. Get dressed. Let's go ask Gabe."

Why not? The worst possibility is he says no. "Okay. Give me five minutes."

Upstairs, I slide on a pair of jeans and a T-shirt. Where are my sneakers? I search under my bed. Maybe I left them by the back door. I run a brush through my hair, then twist it, securing its mass with a butterfly clip.

Nola stands outside my bedroom door. "Are you ready?"

"Except for my shoes. I think they're on the back porch."

"They are. Let's go."

Two minutes later, we're inside Gabe's cottage. By the look of things, he'll be able to open his restaurant in time for the festival, maybe even before.

He waves. "Come on in. You haven't seen what Taffy's accomplished here."

Taffy? The man behind Gabe turns. A broad grin spreads across a jolly face topped by thick, red hair.

"Marleigh, Nola, this is Taffy, my contractor."

"Pleased to meet y'all, ladies."

His Southern drawl is counterintuitive to his looks. "You've moved fast with this." I gesture to the space, where old, whitewashed barn wood covers the walls. "I know it's new, but the addition looks a hundred years old."

"Thank you." He smiles to turns to talk with a crew member, who has tapped his shoulder.

I glance at Gabe. "It's beautiful. I'm so glad you're fulfilling your dream."

And I am. In the past few weeks, Gabe has become a good friend—someone I trust. My heart yearns for what we had before, but he gives no indication his does. I can't risk being hurt again. Friendship is enough.

"Gabe," Nola interrupts my thoughts. "We're suddenly without a contractor. Ours took another job. Do you think Taffy can recommend someone who can take on the barn?"

His smile goes straight to my heart. "I anticipated that possibility."

You did? "How? I mean why?"

His eyes roll. "With all my brother has done, I figured he might try some other way to stop construction. So, I asked Taffy if he'd take a look at the barn, just in case. He has several crews, since he contracts simultaneous projects. We're down to the finishing work here already."

"I appreciate it, but this is a theatre."

Taffy joins us. "Marleigh, I've seen your barn. Anyway, I know Finn very well."

"You do?"

"Don't be so surprised. This is a small industry. Georgia contractors and architects are well acquainted with one another. Finn has a great reputation. As long as he's planned theatres—and he has—I don't need to. With what's been done already, I can have the barn completed in six weeks."

In time for the festival. My heart soars. But the cost. "What's the cost difference?"

Taffy wipes his hand down his pants leg, inspects it, then offers it to me. "The price might be a little more because of the short time. How about we look at your blueprints first, and I'll give you a bid?"

Nola reaches past me to shake his hand. "I'll run back for the blueprints. You stay here, Marleigh. Check out his work." She winks.

Gabe touches my elbow, sending a shiver down my arm. "Let me show you the kitchen."

We enter a room where appliances stand ready for installation. I'm gobsmacked. The walls are tiled to the ceiling. His floor is polished concrete with a drain in the center. All the counters are stainless steel, except one. I run my fingers over its cold marble surface, raising a questioning eyebrow to Gabe.

"The marble's for making bread and pastry."

"You're a baker too?"

Gabe chuckles. "Not in your wildest dreams. I've hired one."

"How did you get so much done so fast? It's been what? A little over three weeks since you started?"

"Taffy didn't have too much to do." Gabe leans against a center island. "Not like the barn renovation. This is an old kitchen, so plumbing was already here. His biggest job was increasing the size of the drain lines to handle industrial use. To expand the kitchen, we needed to remove a wall. Taffy's crew had the wall down, drywall up, taped, and mudded in the same day."

I'm starting to think his contractor can do what he says. With our new donor—"You don't mind us asking to use him?"

"I'm glad you trust me enough to want to." Gabe's eyes are warm, holding mine for a long moment. His lips part. My heart beat drums in my ears. Is he ... Oh, I want—

Nola sticks her head into the kitchen. "Marleigh, can you come in here?"

I blink. The moment is lost, leaving me to wonder if it happened at all.

"Sure." I join them in the restaurant's soon-to-be dining room. Taffy unrolls our blueprints, then nods. "Let's go over there to take a three-dimensional look. You coming, Gabe?"

"No, I need to stay here to make sure they get everything situated in the right place."

As we walk across the yard, I glance sidelong at Taffy. He's brawny—nothing like his name might suggest. "I'm sure everyone asks you, but how did you get your name?"

His laugh is hearty. "It's Welsh. I won't go into all the derivatives and pronunciations, but I was named Dafydd, Welsh for David, after my grandfather. Taffy is the Anglicized nickname. Because my little brother pronounced it that way, it stuck."

And here I thought he was Irish.

"By your accent, I'm guessing you were raised here." Nola says. "I'll bet you had a few fights over your name in your school years."

"Not as many as you might think. I worked hard to excel in soccer. Soon, my teammates had my back."

Taffy opens the barn's door while I flip a light switch. Three naked bulbs illuminate the space. "George didn't get much done beyond the main support structure before he left us."

Taffy stops at a table beneath a light where he unrolls the blueprints. "Not a problem. With Finn's plans, I can see everything I need. He's very detailed, more than most. See this?" He points to a list in one corner. "These are some suppliers he recommends—not a normal inclusion, but in this case being a theatre, it's sure helpful."

Nola and I stand back, silent while he goes through the paperwork. He calls a couple of vendors, tapping on his phone's calculator. After a few minutes and two more phone calls, he rolls up the plans. "I can do this job for close to what George quoted you. I can guarantee the cost won't be more than ten-k over. I'll try for less, but I can have it completed in six weeks. The extra crew causes the price to be a little higher."

Relief weakens my knees. I grab Nola's hand, giving it a squeeze. "The extra cost is worth it. Thank you, Taffy."

"Yes, thank you," Nola says. "Please draw up a contract. We'll sign today."

After a handshake, I follow Nola back to the farmhouse. She nudges me with her elbow. "I get the sense you trust Gabe again."

"I do. He's proved himself." I meet her gaze. "But we don't go beyond friendship, Nola. I can't risk another broken heart."

GABE

Marleigh walks away, and the moment is lost. I'd come so close to taking her in my arms. They ache to hold her. At least she trusts me again. As a friend. I have to keep reminding myself. She's as skittish as a newborn fawn. I hurt her badly. *Lord, heal her heart. Even if she can't be mine, allow her to find love.*

"Gabe?" Taffy's crew chief taps my shoulder. "According to these plans, your stove goes here." He points to the center of the room.

"Right." I rein in my thoughts—focus on the work at hand. "The top half of the wall between the main dining area and the kitchen will be glass. I want diners to be able to see their food being cooked."

After dreaming about this for several years, I designed the kitchen myself. I have my prep stations—hot and cold—on one side, the dishwashing station opposite it, with staging beneath the window to the dining room. The cooking and baking islands are center stage.

The crew leader nods. "They'll like watching. I'll like it." He grins. "I plan to be here opening night."

"You'll be my first guest."

He signals his crew, who move the stove into place. Next, they install the convection ovens. They should have all my appliances in by this afternoon.

I turn in a circle. Satisfaction is a wonderful feeling. *You are a faithful keeper of dreams, Lord.*

With the crew chief well in charge, I walk upstairs to take care of some business. The second-floor addition went up fast. Herb and Boo Higgins only had one bedroom upstairs. When I wanted a second one for an office, Taffy had it completed in two weeks. The rooms still need painting, and there aren't any doors hung yet, but I can work here now.

At my desk, I go online to my food supplier. I place an order for everything I'll need to test recipes. Soon, I'll start looking for my kitchen crew and waitstaff. Now, I make a list of what I need to outfit the kitchen. My dining room alone constitutes another long list.

Twenty minutes later, with my lists in hand, I check with the crew chief downstairs. "If you need me, you have my cell number. I'll be gone two or three hours, but I won't be more than a few minutes away."

He waves me off.

I'll be able to start testing recipes in the kitchen soon. I'll invite Sergio, Finn, and the girls to be my taste testers. On a whim, I call Marleigh.

"Hey, in a couple of hours, if you and Elijah are free, do you want to help me set up all the kitchen paraphernalia I'm about to buy? I'll pay Elijah."

"Sure, but only if you promise to reciprocate when I outfit the theatre." A playful lilt in Beauty's voice sends a thrill down my spine.

"Deal." I'm glad she can't see my goofy grin as I head for Restaurant Depot.

Once inside the Depot, I pull out a flatbed trolly. Heading up one aisle, I load up pots, pans, trays, and more, checking them off my list as they go on the flatbed. Once it's full, I checkout my first round, unload everything into the Yukon, then head back inside for another round.

Shopping takes me close to three hours, a couple thousand dollars, and a very full Yukon. I call Beauty on my way back. "I'm done. Are all y'all ready to work?"

I wish I had Beauty and Elijah today, but he's in school, and she's busy with her renovations. My apartment above the restaurant is finished. The paint is still tacky, but I couldn't wait. I moved in this morning.

I had fun, the other day, watching Elijah help put away all my small equipment. He had the best time examining all the different utensils I use. That boy is so inquisitive—he reminds me of myself as a kid. I wanted to know everything. Beauty was relaxed, laughed a lot, making my heart light.

Since so much is ready in the restaurant kitchen, tomorrow morning I'm going to start planting my garden.

I'll have to use local farms for fresh veg and fruit for the first few weeks, though.

Outside, a horn signals the nursery delivery truck with my order. I lean out the window. "I'll be right down. You can set things on the side of the building." I point to the edge of my fields, then put on jeans, an old T-shirt, and boots.

As I come outside, the driver is arguing with a man who looks familiar.

"What's wrong?"

The guy—I wish I could place him—holds out a cease work order. "You have to stop everything. No deliveries, no nothin'."

"What? Why?"

A snarky grin spreads his lips. "You failed your final inspection."

"How? My contractor said everything was signed already."

The man sneers. "Nope. Plumbing's bad and bar nerfugle murph."

I can't make out what he said. "I beg your pardon?"

"Your friend there," he jerks his thumb over his shoulder toward the barn, "failed her electrical."

He slaps "caution/keep out" tape across the doorways.

"Hold on a minute. I just moved in upstairs."

"Ain't my problem. I just deliver the building inspector's findings."

My hands curl into fists as he climbs into his car, gravel flying when he drives away.

Chapter 24

GABE

With my phone to my ear, I punch in Sergio's number while climbing into my truck. "Hey man, can I bunk with you for a couple days?"

"Sure. What's up?"

"Some redneck from the building inspector's office served me with a cease work order."

"What?" I have to pull the phone away from my ear at Sergio's shout. "I don't believe this. Did he say why?"

"He said we failed our final inspection. Bad plumbing or some half-baked story. Then, he said something about Marleigh's failed electrical, which I know isn't true. We have the best contractor around. I need to get to the bottom of this."

"Do you think it's your brother?"

"I'd stake my life on it." I pound the steering wheel as I realize where I've seen the guy before. "The so-called inspector is my brother's 'muscle' who does Dylan's intimidation for him." How can Dylan get away with this? I stifle a growl of disgust. "Listen I'll see you later. I need to check on something."

"Send me a text when you're coming over."

"Thanks, buddy." I click off, then call the building inspector's office. This has to be another of Dylan's diversionary tactics—not a real cease work order.

When the clerk answers, I cut straight to the point. "I'm calling regarding a construction permit for number fourteen, Level Creek Road. Are there any inspection failures listed?"

"Hold, please. I'll check."

She takes her sweet time. An eternity later, she's back. "Sir?"

I snap to attention. "I'm here. Did you find something?"

"Yes, the final plumbing. Do you want to schedule another inspection?"

"Not yet. Thank you."

Next, I call Taffy. "How fast can you get here?"

"I'm around the corner. Two minutes."

"Good." My need to get to the bottom of this makes me snap. "Sorry. I'm so ticked off right now."

"Can you tell me what's up?"

"Yeah. I just got a stop work order. I know it's phony, but the jerk said we failed the final inspection."

"What?" Taffy's reaction explodes in my ear. "I've never heard such a load of codswallop. I'll be right there."

I get out of my truck, glancing up at the heavens. "We need your help, Lord. I can't figure out how Dylan's guy managed to deliver a cease work order. This whole thing is confusing."

God isn't handing out answers right now, but Taffy's pickup flies into the driveway, skidding to a stop. He jumps out.

"I called Finn to meet us here. What in the Sam Hill is going on?" He reaches back inside the cab of his truck and drags out a clipboard. "I know everything has been done to code or above. I'll stake my reputation on it." He slaps his hand on his clipboard.

"I believe you. Let's go over to Marleigh's and tell her what's happened. I'll explain everything then."

As we walk to Marleigh's, I call Sergio, asking him to join us. He has money invested in both projects. He deserves to know what's going on.

Taffy and I sit at Marleigh's kitchen table while she pours sweet tea. I tell her about the "failures." Her gaze slides to Taffy. I shake my head.

"It's not the work. It's Dylan. Again."

Beauty looks like she might cry or throw up. She sets glasses in front of everyone, while Nola brings a plate of cookies to the table. Willow arrives with Sergio, filling up the last seats.

"Who is Dylan?" Taffy asks.

"My twin brother." I explain his skullduggery. "Somehow, he's managed to get his henchman inside the inspector's office. I'm guessing it involved bribery—his MO."

Marleigh passes on the cookies. "So, what do we do now?"

"If what you say is true," Taffy plucks up a cookie, "I'll call the county office. I have a buddy who works there. While this is a *city* inspector, I can ask my friend to look into it." He covers Marleigh's hand with his free one. "Let me reassure you. Your electrical was done safer and better than code requires. You *will* be ready to open for your festival."

The tension lifts from Beauty's shoulders. She rolls her neck and offers a wan smile. *Poor Marleigh. Ever since she met me, her life has been in turmoil. Lord, forgive me.*

The front doorbell rings. "I'll get it." Nola slips from her chair, returning a moment later with Finn. "I filled him in already."

Although there's room, instead of squeezing into the banquette, Finn pulls out the kitchen's folding step ladder, scoots up to the table, then sits on the top step. "If what Nola told me is true, we need to find out how Dylan pulled it off."

"It's true." Taffy's voice is firm, leaving no doubt he means what he says. "I walk all my projects with the inspectors. If something isn't up to par, the inspector will tell me what's wrong right then—happened once in my career due to some changes in required safety regulations. I was at fault for not knowing about the change. Now, I keep up with the laws." His gaze fixes on mine. "I walked the properties with the inspector. We passed. Both projects did."

His obvious pride in his work restores my confidence in him but highlights my brother's subterfuge.

Finn scrubs one hand over the back of his neck. "So, where does this leave us?"

I like how he includes himself in that "us." He and Taffy are taking personal responsibility for this.

"I know I keep saying this, but I'm so sorry my brother has dragged all y'all into his scheming."

Taffy pops a fist on my shoulder. "No worries. But do you have any idea *why* he wants the land so much?"

I shake my head. "There's no reason I can find. What he says he wants to do is bogus—a cover-up at best. Considering his actions constitute extortion, something has to be worth a lot of money. I even checked with the planning commission to see if he's looked into any building permits in our area, roads with the county, whatever. Nothing comes up."

Finn drums his fingers on the table. "There's one or two ways to get an inspection outcome changed like this. Either a bad inspection by one official, or ..." His gaze travels the group, one by one. "Bribery. This is no small thing. If you bribe a government official, you're liable for up to three times the amount of the bribe and imprisonment for up to fifteen years in the federal pen."

I shake my head. "I know my brother. He never breaks the law. He has people who do his dirty work for him."

I let out a long breath, not knowing how we're going to resolve this. All I can see is my dream going up in smoke. Worse, Beauty's dream is going up with mine.

MARLEIGH

I stop worrying after Taffy reassures me the barn will be finished on time. God knows what we're up against, but he also sent good men to help us. I'm confident in them. Besides, God isn't caught unawares.

Nola now holds my attention. Her playfulness with Finn is interesting. She's flirting. When did this happen? I haven't seen her flirt with any man since Steve died close to five years ago now. It's about time she takes interest in someone again. She did spend a lot of time with Finn when we were designing the theatre.

When she catches me staring, her face turns rosy, and she won't hold my gaze. I'm dying to ask her more, but the business at hand demands my focus.

I glance at Gabe. I feel so bad for him. "Do you think there is any way to get your brother to stop without bringing in the police?"

"No, he's determined—" He snaps his fingers. "Wait. There might be a way. Sergio, maybe I can tell him I've had a change of mind. Go along with his wishes—work with him until I can find out why he wants the land."

I hate to see him put off his dream when he's so close. "What about your restaurant? The festival?"

His shoulders slump. "I don't know. If I do nothing, he won't stop until he takes everything. Maybe we can salvage some of it."

Finn holds up a hand. "No. I don't think that's in your best interest, Gabe. Let me talk with Harry Upton first."

"Who's he?" Gabe asks.

"Harry? He's the city's building inspector. If he says he passed us, then at least we will know for sure someone was bribed. Do either of you have any problem with me talking to him?"

"Not me. I have no feelings for my brother except maybe to be sorry for what never was. He started following Dad's way of doing things when we were little." A grimace hardens his jaw. "I remember the first time. We must have been four or five years old. Dylan gave a neighbor kid a quarter for his bike. Dad thought it was funny, but my brother destroyed my friendship with the kid. Furious, the neighbors painted us all with one brush."

I want to cry for what his childhood must have been like. "Didn't anyone discipline him?"

"Like I said, Dad thought it was funny. When they took me into the business, I went along with the way they worked." He shrugs. "They had a successful business model—find a struggling restaurant in a good location, then swoop in, offer them a way out for pennies on the dollar. Dad made sure the owners didn't have a lot of choice. We'd fix up the place, bring in new management and menu, then sell at a high price." Gabe's sigh is deep. "I couldn't be part of it anymore after seeing them ruin some family businesses which could have been saved with a good consultant. I hated who I'd become."

I reach over and squeeze his hand. My heart wants to say more, but I know the risk. "We're all glad you walked away. We like who you are now."

He glances at me but doesn't say anything.

"So," I clear my throat, "Finn, you'll let us know as soon as possible about what you find? We need to get moving."

Our architect shoves back his chair. "I will. Nola, walk me out?"

"Sure." Her nonchalance as she follows him is a put on. Something's up between them.

The show on television is one all three of us have seen before, so my attention bounces between the basket of laundry resting at my feet and the investigation. A week has passed since Finn contacted his friend at the county.

During a commercial, I click mute on the remote. "Nola, have you heard anything more from Finn?"

"He says an investigation is underway. They do think they've found something." She reaches for the bowl of popcorn and a napkin.

"Sergio is working with them too." Willow tosses a kernel in the air, deftly catching it in her mouth.

"Why?" I grab another pair of Elijah's socks from the laundry basket, folding them together.

"Because Finn's pretty sure there's a bribe involved." Willow picks up a towel. "Sergio can help untangle the money trail if it becomes too convoluted." She gestures to the television set. "Show's back on. Sound, please."

I click the remote. Nola wipes her hands, then reaches for Aysha's jeans, which reminds me about her dress for Jessica's wedding.

"Is your mom okay with Aysha wearing a denim dress for her wedding?"

"Shhh." Willow chastises us.

Nola rolls her eyes. She whispers, "Mom's fine with it, but I'm still pushing for a cute flowered one. However, you know my daughter. At least the denim one has cute ladybugs embroidered on it."

"Ah, let the kid be herself." In the oversized armchair, Willow draws her feet up beneath her. Though she enters our conversation, her gaze doesn't leave the TV screen. "I might laugh if I saw her in anything but denim."

"You and a host of other people, but a mama can hope, can't she?"

Poor Nola. I hand her another pair of jeans. "When she hits middle school and discovers boys, I'll bet you my favorite flip flops she'll change her tune. Then, you'll wish she hadn't." Nola's horrified face makes me laugh. "Not to change the subject—but I am—what's up with you and Finn? You've been too quiet. Details, please."

A possible new romance grabs Willow's attention. She turns off the television.

Nola's face grows pink. "I like him. There's something about him that reminds me of Steve."

I study her. "What do you think it is?"

"I don't know for sure. He doesn't look at all like Steve did—doesn't sound like him either. Their similarity goes deeper. He's solid, has a firm faith—unmovable like Steve's was. I loved that in my husband."

Willow and I both smile. "I'm glad you're taking interest in someone." *God, don't take him away from her too. Please?*

Nola's gaze fixes on something I don't see. "From the moment I met him, I felt something. I've prayed so hard about it. If this isn't of God, I don't want him."

I've prayed that same prayer. *Lord, please don't break Nola's heart.*

"I'm praying for you too." Willow sighs. "I love it when we're all in lo—" She gapes horrified. "I'm sorry, Marleigh. I'm such a dope. I spoke without thinking. Please, forgive me."

She knows my heart yearns for Gabe. "It's all right, sugar." I need to change the subject. I shove our laundry basket toward her. "You can help fold the kids' clothes for penance."

Snatching up a T-shirt, Willow grins. "I think Sergio is close to proposing." Her eyes shine. "What I feel for him is nothing like I've ever felt for any man."

I know Willow can't help herself. She's excited. While those two share about love, I'm struggling to hold back tears. I pick up Elijah's pile of clothes. "I'm going to put these away, then I have some notes to make on Jessica's wedding."

Why is life so complicated? Gabe has won back my trust, but risking my heart again is hard. I haven't healed enough. Yet, I know I love him.

I leave Elijah's clean laundry outside his room. He'll put them away in the morning.

In my own room, I cross to the corner windows. One overlooks the farm and Gabe's cottage. The other frames our barn. Each view holds my teetering dreams.

Keep my faith firm, Lord. I trust in you.

My thoughts calm. I take out my planner for Jessica's wedding. Even though the May date looms large before me, I'm not worried. I jot notes on items left to complete before her big day.

Suddenly, my stomach clenches. What if renovating takes longer? I nibble on my pen. Did I read God wrong? This wouldn't be the first time. I'll be letting Jessica and Walter down. What about Nola with her investment? I shouldn't have let her put her money in this. Has Dylan won?

God, where are you? Help!

From deep within my spirit comes these words, "I have not given you a spirit of fear and timidity but of power, love, and self-discipline."

My fears dissolve. I am at peace.

Thank you. You know the plans you have for me, even though I don't. But they are good. Help my unbelief, Lord.

Chapter 25

Marleigh

Walter sighs, shaking his hand to dislodge yet another sticker. "I give up. I can't work with these small things, honey. I'm getting more stuck on my fingers than on the lids."

I have to bite my lip not to laugh at his Eeyore expression. I had set up a table in our front room to take advantage of the sunlight streaming in, while the four of us put the personalized stickers on the lids of small, scented candles Jessica chose as wedding mementos for their guests. Poor Walter's fingers are better suited to working on financial spreadsheets than crafting.

Jessica peels away one sticker pasted between his thumb and index finger. "Why don't you go see Gabe, my love? Maybe you can help him plant his garden."

She waits until he escapes in search of Gabe, then laughs. "Poor man. I tried to dissuade him from coming, but he didn't want to miss seeing you girls." She reaches for another label to replace the one he mangled. "How are things coming along in the barn? Will you be ready?" She centers the paper disc on a lid, smoothing it in place as she glances at me, her expression changing to concern. "Or should we plan on using our church instead?"

"Taffy promised he'll have it ready." Nola calms her mother with an easy smile. "He said they've gone beyond what the city and county require. He always passes his inspections."

Satisfied, Jessica nods as she reaches for another candle lid.

I'm still nervous. I'll be much happier when we hear back from Finn. "Has Finn told you anything yet, Nola?"

Excitement sparkling in her eyes, she sets the lid aside. "Yes. They picked up a money trail. They think they have the evidence we need."

I draw in a sharp breath and my heartbeat increases. "When did you find out?"

Nola grimaces. "Last night. I'm sorry I didn't tell you, but Finn warned me not to get too hopeful in case the trail dries up."

"Okay, I understand. But now I know, so tell me what they found. Please?"

"Tinley," she turns to Jessica, "Dylan's hatchet-man. He does the dirty work, so Dylan can't be implicated. Anyway, he bribed a clerk into giving him our inspection papers."

Jessica gapes. "Oh, no."

I understand her feelings. "Did the clerk change them?"

"Finn's contact went through the security footage, but all the film shows is the money exchange. Then the clerk comes back and hands Tinley an envelope."

My earlier elation fades. "So where are we now?"

Nola peels off a candle label, pausing with it glued to the end of her index finger. "We have to get a copy of the altered inspection, and make sure the original inspector will testify in court."

My gaze swings to Jessica. Her hands are stilled. She glances at her daughter and then at me. "Girls, I refuse to worry. I'm sure everything will work out as it's supposed to."

She may say she's not worried, but her shaky hands tell another story.

GABE

Sunlight pours into my upstairs office. I'm not supposed to be in here, but with what we've learned, that cease-work order wasn't real or legal. I'm relieved, because I need to be here—if for no other reason than to feel the reality of my dream.

I lean against the window frame, gazing out at my little farm. In the past two weeks, with Walter's help, everything is planted. I'm already seeing small signs of growth. I'm amazed how much I enjoyed the work. God sure gave me the right dream. Who but God knew I'd be a farmer at heart. *Thank you.*

My thoughts turn to the problem at hand. If we can't prove the inspections were altered, my dream—and Beauty's—will evaporate.

My phone rings. Sergio. "Where are you?"

"In the cottage. I hope it's okay for me to be here."

"It's more than okay. Stay right there. Finn and I are coming over."

Ten minutes later, the outside door bangs open, echoing through the old cottage. Footsteps shake the building as they pound on the treads. My door bursts open, hitting a newly painted wall. Sergio's grin spreads from ear to ear.

"We found it." He waves a sheaf of paper in one hand. His other hand holds high a thumb drive.

Finn is on his heels. "Sit and listen, my friend. We have our evidence."

When he closes the door, the doorknob has left a mark in the paint. The news is worth having to do a touch up, but I'm afraid to get excited. I've seen my brother in action. I sit back, but every nerve fiber is at attention. "Okay, lay it out for me."

Sergio slaps the papers on my desk, then rests his thigh against its corner. "Zach Tinley, your devious twin's dirty-worker, waved a couple of grand under the clerk's nose. He caved."

I hold up both hands. "Whoa. Hold on. What clerk?"

Sergio seems giddy over his findings. He must enjoy playing private eye. "The clerk at the building inspector's office. His name's Richard Norwood. Make a note because he's going to have a new address soon."

Alarm bells go off in my head. I jerk upright. "What? We need to keep him here."

Finn laughs. Is he as giddy as Sergio? "His new address will be at the federal pen."

I release a breath. "You two need to slow down and bring me up to speed."

Sergio's expression turns serious. He slides off the desk into a chair. "The permits and inspection office has hidden security cameras. Norwood's a new employee. It's apparent he didn't know about them—or greed made him forget, because Finn's pal at the county was able to review the footage. The film reveals Tinley handing over a wad of hundred-dollar bills to Norwood. There's also audio, although it's a bit garbled. You can still hear him saying, 'more where this came from if ...' Then, it becomes unintelligible. The clerk says something, then you hear Tinley say, 'I don't care how—'"

Finn leans forward, his gaze intense. "None of this implicates your brother, though. However, facing felony charges, Tinley might rethink his loyalty to Dylan."

My brother has ears everywhere. "We need the element of surprise, or Dylan will find a way to beat this. Have you talked to the police?"

"Not yet, I thought we ought to consult an attorney." Sergio pulls a card from his shirt pocket. "Here's the one we used to draw up our contracts. Let's call him—get his advice on how to proceed."

A sense of urgency grips me. "Do it. The faster we get this moving, the less damage my brother can do."

"Do it." Finn echoes my words. "Put the call on speaker."

Glancing between them, I hold up crossed fingers as Sergio taps in the number. When it's answered, he puts the call on speaker.

"Good morning. Heagy, Turner, and Goss. How may we be of service?"

"We'd like to speak with Ward Turner, please. Tell him it's Sergio Landi. I have two others on speaker with me."

"One moment, please, Mr. Landi."

Sergio glances at me. "When Ward gets on the line, I'll explain what we need—."

A gruff voice cuts him off. "Sergio, you old son of a butcher. How are you?"

"Fine, Ward. It's good to talk to you, but I won't waste your time. My friends and I need your help."

"Hang on. I want to record our call, so I don't miss anything. Do I have everyone's permission to record?"

I nod, glance at Finn, who also nods.

"Yes, we're all fine with it. Tell us when you're ready."

"Will each of you state your names, please?"

"Sergio Landi."

"Gabriel Sadler."

"Finn Cavanaugh."

"Thank you. Now, Sergio, why don't you tell me what the problem is."

Sergio explains everything to Ward, including how Dylan impersonated me to the merchants in town.

"The main thing is the bribery," Sergio says. "If we can implicate Dylan in that, then we will be free to move forward with our renovations."

"If their security footage shows what you say, you have a good case on Tinley, at least."

I haven't spoken yet, but my guts are churning. "Mr. Turner—"

"Ward, please."

"Ward, this is Gabe Sadler. We have to stop my brother. He's harming more than just me."

"And you're okay if he's arrested?"

"Yes. He's hurt too many people in his life. He hasn't broken the law to my knowledge before this, but he's bent it pretty far too many times. If something brings him power or money, he'll do anything."

"I understand. I've seen a lot in my years. All you need to do is call the police with what you know, then let them do their work.

I have to know the answer to the biggest question chipping away at my peace. "What do you think our chances are? Will we be able to stop him?"

There is a brief pause, then Ward answers. "Yes. This state takes umbrage to bribing a government official. Make no mistake, a city building permits and inspection office is an arm of the government. You might want to alert your mayor first, though."

His confidence gives me hope. "We'll alert the mayor before we call the police. Thank you, Ward. I appreciate your advice. Please send the bill to me."

After we hang up, I call Mayor Higgins.

"Hello?"

"Miss Boo, it's Gabe. Do you mind if Sergio, Finn, and I come over? We have some sorry news for you."

She hesitates, drawing in a quick breath. "I hope it's not too sorry. I'll see you in a few minutes."

"Thank you." I click off my phone. "Come on, let's go."

"What about Marleigh?" Sergio picks up the papers he laid on my desk.

"You're right. She needs to be here." I follow them out to the farmhouse. When Beauty answers the door, I explain where we're going, and ask if she wants to join us. "I think you'll find this very interesting."

"I would, thanks. Elijah won't be home for another hour."

Five minutes later, we're at the Higgins's new apartment.

"Come on in." She ushers us into her living room. Theirs reminds me of the one I rented for a few weeks. A tray of frosty glasses sits on the coffee table. She gestures to them. "Sorry news should be delivered over sweet tea. Have a seat, take a glass, and let's get on with it."

I have to chuckle. Our mayor is down home people who gets right to the point. I shoot a quick glance around the apartment. "Is Herb here?"

The mayor peers at me. "Is this so bad you think I need reinforcements?" She calls over her shoulder. "Herb? Can you come in here?"

"Comin'."

I settle on the sofa next to Beauty, while a relaxed Herb saunters in. Gone are his former signature overalls. In their place are khakis and a collared shirt. Relaxed, he picks up the last glass of tea.

"These young'uns have sorry news for us, Herb."

"Ah." Herb sits next to his wife. "Well, we have our tea, let's get on with it. Gabe?"

"Sergio brought us some information—"

"Then, let him tell us."

Sergio startles, then clears his throat. He isn't as used to Miss Boo's directness as the rest of us. "The city's building and permits clerk accepted a bribe to change our inspections to show they failed."

Miss Boo chokes on her tea. "You can't mean Harry Upton. He's been—"

"No, ma'am." Sergio shakes his head. "Not Harry. It's the clerk, Richard Norwood."

Herb frowns. "Don't know him. Must be new."

The mayor eyes us. "Are you sure about this? You realize you're talking about a felony, don't you?"

"Yes, ma'am." Sergio's answer leaves no room for doubt.

Finn sets his glass on the tray. "If I may, ma'am, I'm friends with Harry Upton. I went to him first. He verified he passed both inspections. He'll testify in court too. Then, I went to your IT manager. He was able to view the security camera footage, which is clear as can be."

The mayor's blood pressure must be rising. Her face grows red. "Herb, pull up that date on the security camera. I want to see it with my own eyes."

Herb opens a laptop sitting on the table. We all gather around. He pulls up the date and time. A moment later, a scene unfolds before our eyes. We watch the footage through twice. It's unfortunate Norwood's face is the only one visible.

"Herb, call the police. I want him arrested now." She startles as if she realizes what this will mean. "Gabe," her voice softens. "Does this involve your brother?"

"Yes, ma'am. I'm sorry to say it does."

She glances at Beauty, then back to me. "Are you *sure* about having him arrested?"

"I am." I hope I sound resolute. As little relationship

as I have with him, the fact remains he is my brother. My identical twin, but he wedged enmity between us from the day we were born.

"Marleigh, where are you on this?" Miss Boo asks.

Nodding, Beauty catches my eye. "I'm with Gabe."

"Thanks." I reach over and squeeze her hand. I'd love to keep holding it, but I'm just beginning to regain her trust. It's too soon. I let go, lacing my fingers in my lap.

Herb pulls out his phone, dials, then clicks "speaker."

"This is City Councilman, Herb Higgins, of Sugar Springs. I need to report a crime."

"Is this an emergency?"

"No. I'd have called nine-one-one if it was."

"Sorry. Can you tell me a little about it?"

"A clerk at the city building inspector's office took a bribe and changed the outcome of an inspection."

"We will send an officer right out. Should he go to City Hall?"

"No, have him come to our place. Then, I'll walk him to the scene of the crime if need be." Herb gives him their address. "Thank you. When should I expect someone?"

"Within the hour."

"Ten-four."

He chuckles as he swipes off his phone. "I always wanted to say that."

Miss Boo swats his arm. "You're a mess. But thanks for making the call for me." Her gaze takes in each of us. "Things will heat up pretty fast. I know the bank didn't want any publicity from prosecuting your brother, Gabe, but I have no such proclivities. No siree. I welcome everyone knowing Sugar Springs won't sanction lawbreakers."

While we wait, Miss Boo shows Beauty around their apartment, focusing on her curio cabinet in the foyer. They return to the living room with a plate of cookies, another glass, and a pitcher of sweet tea. The treats are homemade sugar cookies.

We're all on tenterhooks while we wait for the police to arrive. I pace. Herb shows Sergio his framed map collection, Finn inspects the balcony, while Beauty talks with Miss Boo, who reaches out her hand, stopping my pacing. "With the business at hand, will you be done in time for the festival?"

I nod. "Taffy promised we will, as long as nothing else goes wrong." I hope she's reassured.

Herb steps close. "I'll send Harry over tomorrow for a new inspection. I'll accompany him myself to make sure it's logged in as passed. This Norwood fella should be out of there by then, anyway."

Beauty looks at her watch. "I need to go get Elijah." She turns to me. "Will you let me know the outcome?"

I nod, then look around the room. "Let me treat everyone to supper tomorrow night at my place. I'd like to try out some new menu items I've developed." I smile at Marleigh. "Kids and roommates included."

She lays her hand on my arm, sending a shiver up my spine. "Thank you. We'd all like that."

A few minutes after she leaves, the doorbell rings with a hollow tink-tonk. The door may be high quality, but someone failed on their bell. Herb opens the door, then escorts a detective into the living room.

"Good evening. I'm Detective Mike Freeman, Gwinnett County Police. I understand we have a case of bribery?"

After we explain everything, Detective Freeman takes our names and contact information. Herb provides him a digital copy of the security camera footage.

Mike closes his notepad. "It's unfortunate they can't make a positive identification of Tinley, but I'll get a warrant for Norwood's arrest. By the time y'all finish your supper, he'll be in the county jail. With luck, he'll ID Tinley." He turns to the mayor. "I'll call you when he's been picked up."

I'll breathe a lot easier when Norwood is behind bars, but will he identify Tinley? More importantly, will Tinley tell the police who he works for? My guess is there are no tax reports for him. Dylan will have paid him cash under the table.

We're not out of these woods yet.

Chapter 26

GABE

Before the sun peeks over the horizon, I have my bag packed and stored in my Yukon. Herb scheduled Harry Upton to be at the farm this morning by seven. I pull into the driveway at six-fifty-two. I can't wait to move back in.

After getting the cottage unlocked, I sit in my truck. Right at seven, Herb arrives with Harry. I jump out, meeting them at the door.

Harry, dressed in khakis with a brown shirt, reminds me of someone, but I can't think who he could be. When he smiles, his eyes twinkle. Of course. He's the town's Santa. He sure has the hair and beard for it, although his hair is pulled back in a ponytail today.

I thrust out my hand. "Thanks for altering your schedule, sir."

While shaking hands, he gives the cottage a once-over. "Not a problem, given what's happened." He turns to Herb. "Are you adjusting to apartment life?"

Herb barks a laugh. "I'm enjoying not being a farmer." He points to the acres I've worked so hard on with Walter. "Looks like young Gabe is taking to it, though."

"You're right." I can't help my grin. I find work so gratifying. "Come on in, gentlemen." I hold the screen door open. "Here's my kitchen—where the last inspection derailed."

Harry looks at his paperwork. "I have the original report right here. Your plumbing passed—so did the barn's electrical. But for our case against Norwood and Tinley, I'm reinspecting both officially." He sets his clipboard on the counter and gets to work. Though he's thorough in his inspection, the task takes him no longer than fifteen minutes. I follow him like a puppy dog, anxious to see how he inspects everything.

When he's done, he initials the papers. "You pass—again. Knowing Taffy like I do, I almost didn't need to inspect it." He hands me our notice to post. "Norwood was a buffoon. If I don't miss my guess, his credentials were false. I don't like being hoodwinked." He slaps the clipboard against his thigh. "You can move back in, and work can continue. I'll go inspect the barn now."

"Thanks, Mr. Upton." I send a text to Marleigh letting her know. A moment later, I receive a smiley face. She meets Harry in the yard.

I snatch my duffle bag out of my truck, then take the stairs two at a time. As soon as I put my clothes away, I return to the kitchen and call Taffy.

"We're back in business."

"I'll have a crew there in an hour."

"Wow, thanks. I owe a lot of y'all dinner. With my kitchen ready, I can experiment. Come by at six. I'll feed your whole crew."

"You're on. The guys will appreciate it."

I lay down my phone and sharpen a knife. I want to make a meal for everyone. There's Marleigh, Elijah—I count them off on my fingers. Sixteen. Herb will let Miss Boo know, so I bang out a text to the guys, asking them to alert the ladies.

Now, it's time to get to work. I grab what I need from the fridge, then start chopping, dicing, and measuring spices.

I'm in my element. For a moment, I pause my knife. *Thank you, Lord, for keeping my dream alive.* I return to my work. Soon, I have all my herbs and spices chopped and measured. Each is put in a *mise-en-place* bowl. Several other little containers sit empty beside those, awaiting their ingredients.

"Knock, knock." Beauty's voice drifts from the screen door. There is a peaceful quality in it. Warmth spreads through my body, and I haven't even turned on the stove yet.

"Come on in." I lean against the counter, basking in her radiant smile. "I guess you passed."

"I did. Taffy called and said his guys will be back to work in an hour."

"I'm glad. He ... uh ... called ... uh ... same here." Why can't I articulate anything?

She runs her fingers over the countertop. "He's good, isn't he? I mean the way he seems to care about this job."

"Yeah, he is." Oh boy, do I sound lame. "I don't know how he gets the men to work so fast, but I won't argue." What an idiotic thing to say.

Beauty gestures to the diced shallots. "What's this?"

Pointing to each bowl, I sing, "Parsley, sage, rosemary, and thyme."

She laughs. I love making her laugh. I love her laugh.

I love her.

"I mean why the little bowls?"

"Ah. Mise-en-place."

"What?"

"Mise-en-place means 'everything in place.' All the ingredients needed to make a dish are measured and put in separate small containers to add when they're needed. Saves time in a commercial kitchen."

She shakes her head. "Why have I not known this?"

I shrug, grabbing a carrot to peel. "Do you watch cooking videos?"

"No, but maybe I need to start."

Or spend time watching me.

"Can I help?"

Blood courses from my heart to my brain. I move aside to make room for her. "You sure can."

"Why don't I do these?" She takes the carrot from me. When her fingers touch mine, an electric charge zips up my arm. I can't seem to let go of the silly vegetable.

She wears a sassy grin. "I do know how to peel a carrot."

Chuckling, I release my hold. "Okay. When you're done peeling, cut them in coins."

She blinks and tucks a wayward strand of hair behind her ear. "Coins?"

"Sorry. Culinary term. Just slice them about one-quarter-inch thick."

"Coins. It's an apt description, I'll give you that."

Beauty's in a playful mood. With my heart beating a rapid staccato, I pick up two large onions, remove their paper-skins, then chop them in half. She stops her slow, meticulous peeling to watch as I dice the onions.

"Wow. You're so fast, I didn't even get teary-eyed. How do you manage to not cut off your fingers?"

"It's all in how you hold your hand. See?" I demonstrate. "You curl your fingers under so the blade never gets near the tips."

She attempts to curl hers while still holding the carrot in place. She doesn't have the hang of sliding her fingers back.

I grin and flip my knife, its handle landing flat in my palm. "If you continue to practice, you'll get it. Carrots aren't the easiest thing to learn on, though. Believe me, in culinary school, there were a lot of cuts until I learned."

In record speed, I chop several ribs of celery, while she continues to work on her first carrot. I resist the urge to come up behind her, put my arms around her, and show her how. Although, with a knife in her hand? Might be dangerous. She doesn't trust me that much. Yet.

When the vegetables are ready, I pull out a large frying pan to caramelize the onions. I turn the flame on high to get the pan hot. My phone vibrates on the stainless countertop. The Swedish chef ringtone garbles.

Dylan.

MARLEIGH

Curl fingers. Slice. Move fingers back on carrot. "This is frustrating." I glance at Gabe, but he's frowning at his phone. I remember that ring tone—his brother's. Hair on the back of my neck stands up. Gabe meets my gaze, putting his finger to his lips, cautioning me to keep silent. I lay my knife down and nod.

He turns off the flame beneath a frying pan before answering the phone. "Dylan." Gabe's eyes narrow. "Hold on. This isn't a contest."

I wish he'd put it on speaker. I strain to hear but the other voice is muffled—a masculine voice, but unintelligible. Easing onto a stool, I try to keep my leg from bouncing. Outside, birds are chirping. In here, the air crackles with tension.

Gabe's brows come together in a frown. "Dylan, Calm down. This isn't—"

He turns his back to me and lowers his voice, but I can make out, "Don't threaten me ... No. Look, let's get together. Maybe we can come to an agreeable end to this. Where are you?"

Gabe startles. He lays his phone on the counter. His shoulders rise, then lower. He turns. I can't read his expression but judging by the whiteness around his lips, it can't be good.

"What did he say?"

"You don't want to know." He swallows, then crosses to me, and gently grips my upper arms. "You need to watch your back. We both do. Don't go anywhere without someone with you or knowing where you are. Keep in close phone contact."

Elijah!

I pull from his grasp. "Gabe, you're frightening me. Is Elijah in danger? What did Dylan say?"

"I'm not sure Dylan knows about Elijah, but we should assume he does. Sugar, my brother doesn't like to lose. I'm going to call the police and the marshal's office. We'll get a restraining order. I'll also ask them to keep watch over you."

"What about you?"

"I'll be okay if the police are watching my property."

The morning started out so good, but now I'm looking over my shoulder with every sound. I search Gabe's eyes.

"I'm so sorry, Marleigh. I hate that my brother's drawn you into this."

He reaches for my hands, and while I find his touch comforting, I wish he'd take me in his arms. I still love him. I have no idea if his feelings go beyond friendship, but I love him. I shake my head.

"It's not your fault, Gabe. Even if you hadn't wanted a restaurant here, I bought this property for the barn. I'd be in this mess even without you." I pull away to put a little distance between us. My heart needs the safety. "In fact, you might have been my adversary."

"What? No way."

"No, think about it. What if you were still involved in your dad's business? You'd be helping your brother."

He gives a vehement shake of his head. "No way. Once I saw you, I—" He turns and places his hands on the stainless counter, leaning on them. "No. I wouldn't be working with them."

I reach out to touch him but pull back. I don't dare.

"Gabe, if I have to be in this, I'm glad it's with you. You know how your brother operates. Do I make sense?"

He sighs and turns, now leaning his back against the counter. "I guess." After a moment, he offers a half smile. "I'll talk to the police. But after I do, I have several recipes to prepare for all y'all tonight."

While Nola talks with Aysha, I sit in my room with Elijah standing between my knees facing me. His little face is serious as he cups my cheeks with his hands. "Marma, tell me what's wrong. Maybe I can make it all better."

I don't want to frighten him. How can I say this? "I've always been honest with you, so ... you know Mr. Gabe has a twin brother, right?"

"Yeah." He lowers his hands and furrows his brow. He's trying to work out how Gabe's twin has anything to do with us.

"He wants this farm."

"But we own it. Except for the restaurant. Mr. Gabe owns that."

"You're right. But Dylan—Mr. Gabe's brother—doesn't care. He thinks we stole the farm from him."

"You don't steal. The Bible says not to. Can't you tell him?"

With a grimace, I shake my head. "Sugar, I'm afraid there's no talking to him. Mr. Gabe tried. He said his brother has let greed become his god. The thing is ..."

I pause to draw a deep breath. *How can I say this without scaring him, Lord?* "I don't trust Dylan. The police are looking for him, but until they can arrest him, we need to be very careful."

He nods and scoots a little closer.

"And careful means you and Aysha must have an adult with you anytime you are outside our house."

"Is he after Aysha too?"

"No, but if someone tried to kidnap you, they'd grab her too."

His frown disappears. He squares his small shoulders, and his little face scrunches into what he thinks is a "man" expression. He jabs his thumb to his chest. "I'll be extra careful. I won't let anything happen to Aysha."

I hug him. Then, because I don't want him living in fear, I try to keep things normal. "Good. Now, we're going to Mr. Gabe's restaurant for supper in about an hour."

"He ain't open yet."

"Isn't, but you're right. He's trying out some recipes on us."

His face lights up. "Oh, boy. I like his cooking."

While he runs off to find Aysha, I ask God to set a guardian angel over Elijah, then seek out Nola. She's in the kitchen pouring a glass of sweet tea.

"How did Aysha take the news?"

Nola holds her glass under the fridge's ice dispenser. "Ha. She told me she'd keep a close eye on 'Lijah. She wasn't gonna let anybody kidnap him." Ice splashes into Nola's tea.

"He said the same thing about her. I guess those two are mentally stronger than we give them credit for." I open the fridge and search for a Coke Zero. "Gabe doesn't think Dylan would go after the kids, but I'm glad I made you Elijah's legal guardian if anything happens to me."

Nola's expression sobers. "You don't think you're in physical danger, do you?"

"I don't know. From what Gabe says, when his brother found out I bought the land and sold five acres to him, Dylan went crazy. He refuses to give up. Still, he has to know if anything happens to me, he'd be the first suspect. He's not stupid."

Nola reaches over the sink and closes the window curtains. "No, but I read once about how greed is a bottomless pit. A person tries to satisfy the itch without ever getting enough."

I shiver. "Unchecked greed would drive a person insane."

Nola locks her gaze on mine. "Exactly."

Chapter 27

GABE

The kitchen is warm, but it's not from the oven where our main course is roasting. How I wish I could go back to the day Beauty told me her dream. If I'd been slower to react, she wouldn't be in this mess, and I never would have hurt her like I did. My knee-jerk reaction—a result of the way Dylan always one-upped me—will haunt me forever.

Will Beauty ever trust her heart to me again?

A timer buzzes, signaling thirty minutes before we sit down to eat. I pull the prime rib from the oven, then set it on the carving station to rest. After my vegetables go in to finish, I drain the potatoes. I'll mash them in a few minutes.

Right now, I need to set up tables for us to eat in here. I push two rolling, stainless steel work tables to a wall in the hallway. Then, I move three large tables from the dining room to the kitchen where they can watch me fix their dessert, arranging them in one large rectangle.

Sergio and Finn can help bring in chairs when they get here. I glance at my watch. They should be coming through the door about ...

"Hey, buddy." Sergio saunters in.

... now.

"Finn's right behind me." Sergio glances around the kitchen. "Man, things smell good in here. I detect beef … garlic … and …" He wiggles his nose, sniffing, then shrugs in defeat. "… Something else. Can I do anything?"

"When Finn gets here, can y'all—"

"Can we what?"

Those two have been spending too much time together. They could be a comedy duo. "You can bring in chairs from the storage room, please. Six on each side, two on each end. There're sixteen of us."

While they set chairs, Marleigh arrives with Elijah. He runs to me, throwing his arms around my hips. His head tilts back as he looks up. "Hey, Mr. Gabe. What's for supper?"

I glance at Beauty. My heart soars when she smiles and doesn't discourage Elijah. Could this mean—? The room grows Ethiopia hot.

I give Elijah a quick hug. "Can you take this basket of rolls to the table?"

"You betcha. I'm strong." He lifts the basket, then sets it on the table, pushing it away from its edge.

I share a smile with his sister, who hopes to be his mama soon. I wouldn't mind being his daddy. Whoa—that takes me aback. Yet this feels right somehow. My chest tightens. This is what I want—to marry Marleigh and help raise Elijah. The possibility is a lot to digest right now.

Taffy's crew joins us. Thankfully, chaos distracts me, covering the moment. I need to chew on my last thought for a while. Alone.

Nola, Aysha, and Willow arrive, along with Jessica and Walter. Every one of these people have become my family.

While I finish making my salad dressing, the ladies help by setting salads at each place. Finally, I bring small tureens of dressing to the tables.

"If y'all would like to be seated, please, we'll begin." I want to tell them what they've come to mean to me—without getting sappy.

With everyone in place, I look over my friends. "When this dream was just a kernel, I was working with my father and brother, growing more dissatisfied each day. All y'all know their story. But the journey to this moment has been filled with pitfalls and roadblocks. I guess you know that too. What I'm trying to say is each of you has had a hand in making this dream come true." I swallow the hitch in my voice. *Help me, Lord.* "Most of all," I pick up my wineglass. "I want to thank Marleigh. If you hadn't agreed to sell me this parcel, I'd ... well, I don't know where I'd be—for certain not seeing the fulfillment of my dreams. Thank you." I glance around the table at everyone. "To Marleigh, who held fast to her dream."

Every voice joins in, "To Marleigh!"

Beauty turns a beautiful rosy red, almost matching the rosé in her glass. Her gaze meets mine. She nibbles her lip.

With a grin, Elijah eyes me, then shouts, "Speech, Marma!" Does he have some idea of my feelings?

Marleigh lets her gaze travel the group. They rest a moment on me. "Like Gabe, all of you have played large parts in getting us to this place. From Elijah," she leans down giving him a peck on his cheek, "who was the first to tell me to chase my dream—reach for the stars. Finally, to those whose skills are transforming an old barn, thank you from the bottom of my heart."

Once again, glasses clink together as everyone acknowledges her words. *I hope she finds happiness, and I'm working alongside her.*

For the rest of our evening, I show off a bit with my culinary skills. It's all to impress one beautiful woman. I can only pray my efforts help my sorry case. When I strike a match to a pan of bananas Foster, then spoon the flaming confection over their ice cream, she's wide-eyed. Elijah and Aysha bounce in their seats.

All in all, I'm happy I get to treat my friends and try out a few tweaks on old standby recipes. The new versions will go on the menu. With a thankful heart, I glance around at everyone chatting. As my gaze falls on Beauty, she's telling Finn about the first show she wants to produce.

A seed of an idea plants itself in my mind ... and my heart. Can I pull this off? More important, will it work?

MARLEIGH

The afternoon light pours through the open barn doors, illuminating the space in a magical kind of glow, reminding me theatre is where people suspend disbelief.

Overhead, work lights hang from the rafters. Taffy points at timbers above us, running from side to side in the barn. "Those beams are where we'll hang the chandeliers you want." Closing one eye, he cocks his head. "I thought your cheese had slid off your cracker when you showed me pictures of them, but ..." He chuckles. "I have to admit, they'll add some glamor to this place. And a bit of whimsy." His arm swings, pointing to beams traversing the length of the space. "Up there, we'll add Fresnels to augment the chandeliers if you want more light."

"It's perfect. Thank you, Taffy." I roll up my copy of our plans. "When do you think we'll be able to move in?"

"Everything is moving in our favor right now, so barring any problems, I feel good saying by mid-May."

From your lips to God's ear. I leave the barn in search of Nola at home.

Home. No longer a rental. Mine and Elijah's. I sank everything Mom left me into this property, leaving a minimal mortgage payment. Investors plus our loan will carry our renovations. Even if everything fails, I can still provide a home for my boy.

I open the back door. "Nola?"

"In the office."

I join her, laying our blueprints on the corner of the partner's desk we share. "Taffy said we'll get cleared for move-in by mid-May. We need to hold auditions soon. Do we know anyone who has space we can use—or rent if we have to?"

"Hmm." She flips through cards in her rolodex. I don't know anyone else who still uses one, but she attaches sticky notes to them. Not a bad idea.

She sighs. "No one. Hey, why not ask Miss Boo if we can use the community room at city hall?"

"Great idea."

I call Miss Boo. She checks the schedule, then books us for two nights, two weeks from now. Next, I go online to secure rights to the show, order scripts and musical scores.

"I got it. Our first show is set in stone."

Nola's grin is wide. "Did you think this would ever come to pass?"

"I had my doubts for a while." I pinch myself. "It's not a dream, but I suppose it's the fulfillment of one. Now, it's time to announce auditions."

I post our auditions on several online sites for sharing theatrical news, including a link to sign up for a time slot, plus one to attach their videoed monologue and song.

I close my laptop. "Now, we wait."

Nola stretches. "Are you going to be home tonight?"

"Uh-huh. Why?"

Her wide smile rivals Julia Roberts in *Pretty Woman*. "I have a dinner date with Finn."

At last! I jump up and hug her. "I'm excited for you."

She blushes. "It's only dinner, not a proposal."

"Maybe, but I see how he looks at you. Anyway, I'll be here. I think I'll take the kiddos to Albano's for spaghetti. It'll be a treat for them."

"They'll love it." She leaves the office but stops in the doorway. "Are you going to give parts to our two?"

"Of course. I can't leave them out of the first show in 'our' theatre."

"Aysha will jump over Jupiter. She says that's farther than the moon."

I laugh. "I don't doubt she's right."

After Nola leaves to meet with a client, I pull out an old script to copy pages for audition sides. I make enough for each person in every scene. Afterward, I turn to the songs.

A music director. I forgot to call someone, but I know who I want. Loreen would be perfect. She's one of the best in Atlanta. A quick call secures her. An hour later, my desk has piles of printed scenes. We're ready for auditions.

Elijah and Aysha aren't downstairs yet. I sent them to get ready a half hour ago. What are they up to? Because they so often tickle my funny bone, I tiptoe upstairs, stopping outside the bathroom. I peek between the door hinges. They're sitting next to the tub, leaning against it. They are deep in discussion. I pull back and listen.

"You're lucky. At least you *had* a daddy once. I never had one."

Elijah's lament pierces my heart.

"Yes, you did. You have to have a daddy to be bornded." Aysha's precocity cracks me up.

"Well, I never knew him." For a moment, neither speaks. "Do you ever wish you could have a new daddy?"

I lean closer.

"Yeah," Aysha says. "Daddies are fun."

"Do you know who you want for your daddy?"

"Mr. Finn likes Mama. I like him. He makes funny noises."

Elijah whispers, "I like Mr. Gabe. He'd make a cool daddy, but I don't know if Marma feels safe with him."

I can't bear anymore. I tiptoe back to the top of the stairs. "Elijah? Aysha? Are you two ready yet?"

Scrambling feet hit the tub, then patter on the tile. "Yeah, we're ready, Marma."

"Then, let's get a move on. I'm hungry. Besides, I have a surprise for you two."

They jump up and down. "Yay! What is it?" Elijah asks.

"Over supper, I'll tell you."

Twenty minutes later, while they twirl spaghetti, I tell them about the show. "And there is a part for you two to share."

Aysha frowns. "How can we share it? Oh, wait I know." She drops her fork. "I'll bet it's a animal—one of us can be the front and the other one its bum." She giggles.

Elijah's horrified expression makes me laugh.

"No, you'll trade off performances."

Aysha shoves a forkful of spaghetti into her mouth. "Dewemouf dition?"

"Swallow first, please. Then, talk."

She swallows and grins. "Do we have to 'dition?"

"No. Since I'm director, I can cast you both without an audition."

My boy, with a three-inch piece of pasta dangling from his lips, grins at his partner-in-mischief, leaving me wondering what shenanigans the two of them will come up with.

Willow and Nola next take seats at one end of the community room. Loreen has joined us to get a feel for how we work. Earlier today, I sent her the audition videos. Tonight, she will put the actor to the video. A moment later, the doors open for the first wave of auditioners. I can see others in a line snaking around the edge of the building. Miss Boo has requested more chairs from maintenance to be placed inside the lobby.

Finn and Sergio help us by collecting each applicant's résumé. Gabe wanted to help, but he had already scheduled interviews of prospective employees. It's for the best. I need 100 percent of my attention for finding my cast.

Finn hands us a stack of papers. Willow and I pair up actors by their paperwork for our first round. We hand our list to Finn.

He looks at the list of pairs. "Ava and Derek, please come pick up side four. Take a minute to look over the script, then begin."

Willow and I watch body language as they study their scene. I make a note as does she. We'll compare them later tonight.

"We're ready," the male actor says.

I nod. "Begin."

About halfway through, I stop them, give a couple of changes I'd like to see them try.

As they begin, Nola leans toward me, whispering, "Why did you ask them to change it? I thought they were good."

I lower my voice. "They were. I want to see how they take direction. What I asked them to do doesn't fit the scene, but actors I want will do what they are asked anyway."

Wide-eyed, she turns her attention to the pair. She makes a note how the female gave us what I asked, but the male didn't make any change. She'll get a call-back, but no matter how good the male actor is, if he won't take direction, he won't get cast—not in my show.

"Thank you. Please make sure we have your contact information. We will notify you tonight if you are being called back."

The process takes an hour to get through each group, and we don't finish until eleven-thirty. After all the auditioners have left, Sergio makes sure the doors are locked. The six of us sit around the table to discuss each audition.

Sergio adds good comments from an audience perspective. I pull up videos on a few, getting Loreen's fresh notes about their singing. We have our call-back list cemented by one in the morning. Willow sends texts to each. After Loreen leaves, Finn and Sergio walk us home.

Before going to bed, I check my messages. There's one from my lawyer. I click play.

"Marleigh, this is Billy Williams. Your adoption hearing is April twenty-fourth. Be at the county court by ten. Have Elijah with you."

My heart soars. I want to wake up Elijah to tell him, but, instead, I'll go to bed and dream about being my boy's forever mama. I drift off to sleep, dreaming of us picnicking by a river.

After what feels like a short nap, loud pounding awakens me. I jump out of bed and rush to the window. Bright lights flash all over the yard. It's two-fifty-five in the morning for crying out loud. Who is making such a racket? Better, why? I grab my robe, shoving my arms in its sleeves as I run downstairs. I open the door to two large policemen.

"Can I help you?"

The largest police officer—I glance at his badge, Andrew Harris, stalks forward and grips my upper arm. His other hand holds a gun—pointed at me.

"Marleigh Blue Evans?"

"Yes ...?"

"You're under arrest on suspicion of arson."

Chapter 28

MARLEIGH

I'm going to lose Elijah. They'll never let an arsonist adopt. God, help me! I want to flee, but my legs refuse to work. I'm shaking so hard I'll collapse if Harris lets go of me.

Nola clambers downstairs rubbing her eyes. "What's going on?"

"They're arresting me."

She gapes.

Gripping my arm, Harris glares at her. "Stand back. Who are you, ma'am?"

Squaring off with him, she plants her fists on her hips. "I'm her business partner and roommate. What's this about?"

"She's wanted on suspicion of arson."

"You're crazy! Marleigh isn't an arsonist."

I can't believe this. "Officer Harris, where was this supposed to have happened?"

He holsters his gun, but the other cop pulls out his weapon, holding its barrel six inches from me. Nola gasps.

I frown at him. "Are guns necessary?" His name tag says Juan Garcia. I commit both his and Harris's name to memory.

Harris crosses his arms. "Last night. In Atlanta." He pulls out a slip of paper but doesn't look at it. "You have the right to remain silent. If you—"

"I know my rights. You have this all wrong. I held auditions last night. At city hall. There were over a hundred people there. My friends can tell you. Willow? Where are you?"

"I'm over here calling my uncle." Her voice comes from behind me, near our office, but I don't dare look. "We'll get this straightened out."

Harris glares at Willow, then turns his attention back to me. "Anything you say can and will be used against you in a court of law."

"How could it be used against me? I haven't *done* anything."

Garcia grabs my right wrist, pulls my arm behind my back, then snaps on handcuffs.

Please let Elijah stay asleep. I don't want him traumatized.

"You have a right to an attorney. If you cannot afford—"

Willow gets in Harris's face. "Look, Officer Harris, my uncle is your commander. He wants to talk to you." She thrusts her phone at him.

He scowls. It's clear he's annoyed at the interruption. I don't think he believes her, either.

"If you cannot afford one, one will be appointed to you by the court."

He grabs Willow's phone and slaps it to his ear. "This is Officer Harris." He frowns. "But, sir, that's not standard proce—yes, sir ... no, sir ... I see ... yes, I understand, sir ... I will, sir." He inhales a deep breath, hands Willow's phone back to her as he turns to his partner. "Remove her cuffs."

Garcia narrows his eyes. "And why would I?"

Harris clamps his lips together, speaking through clenched teeth. "Because the chief said so." He locks his gaze on me. "You still have to come in for questioning, though, so don't try anything funny."

None of this is funny. "Can I at least put on some clothes?"

Harris looks at Willow, her expression warns him off.

"Yes. Just don't try anything."

Upstairs, I yank on jeans and a T-shirt. I hurry back down, although I'd rather hide. As they lead me out, I call over my shoulder, "Nola, take care of Elijah."

Garcia tightens his grip on my arm, jerking me to a stop. "Who's Elijah?"

My blood turns cold. Shoot! I never should have mentioned him. "My five-year-old brother. I'm his legal guardian."

He glances at Harris. "Shouldn't we take the kid to DEFACS?"

Willow jumps in front of him. "Don't even think about it. He stays with us."

Harris stares at Willow but doesn't challenge her. "Put Evans in the squad car," he says. "The kid's fine here."

Smart man.

With a defiant stare at the officers, Willow puts a hand on my shoulder. "Don't worry, Marleigh. Nola and I will call everyone who was at auditions last night. They'll all vouch for you."

I toss a grateful smile to her as they lead me away, but I continue to pray while they put me into the back seat. *Stay with me, Lord. I need you.*

"Can you tell me anything? How am I supposed to be involved?"

Harris, who's driving, shakes his head. "No ma'am. You'll be told at the station."

Fine. I'll wait. But fear is gaining a stronghold.

Fear not. For I am with you.

Thank you. I know you aren't taken by surprise, Lord, but I sure would like to understand this.

Fear not. For I am with you.

Okay.

I hope God isn't upset with my lack of enthusiasm.

A few minutes later, we pull up to a back door at the police station. Garcia escorts me inside. He points to a bench.

"Sit there and don't move." He crosses the room and sits at a desk. His eyes don't leave me.

Harris disappears down the hall. This place isn't anything like I expected, resembling any office building instead of a jail except there's no carpet.

"Miss Evans?"

I glance up. A man stands before me, dressed in a suit. "Yes?"

"I'm George Goss." He hands me a card. "From Heagy, Turner, and Goss. Sergio Landi called me to help you."

Thank you, Lord.

"Thank you." How did he get here so fast? He must sleep in his suit.

"Your roommates told me everything, where you were last night, who you were with, so this shouldn't take too long." He speaks with Officer Garcia, then comes back to me. "Let's go into the commander's office."

I follow him, still in a state of confusion, but less fearful with him here. We enter Willow's uncle's office. He motions us to sit.

"Marleigh. I'm sorry about all this, but you were accused of starting a fire at the Atlanta Apollo Theatre. Your shoe—" he holds up the broken-heeled shoe Candace said she'd take to be fixed for me— "was found next to a can of gasoline."

Things begin to click in my brain. I shake my head. "No. First of all—"

"Hold on, Marleigh." Mr. Goss glances at Captain Raines. "May I record this?"

Willow's uncle shrugs. "Sure, we are."

Mr. Goss taps his phone, then nods at me. "Go ahead."

"First, I wasn't in Atlanta last night. I was at city hall in Sugar Springs holding auditions for a show. There are seventy-two people, or more, who spoke with me—let alone saw me. Secondly, I broke my shoe months ago. I had both the heel and shoe in my office to take to a shoe repairman. Candace DeMille said she would take it for me." I went on to explain how she fired me. "In my haste to get to Elijah, I forgot all about it."

Captain Raines cocks his head to one side. "There's something missing. Why would she accuse you?"

"I'm opening a theatre."

"A theatre's enough for her to accuse you of arson?"

Anyone opposing her is in her sights. "There is one other thing. I wouldn't make my financial reports to the board match hers, which were much lower than the actual ticket sales."

The captain frowns. "Cooking the books?"

I nod. "So it appears. She was insistent I make mine correspond to hers." With a rush of clarity, the pieces fall into place. *Dylan.* "There's one other reason maybe." I glance at Mr. Goss. "Gabe Sadler found out his brother's henchman was her boyfriend. There's a possibility he had something to do with me being accused. He wants my land."

My attorney rubs his fingers along the whiskers under his chin. Poor man dressed but didn't shave.

"I'm aware of some of the problems he's caused for you and your partners." He turns to Captain Raines. "Sir, I think we need to get further investigation on this fire. Were there any security cameras?"

A commotion in the hallway filters into the captain's office. Officer Harris sticks his head in the doorway.

"Excuse me, Captain. There are at least fifty people out here telling us Miss Evans was with them last night. What do you want me to do?"

"Get their names and numbers. Thank them for coming in."

"Yes, sir." With a glance at me, Harris leaves.

Mr. Goss stands. "So, there's no reason to delay Miss Evans any longer, right?"

"None." Willow's uncle shakes his head. "Again, I'm sorry, Marleigh. I hated to even send men to detain you, but with an accusation, I had no choice." He stands, holding out his hand, which I take. "Please stick close, though. We might need you to be a witness."

"I understand." My attorney and I leave his office.

In the lobby, he stops. "Marleigh, I'll follow up with the captain. I'll call the fire marshal about the investigation. If they have outside security cameras—which most public places do nowadays—this may be solved quickly. Either way, you're exonerated."

If whoever did this isn't caught ... Gabe stands by a window. I look back at Mr. Goss. "Thank you. My biggest worry is how this will affect me adopting my little brother. I'll be much happier when this is behind me."

"You weren't booked. You should be fine. I'll be in touch." He glances across the lobby at Gabe, then smiles and leaves.

After he's gone, the lobby is clear of people—except for Gabe. My heart swells as his steps eat up the floor.

"Are you okay?"

I am now.

GABE

I give my name and phone number to an officer, while keeping one eye on the hallway for Marleigh. I glance at Officer Harris.

"Can you tell me if Marleigh Evans is being booked?" *Please God, don't let them book her.*

He peers at me, searching my eyes. I guess he decides I'm okay because his lips stretch into a half smile. "No. She has an ironclad alibi. Even the mayor called us. She'll be out shortly."

I take a seat on a bench, then jump up and pace. I've never been so angry with my brother. I know his hand is in this somehow. Just like with Norwood. I pause, staring out the window. Wait. Norwood was arrested. Did he identify Dylan's henchman, Tinley? I blow out a large breath in frustration.

A door opens. I turn. Marleigh and the man I assume to be her attorney come out. Her shoulders slump. Her feet drag.

I wait for them to finish talking. After a moment, he gestures toward me. Marleigh turns her head with a smile. When he leaves, I hurry over to her.

"Are you okay?"

A small smile lifts her lips. "Yeah, but I'm so tired I can hardly stand anymore. I guess the adrenalin stopped pumping."

I put her hand through my arm. "Let me take you home."

"I appreciate it."

We head to the parking lot where I point to my Yukon. "I'm over here. I'm positive my brother is involved in this. I'm sorry he's aimed his arsenal at you. I'll do whatever I can to make it right, Marleigh." I open the car door for her.

She places her hand on my arm, stopping me. "Gabe, I've told you before I don't blame you for any of this."

My heart swells. We've come a long way. Dare I hope she trusts me again?

"I'm grateful, but let's face it. If it weren't for me, you wouldn't be dealing with all this." I close her door, walk around, and climb inside. "I'm praying Norwood identified Tinley. If so, there's the tie to Dylan."

"And to Candace."

I stare at her. "You're right." I shake my head to clear it. "This is so crazy. All of it." I start the engine. "Dylan's gone off the deep end."

She lays her head against the back of the seat and doesn't say anything. Poor kid. She's already asleep.

"Did I tell you Candace was stealing from the Atlanta Apollo?"

Her quiet whisper surprises me. "I don't think you did."

"Well, the day Elijah was hurt, she wanted me to change my financial report to match hers. Both reports get presented to the board of directors and comptroller. But I always received the ticketing company's final sales report. My report was compiled from their numbers."

I glance at Beauty. "And you told her no? What did she say?"

"I didn't have a chance to tell her. Elijah's school called about his accident. She said if I left, I was fired." She lifts one shoulder. "I left."

"I wonder how she went on with the directors."

Beauty sits up. "I'd have loved to be a fly on the table. I'd like to know how long it's been going on. I worked there for several years, but I'd never done financial reports until a few months ago. The comptroller asked me to start doing them."

"Sounds like they may have suspected her already."

"Yeah, but I was hoping he was setting me up for a promotion, and she was on her way out."

I glance at her. "I'm glad you didn't get promoted. You might not be getting ready to open your own theatre."

Her smile stretches wide. "Yeah." Closing her eyes, she leans her head back.

Somehow, we have to prove Dylan is tied to this. He's always had Tinley to do his dirty work, but the work has never been as nefarious as last night's. Does Dad have any idea what Dylan is up to?

Chapter 29

MARLEIGH

Gaping, Elijah stares, his eyes alight with hero worship. "Wow! Real handcuffs? Were you scared?"

I'm glad *he* thinks it's exciting. "For a minute, yes, but I knew God would take care of me."

He nods. "Can I go see the theatre?"

Five-year-olds. Here I worry about him being traumatized. "You can, but—"

He huffs out a loud sigh. "I know. Don't get in anyone's way."

I pull him into a hug and kiss the top of his head. He allows me to snuggle him for a hot second, then pulls away with a saucy grin, and races out the door. I stand in the doorway, my gaze following him until he's safely inside with the barn door shut.

Crossing her arms, Nola shakes her head. "Your boy's a piece of work. He's so well adjusted, last night didn't upset him at all, but adds to your hero status. So, tell me what happened after Mr. Goss arrived."

"He told me y'all explained where I was. I heard Officer Harris was overwhelmed when all y'all showed up to tell them I was at auditions."

"The place filled with actors so fast, it was hilarious." The toaster pops. "Willow got right up in Harris's face yelling he should have listened to her. Funny stuff."

Everyone needs a Willow in their life.

I plop my toast on a plate. "And to think, just a few months ago, we were protecting her from boyfriends. I'm just glad we held those auditions last night, so y'all could prove I'm not an arsonist. All I could think of was not being allowed to adopt Elijah if I went to jail."

I slide onto the banquette bench and pick up the mug of steaming coffee Nola has waiting for me.

"I'd be scared too." One of her perfectly plucked eyebrows raises in query. "Toss some bread in the toaster for me?"

I pop in the bread. "You know the prosecuting attorney will ask us to give a deposition. There's a possibility we might have to appear in court. Are you up for it?"

"If testifying will stop Dylan Sadler's rampage, I'd show up dressed as one of Cruella's dalmatians."

Coffee squirts out my nose. I slap my hand over my face and wipe as she eats her toast. "You're a mess."

"Got you to laugh."

"Yeah, you did. Thanks. So, rehearsals have gone well this week, but I'm anxious to get into the barn. Do we have our new rehearsal schedule ready for next week?"

"Already done. Cast and crew have been emailed." Willow enters the kitchen. "Stage Manager reporting for duty."

"Oh, you remind me." Nola taps a note into her phone. "You're on salary starting today. Have you quit your other job?"

Willow's grin is Grand-Canyon-wide. "Sure did. They offered me more money to stay, but they can't beat being partners with my besties."

My jaw slackens. It's official. I stare at her and Nola. "We've done it. We've made our dream a reality."

By one accord, we reach out, clasp hands around the table, and offer thanks to God.

At "amen," adrenaline courses through my veins. "Willow, who is designing our set? This first show needs to be killer. Are we behind schedule?"

"Nope." Willow opens her computer. "I contracted LaShawn Irwin. He's terrific. He'll cost a bit, but he will come to rehearsals to make sure the set will work and there aren't any bugs."

Nola rises, sets her plate in the sink, and starts another cup of coffee. "Let's move this to the office. I want to nail this budget."

Moments later, we're armed with coffee and seated around the desk with our own research results in front of us.

"I have some news to make you happy, Marleigh." Willow's trying to act nonchalant, but it isn't working. Her excitement is contagious.

"Tell me."

"Besides Angel, we now have Mitch on staff. In fact, they're both coming today, so they can play with the systems. They're anxious to see their scene shop too."

I cross my fingers in my lap. "Do they know our systems aren't quite like the ones at the Apollo?"

"Yeah, but they're thrilled to be away from all the offstage drama there. Besides, with Candace now in jail—"

"What?" I gape at Willow.

"How do you know this?" Nola stares at her.

"Sergio has an ear to the police department. The Apollo's outdoor security cameras caught her distinctly. They arrested her this morning."

I can't believe how fast an arrest happened. "What about Dylan or what's-his-name?"

"Tinley," Nola supplies his moniker.

"Yeah, him. Was he there too?"

"There was a man with her, but his back was to the camera." Willow opens her email, reading Sergio's message to us. "'I think Candace will confess, since the police have that video evidence. I'm pretty sure she'll identify Tinley. She's vindictive—won't go down alone for anyone. We need to pray he outs Dylan.'" She closes her laptop. "So, there you have it."

"Does Gabe know?" Poor guy. I can't imagine how he feels.

"Sergio called him before he told me. He said Gabe is relieved."

Nola corrals our thoughts. "Okay, we'll all pray. Right now, we need to get *our* act together."

She's right. I open the costuming document on my laptop. "For this show, let's rent. The estimated rental is twenty-four hundred. To make them would be over six-thousand."

Willow peers at my screen. "You have all the characters listed and any costume changes?"

I wrinkle my nose. "Of course. There are eighteen roles."

"Then, I agree. That price isn't bad. There is also the advantage of not having to store a lot of show-specific costumes."

Nola keys in a notation on her computer, then reads through our marketing costs. "Since most will be on social media, PR is low budget. I've arranged a few interviews with local papers. Even with artistic and technical costs, I think we can afford fifteen hundred for a set designer. I'm sure he can make more elsewhere, but …"

Willow picks up her phone. "LaShawn has a heart for community theatre." She grins. "Anyway, he owes me a favor. As soon as I told him what we're doing, he said to count him in. This won't be hard at all, since he's done this show before. He'll send the CAD drawing over this afternoon."

I turn Nola's monitor toward me, so I can view her spreadsheet of budget and projected ticket sales. "Wow! If we do even eighty percent, we stand to make a good income. We'll cover production costs, salaries, and fund our next show."

After palm-stinging high-fives, we cross the yard to the barn. On our way, we pass Gabe who's in his herb garden. He waves, then bends and clips off some leaves, dropping them into a basket at his feet.

We open the door, stepping inside our dream. There is activity all around us. Men are on the catwalks adjusting lights. Our huge grand drape hangs open, its red burlap cohesive with the barn.

Taffy orchestrates the chaos with the aplomb of a music director. After a moment, he joins us. "The guys are busier than a funeral fan in August. We're close to finishing. Your seats arrive today, the installers will be here tomorrow. We've received sign-off on all plumbing and electrical."

I breathe a sigh of relief. "Thank you, Harry Upton."

"Exactly." Taffy inspects his clipboard. "Once your seats are installed, the fire marshal will come to do a final inspection. He tested your sprinkler system last week."

All his information makes my head spin. "Do you think we'll have occupancy next week?"

The man's smile warms my heart. Taffy cares about this job—even made our theatre personal. He bows with dramatic flair, making me giggle. "As promised, m'lady."

I throw my arms around his neck. "You're the best. You and your family have box seats for opening night."

"Thank you. They're really excited to see the show, my daughter more than anyone. She's a true theatre buff. Now, if y'all will excuse me, I have work to do ... finishing your theatre."

Nola, Willow, and I wander throughout the barn, inspecting our dressing rooms, costume closet—which is not a closet but a good-sized room—and every nook and cranny of our theatre.

"Marma?" Elijah finds me by the sound booth. "Wow." He points to our large soundboard. "That's cool."

Willow pulls him around to sit on her lap. "Want to see how it works?"

"Yeah!"

She takes his hand showing him how to move levers and turn dials. "You never touch the board if I'm not here, though. Got that?"

"Pinkie promise." Elijah holds up his right pinkie finger to loop through hers. He adores his two "aunties" and wouldn't disobey them. How did we ever get so lucky with this boy?

I slide an arm around his shoulders. "Did you come looking for me for a reason, sweetie?"

He thinks for a moment. "Oh yeah. Mr. Williams is in his car outside the house. I told him I'd come get you."

We gals make eye contact. My adoption attorney. "Let's go."

We find him tapping his foot, a dour expression on his face. My stomach pitches. Has he brought bad news?

GABE

I've cut all the thyme I need for this recipe. I'm turning toward the basil when Beauty, Willow, and Nola cross the yard toward the barn. I raise one hand to wave, but they don't stop to chat. There's a lot for them to do.

Sergio says it's best for me to open before the theatre to work out any kinks in my menu. Finn agreed with him. I've decided to offer four theatre-menu items—food we can cook fast to get people in, served, and over to the theatre before the curtain rises. I plan to open a week from Friday night.

After harvesting what I'm able for today, I carry everything into the kitchen. I'll be glad when I can provide all the produce we need from my own garden. That's still a few months away.

I check my inventory, call suppliers, and place orders. I'll be ready for next week. The kitchen door opens.

"Ah, Raul. Glad you're here. I need to go over the menu with you. Then, we'll decide which recipes to use."

He grabs an apron from a hook by the door and loops it over his head. "I'm ready, Chef. What do you have?" His gaze sweeps the kitchen as he ties his apron strings around his waist. "It's looking great in here."

"Thanks. By the way, have you hired two line cooks yet?"

"Yes, Chef. Carlos and Enrique. When do you want them to start?"

"Tomorrow. We open a week from Friday."

Raul's eyes pop wide. "Wow. But there's no reason we can't do it."

He possesses the attitude I need in my kitchen. "Then let's get busy."

For the next hour, we discuss recipes. Raul has some good suggestions to add to the menu. He'll make a good *chef de cuisine* in time.

After we have the first week's menu hammered out, we start cooking. Soon the kitchen smells tantalizing from meat sizzling on the grill.

My phone vibrates in my pocket. I pull it out to see who it is. Dad.

"How are you? How was your cruise?"

"What's this I hear about you and your brother? When are you going to get with the program?"

So much for pleasantries. "Look, Dad, I'm getting ready to open my restaurant. I don't have time for this. I'm *not* working with Dylan ... ever. We don't agree on business practices. I have to go."

"If you—"

I tap the off button. My phone rings again. I turn the device off before heading to the grill.

MARLEIGH

With my heart beating in my throat, I hurry to my attorney. "Mr. Williams, what's wrong?"

"What? Oh." His brow smooths, and his frown disappears. "Another client has a problem. I came over to tell you everything is moving forward for you to adopt Elijah."

I want to Snoopy dance in front of him, but I resist. Still, my feet are itching to move. "What did they say?"

"The judge looked into the recent accusation. He saw you weren't booked, so he spoke with the police too. You and Elijah will appear in court in two weeks for his adoption. Congratulations."

My heart soars. Elijah is about to become my son. Forever. "Thank you so much. You'll be there with us, won't you?"

"Oh, yes, I'll be there. On another note, I'm coming to see your first show. Bought tickets yesterday as soon as your box office opened."

"Our box office? How did you find out?"

"Your website."

I swanny, I didn't know Nola had our website up, but we've all been running in concentric circles this past week. After my attorney leaves, I go into the barn again to meet with Jessica and Walter.

Nola and Willow have them in our new wedding consultation room on the second floor seated at the conference table.

I join them. "Sorry I'm late. I had to meet with my adoption attorney."

Nola's brows draw together. "Is everything all right?"

"Yes." I squirm in delight. "We go to court in two weeks."

They all jump up, congratulating me with hugs.

Jessica shakes her head in wonder. "I don't know how all y'all manage to keep your heads on straight. You girls amaze me."

Nola laughs. "Well, I'm about to amaze you even more, Mom. Everything is ready for your big day. We get occupancy next week. Your wedding is the Saturday two weeks before this show opens. The timing is perfect."

Jessica clasps her hands in front of her. "I'm so delighted. I love the idea of your set behind us. *Beauty and the Beast* is such a romantic show."

I still have some doubts about displaying the set. "I think we should have the curtain closed for the ceremony, then open it for your reception, if you still want to."

She exchanges a glance with Walter. He takes her hand in his. "I told her our guests should watch us—not look at the set."

She gazes at him for a moment then nods. "Okay. I agree."

I love compromise. "All right. Now, everything is finalized." I run my finger down our check list. "Caterer—

check. Flowers—check. Cake—check." I continue through the lengthy list, thankful nothing has been missed.

I glance at Nola's mom. "How are you holding up?"

"Since you and my daughter are planning all this, and Willow will be our stage manager, I'm not nervous at all. I'm looking forward to it." Jessica beams at her fiancé. "Now, we want a tour of this place."

We chat about Gabe's opening on Friday night, as we show them around.

"His restaurant should help you girls too," Walter says. "Maybe a dinner theatre?"

Chapter 30

Gabe

My nerves are strung taut. I pop an antacid into my mouth and talk around it. "Is everything ready?"

Raul, the line cooks, my maître d', and wait staff all nod as one.

"All right. Please, promise you'll forgive me if I bark at y'all tonight. This is make-it or break-it for me ... for us." *My future is at stake.* "Two restaurant critics will be in attendance, but even if you figure out who they are, give them no better treatment than any other guest. Agreed?"

Like a Greek chorus everyone nods, and in unison, they reply, "Yes, Chef."

I glance at the clock. "We open in an hour to a packed house. Reservations are full." With adrenaline coursing through my veins, I rub my hands together. "Let's get moving."

Bernardo snaps his fingers for his wait staff, who follow him to the dining room. Raul found the best maître'd in Atlanta for us. I thought Mateo had the corner on staffing, but I believe mine is every bit as good as his. Maybe better.

Mateo called saying he would be here tonight. He took me under his wing after I graduated from culinary school.

For him to leave his own restaurant in the hands of his staff to come to my opening speaks volumes. I want to do the same someday for another chef. Maybe Raul.

Beauty and the gang have reservations too. Just knowing they're here will help keep me calm through the evening. For the fortieth time, I run a mental review of my menu while the staff continues prepping.

As the kitchen grows warmer, I prop open the back door, securing its screen door. Through the window to the front-of-house, I can see Bernardo seating our first guests. His whole attitude is welcoming. It's contagious, and the servers follow his lead. Word is he has a photographic memory for names and faces. I have a happy crew with him leading the front-of-house staff. Add to that Raul heading my kitchen staff, it's a double win. I exhale a large breath and return my attention to cooking.

Within a few minutes, servers approach the window with the first orders. The choreography in the kitchen works as it should. I know problems will arise at times, but my crew members are a team already.

Thank you, Lord.

An hour later, Bernardo slips into the kitchen. "Chef, there is a gentleman who insists on seeing you."

"Do you think it's one of the restaurant critics?" I pass my sauté pan to Raul, then slip off my apron.

Bernardo frowns. "No, Chef. I placed them at table six."

Something's amiss, I can feel it. So does my maître d'. Table six is hidden behind a divider. We set it aside for private dining. My stomach squirms. So much for wanting things smooth on opening night. However, I always want to be available to patrons.

"All right. I'll come. Thank you."

He nods, then doubling as *sommelier*, he arms himself with our house white and red wine bottles to refill our guests' glasses.

I wink at Beauty as I wind my way to table six. When I round the corner, I'm gobsmacked. My parents. Tentative delight warms me. Have they had a change of heart?

"Mom. Dad. I'm so happy to see you. Welcome."

My mother picks up her wine glass and drains it without a word. Her face could be carved in stone. No expression. I turn my attention to my father, who scowls. What—?

"Let's not waste time on pleasantries, Gabriel. I want you to drop all these ridiculous charges against your brother."

I should have guessed their appearance is about Dylan. So much for change. "First of all, I didn't file any charges against Dylan."

I'm afraid my father will snap his wineglass with his white-knuckled grip on its stem. "Well, somebody did, and you can stop it. Stand up for your brother. Tell them it's not true."

I make sure my back is to the other diners. "You're asking me to lie? Dylan *did* do the things he's accused of, Dad. He put a lot of people—not just me—in jeopardy. His own actions brought the warrant."

A loud curse explodes from his mouth. Heads turn toward us.

"Please lower your voice." I need Bernardo. I raise and lower one hand as my father speaks through clenched teeth.

"Your brother has found the way to make our company rich beyond your dreams. Now, you must step up to the plate—withdraw the charges. We need this property. We need those diam—"

My mother's fingers cover her lips in a fast motion, her age-old signal for dad to shut up.

And now I know.

"The company is not what it used to be, Dad. Dylan ruins lives for his own gain. Don't you see that?"

My mother's face morphs into something ugly. She scowls. "You were always such a disappointment."

Ouch. Why do I keep hoping they'll change?

Dad slaps his napkin on the table, overturning his wine glass. In slow motion, its red stain spreads over the tablecloth. He stands and jabs his finger into my chest. "You are no longer my son."

My last hope dies. While we've never been close, they are my parents. Or were.

My father's attention leaves me. He scowls over my shoulder. I turn my head. Behind me stand Bernardo, Finn, and Sergio.

My mother slips her hand through Dad's crooked elbow, then, like an imperial pair, they exit.

Disowned.

Never have I felt—no that's wrong. They emotionally abandoned me when I became a Christian and joined a church at age ten.

I am a Father to the fatherless.

Yes, you are. Thank you, Lord.

Bernardo picks up my mother's empty wine glass, tapping its side with a knife. "Ladies and gentlemen, tonight's dramatic interlude was brought to you by ..." He sweeps an arm toward my friends' table. "... the SS Spotlight Theatre for your entertainment. To see more, be sure to purchase tickets to their production of *Beauty and the Beast* in the new theatre next door."

Out of the corner of his mouth, he demands we bow. Realizing what he's doing, Finn, Sergio, and I grin while performing sweeping bows. Bernardo leads the applause. Chuckles begin to swell as murmurings abound.

"I thought it was real!"

"How much fun."

"I love dinner theatre."

"Was this one of those?"

My maître d' has diffused an embarrassing situation. He signals the busboys, who make quick work of clean-up at my parents' abandoned table. At the same time, he takes my elbow, guiding me back to the kitchen, while Finn and Sergio return to their table.

I clear my throat. "Thank you."

Bernardo nods. "Leave the rest to me, sir."

MARLEIGH

I've never had reason to doubt Gabe about his parents, but I didn't understand. At times, I'd wondered if his was more a matter of perspective, but after hearing what I did tonight, witnessing their cold, hateful exit, my heart breaks for him.

If only we could be a family—Gabe, Elijah, and me. I think he's given up on us, though. I wish we could go back to when he revealed his desire for the farm ... but as Aunt Susan used to say, "Were ifs an' buts candy an' nuts, we'd all have a merry Christmas."

I can't go back. Gabe didn't break my heart. My own actions did.

Forgive me, Lord. I'm not asking you to change anything for me, but please let him find someone who will love him for who he is and make him happy.

A half-hour later, Gabe joins us.

I reach for his hand. "My friend, you have outdone yourself. Everything was wonderful." I squeeze, then release his fingers.

A slow, easy smile draws his mouth upward. "Thank you. That means a lot." His gaze sweeps our table. "Unless you have other plans, how about staying for coffee and dessert on me? I'm hoping all y'all will wait for the critics' reviews to come out."

I've never seen him this antsy. "I'll stay."

The rest agree. Nola calls her mom, telling her we'll be late and to go to bed in the guest room.

"What did your old boss have to say?" Sergio asks.

"Two thumbs up."

"We both will be successful if our theatre opening is anywhere near as good as tonight." Before I make a spectacle of myself embarrassing Gabe, I pick up my water glass and sip its iciness.

"I want to thank you guys," Gabe claps a hand on Sergio's, then Finn's, shoulder. "I'm not sure what my dad would have done if not for y'all and Bernardo."

I feel so bad for Gabe—to have his own parents sabotage his opening night.

"However, I now know why."

Finn snaps his gaze to Gabe. "Why what?"

"Dylan." Gabe pulls over a chair and sits, lowering his voice. "Dad dropped—albeit by accident—a tidbit of information revealing the reason for Dylan's crazed behavior. Sugar Springs is part of the Georgia Piedmont and—get this—there are minable diamonds and gemstones here. I'm guessing they're industrial grade, but any or all of them could yield a fortune."

Sergio's eyes pop wide. "I never knew that. I wonder how he learned about it."

I knew. "I heard about the diamonds in a college class on geology."

Willow does a double take. "You? Geology?"

I shrug one shoulder. "A passing interest, plus I needed a science credit."

Finn nudges Gabe. "Are you thinking about mining?"

"And ruin the beauty of this peaceful place?" He cuts his eyes to mine. "All this land except my small plot is yours. Would you want to mine it?"

Gabe *has* changed, more than I realized. There is no greed, no pretense in him. "Never. We'd lose more than we'd gain."

The restaurant empties with a lot of compliments and congratulations. My staff cleans up while we linger over coffee and a decadent black forest cake.

A little after one in the morning, Raul approaches the table. In his hands is his cell phone, its screen reveals the restaurant critic's column. With a flourish, he bows, handing the phone to Gabe.

"Congratulations, Chef."

For a moment, Gabe's gaze lingers on Raul, then with a deep breath, he takes the phone and reads.

"Former Chef de Cuisine at Wild Azalea, Gabe Sadler opens his SS Garden Table. Chef Mateo's loss is Sugar Springs' gain. The venue is uniquely comfortable. Service is outstanding with maître d' Bernardo Cervantes leading the waitstaff. The cuisine is as good as any five-star restaurant—quite a feat for opening night. If Chef Gabe's SS Garden Table follows tradition, you can expect them to grow even better with time. This reviewer gives Chef Gabe four-and-a-half stars, but only so he has room to grow into a full-fledged five-star establishment."

Gabe sets down the device to our applause.

"Congratulations, Gabe." I'm so happy for him. I want to throw my arms around his neck. Instead, I sit on my hands.

His eyes shine. "Excuse me, please. I need to congratulate my staff."

I'm not ready to say good night, but I realize he needs to close up.

And I need to discipline my heart.

After saying good night and checking in on Elijah when I get home, I close my bedroom door. A light still glows in the kitchen of the restaurant. Gabe's night was a success even with his parents' added drama. For his sake, I pray they will have a change of heart.

A lot rests on our theatre's debut too. Everyone close to me is invested. It has to be a success. My future and Elijah's—to say nothing of Nola's and Willow's—depend on it. Rehearsals have been going well, but everything must go as planned.

I can't afford to let my guard down.

Chapter 31

MARLEIGH

I awaken to bright sun pouring in my window. I stretch, my eyes popping wide open. Today's the day Elijah becomes my son forever. I throw off my covers and take a fast shower.

When I open Elijah's door, he's fast asleep, sprawled sideways in his bed with his covers kicked to the floor. I sit on the side of his bed and rub his back to awaken him. My heart beats fast in anticipation.

"Wake up, sleepyhead."

He yawns as he stretches, then reaches up for a hug. I wrap him in my arms. *Lord, how I love this little boy. Thank you for making him mine.*

"Are you ready for our big day?"

He yawns again. "What is it?"

He isn't awake enough to remember. I tickle him. "It's our adoption day!"

He slips my embrace and jumps on his bed.

"Yay!" He jumps again, then leaps off the bed toward his closet. "Do I get to wear my suit?"

The blue, three-piece suit has hung in his closet, worn only once before. He'll outgrow it before it wears out.

"Yes, sweetheart. You can wear your suit today. I'll go start pancakes."

"Honest? Pancakes on a Tuesday?"

"Well, this is the most special Tuesday ever." I want everything to be special for him.

He throws his arms around my neck. "I love you, Marma."

I remember when the social worker brought him to us. He was so tiny, less than a week old. I fell in love with him the first moment I held him. I told Mom I would spend my life loving him. She warned me not to get too attached. He might get adopted, after all. I prayed we would be the ones to adopt him.

And God honored my prayers. Twice.

I squeeze him. "I love you to Mars and back."

At the courthouse, my adoption attorney greets us. I introduce Mr. Williams to Willow, Nola, and Aysha, who have come to watch us become a forever family. They take seats as Mr. Williams goes over what the judge will ask both of us.

There are several others there to finalize their adoptions, although they all appear to be babies. When it's our turn, Elijah clings to my hand as we approach the judge.

The man glances up with a smile. "Hello, Elijah."

My boy smiles back but doesn't let go of my hand. "Hello, sir."

The judge glances at our papers, then his gaze meets mine. "This is an unusual adoption. Little Elijah has had a lot of loss in his short life."

"Yes, sir, he has, and I want to make sure he doesn't have any more." I hope I'm not out of place. I cast a worried glance at Mr. Williams. A nod is my assurance I didn't make a huge *faux pas*.

"Elijah, are you happy with your sister, Marleigh, becoming your mama?"

"Yes, sir, but she already is."

The judge tilts his head. "How do you mean, son?"

Elijah swings my hand back and forth. "She's always been my Marma. I don't remember any other mama."

Now the judge gazes at me. "Mar-ma?"

"That's what he calls me, because he says I'm his sister-mama."

He crooks his finger for Elijah to approach the bench. My boy looks up at me for my answer. When I nod, he walks to the judge, who lifts my boy onto his knee, chatting with him. My heart swells with Elijah's giggles and the judge's chuckles.

At last, he asks, "Elijah, when I grant your adoption, what are you going to call her?"

His expression is one of incredulity. "Marma, of course."

"Not Mama?"

"Sir, she's more than just a mama. I don't know how to say it, but she just is. She's Marma."

When the judge sets Elijah on his feet, he runs back to me. The judge reminds me an adopted child can never be disowned. As if. I promise to love him and raise him the same as any other child I might have in the future. The judge then declares our adoption final.

Like every other family there, we hug, laugh, cry happy tears, then hustle out the exit. My heart is so full, it might burst. Outside, I kneel, holding Elijah in my arms for a long moment. There were times I was afraid today wouldn't happen.

Thank you, Lord!

After a kiss, my son—*my son!*—squirms in my arms and wiggles free to run with Aysha. He's right. Nothing has changed. Our lives are the same, but somehow the sun shines brighter.

When we're all in the car, Elijah announces our special adoption dinner has to be at Gabe's for the Elijah burger.

I glance at him. "The Elijah burger?"

"Gabe said he's doing a special hamburger and naming it after me."

Willow giggles. "Sounds like Gabe."

"Then, let's go. Do you think we need to call ahead?"

Elijah clicks his tongue in exasperation. "I made us reserbations."

There is no way I'm correcting him today. "Well, thank you, Son." I'll never get tired of saying "son."

When we walk into the Garden Table, Bernardo greets Elijah with a bow.

"Mr. Elijah, your table is ready, sir."

He giggles, glancing at me, then back at the maître d'. "Thank you, Mr. Bernardo."

We all choose the Elijah burger. When the food arrives, I open mine to see why Gabe named the sandwich after my son. The cheese is Colby. Of course. There are four pickles, no tomato. Ketchup, no mustard.

The perfect Elijah burger.

Gabe approaches the table. He squats beside my son. "How is it, buddy? Did I get the Elijah burger right?"

Elijah's grin—mouthful of food and all—is the answer. He sets his sandwich back on his plate, then high-fives Gabe.

"Thanks."

"You're welcome." Gabe turns to me. "How's the show coming along?"

"Great. We have a super cast. I think we will have a hit."

"We're busy, so I have to get back to the kitchen, but I have reservations for your opening night."

"And not be here?" What chef abandons his new restaurant to see a show?

"I wouldn't miss your opening night for anything." He smiles, squeezes my shoulder, and disappears into the kitchen.

The kind who believes in dreams.

Aunt Susan used to say she was as busy as a one-armed wallpaper hanger. I never fully understood her. Until now. The theatre takes all my time with rehearsals, set building, costuming, besides a million other details. Being Elijah's mother takes all my time. Then, there's Jessica's wedding smack dab in the midst of all the craziness.

By Friday evening, my nerves are stretched like a rubber band. We three gals sit at the conference table for a last-minute review of the wedding rehearsal and ceremony the following day.

"Everything is going according to plan, Marleigh." Willow ticks off her list. "Everyone will be here within thirty minutes for the wedding rehearsal."

The rehearsal supper. Oh, no! "Willow, where is the rehearsal supper? Did we plan one?"

Nola lays her hand on my arm. "Marleigh, relax. We have it covered. We're going to Albano's—a favorite of Walter's."

Relief floods over me. I look at my friend-slash-CPA. "We need to hire a bona fide wedding planner. I can't keep doing this. I'm so outside my wheelhouse, it isn't even funny." My attention returns to Willow. "All right. Then, let's get into the theatre to make sure all the decorations are ready."

She giggles. "No, Marleigh. The decorations go up tomorrow morning."

I stare at her. "Nothing for tonight?"

"You were in my wedding. Don't you remember?" Nola pulls out her phone and opens the photo app. "Look at these. This is my rehearsal. The next one is my actual wedding."

How could I forget her wedding? "In my defense, yours was the one and only wedding I've ever been in. Okay," I stand. "So, let's raise the curtain on Jessica's wedding rehearsal."

The theatre house looks the same as always. I glance at Willow. "How is this going to be transformed by five o'clock tomorrow afternoon?"

"Oh, ye of little faith. The caterers are handling the whole shebang. They have tables and chairs for the back of the house. Walter is paying Mitch and Angel to remove our theatre seats over there. They will store them in those side storage rooms." Willow points to the side walls of the theatre house. "Don't you remember Taffy showing us how fast the seats can be removed and stored?"

How have I been so out of it? I'm questioning my mental capacity right now. "What else have I missed? Or forgotten?"

Willow shakes her head. "Nothing for you to worry about. I handle logistics. Nola handles the money. *You* handle the artistic stuff. We're a team." Once again, my friends calm me.

"I've been so used to having to do everything when I worked for Cruella." I grab both their hands. "Thanks for reminding me—for always being there."

Nola winks. "We have each been there for each other in every life crisis we've had. We're the original three musketeers."

Willow pushes on a seam in the side wall, opening our disguised seat-storage rooms. "Did I ever tell you my grandma was one of the original Mouseketeers?"

"No way. Which one?"

A giggle bursts from her lips. "She was in one single show. She could solo tap dance with the best, but as soon as you put another person onstage with her, her right foot became another left one. She managed to create chaos. They let her do the one show as a guest, keeping the chaos as comedy." Willow shrugs one shoulder. "She was kind of like an early Carol Burnett."

The back door opens. Two couples from the wedding party enter, chattering and laughing. They stop just inside the doors, where one woman stops, gaping.

Her husband taps his jaw, signaling her to close hers. She laughs. "Well dang, I cain't believe my eyes. This was a dirty ole barn last time I was here. I thought Aunt Jessica had slipped north of the gnat line to hold her weddin' in a barn."

Nola's cousin isn't alone. Nobody has been in here except the bridal couple. After everyone arrives, Nola gives them all a quick tour of the main facilities, pointing out restrooms and dressing rooms.

Willow consults with the preacher. When she's done, she shouts, "Places!"

One silver-haired woman looks at Willow like she has two heads. "Places? Whatever do you mean?"

My eyes roll before I can stop them as Willow struggles to hold in her giggles. The woman blushes when Nola explains we wants them to take their places for the rehearsal.

"Well, snap my garters, I never heard that before." She turns to Walter. "Why didn't I know, Bubbah?"

Ahh. Right. She's Miss Lainey, Walter's sister.

He grins. "Because yer a country hick an' ain't got no culture."

She swats his shoulder.

Jessica's smile is indulgent. "Don't be fooled by their banter. Miss Lainey is more cultured than Walter."

I take stock of Walter's sister, then take her arm, leading her to a seat. "Miss Lainey, have you ever been in a play? I believe you have some raw talent."

Her gaze roams over me like she's auditioning me. "Never. Might be fun. What do you have in mind?"

"You make me think of Diane Keaton."

"Me? How?"

I study her face. "You resemble her a little, but more than looks, it's attitude. I just have a feeling yours would translate well to the stage."

"Well, I'll be dipped and rolled in cracker crumbs. Wait until I tell Bubbah. He'll get real tickled."

Outside the barn doors, we all throw the last of our rose petals at their car as the bride and groom drive away. I cross my arms with a sigh. "The wedding came off without a hitch." We congratulate each other.

Willow's ringtone, *Give My Regards to Broadway*, makes her jump. She slides her phone from her pocket. Glancing at the caller's name, she answers with a frown. "Hello? What!" Her gaze cuts to me, then with a burst energy, she spins, and heads back into the theatre.

Nola brows draw together. "What lit her tail on fire?"

I shrug. "No idea, but let's go see what's up."

She's pacing the floor, one hand slap on top of her head. "How bad?"

Bad? I grab her arm. "Is it Gabe? His brother?"

Her negative head shake is absolute. I exhale. "Then, what?"

She holds up one finger for me to wait.

"Okay ... tell her what I said." Willow slides her phone back into her pocket. She stares at us and takes a big breath.

"Serey, our leading lady? She's been in a car accident. Her leg is broken in three places."

"Oh, no. Poor Serey." I'd be devastated. "I'll bet she's heartbroken. She loves the role of Belle."

Willow nods. "But that's not all. Her understudy was driving. She broke her back."

Chapter 32

MARLEIGH

"Oh no! What are we going to do? I can't think of anyone who can learn her role—" My gaze scans this beautiful barn-slash-theatre. All I see is my dream flying out the window.

"You."

What?

Nola crosses her arms. "Don't look at me like you don't know what I'm saying. You've done the role before, besides as director, you know Belle's choreography and blocking."

"Nola's right. You've never forgotten the songs. I hear you sing them all the time. You can have the script memorized again in a week." Willow taps her temple. "I know you."

I shake my head. No. But they ignore me, talking to each other.

Willow ticks off to-dos with her fingers. "I'll have a seamstress come tomorrow night to check her measurements against Serey's. Marleigh's close to Serey's size. The seamstress can make any necessary alterations."

My heartbeat pounds in my ears. "I can't. It's been too long since I've done this show. I—"

Nola's hands land on my shoulders. "Marleigh, listen to me. Take a breath." She waits.

I take a slow breath and release it. Doesn't help. An entire flock of flop-buzzards are circling in my stomach waiting to devour me.

"Girl, we have no choice. We can't postpone the show. The festival—which was *our* idea—starts in two weeks. This production kicks off the festival—it must go on. *You* are the only one who can do it. Now, pull up your big girl panties and get to work."

She's right.

"Why do you always have to be so logical?" I give her the stink-eye. "Okay, okay, I'll do it, but you two are going to have to help me."

They cheer, high-fiving each other.

"Hey, what about me?"

They pull me into their circle. No matter what, we've always been there for each other. My nerves quit twitching. The flop-buzzards go in search of someone else, and my heartbeat returns to normal.

Willow gives me one more hug and pushes me toward the door. "You need to start now. I'll grab your director's script from the sound booth. Don't worry, I'll bring it home after I change the website. That'll take me five minutes. Then, we begin drilling you."

In our home office, I use my phone to send an email to the cast, letting them know what happened. They'll want to send both women messages.

Willow arrives with my script, dropping it on the desk.

"Thanks." I open it to Scene One.

Nola follows her in and drops into a chair. "By the way, we should send flowers to both ladies. They're at Northside Hospital."

"Spring bouquets. They'll love those." I turn a page in my script.

"Great, I'll order them right now." Nola picks up her phone.

Elijah knocks on the door jamb. He knows better than to barge in when we're working. "Marma?"

"What do you need, sugar?"

"I'm hungry."

"You just had supper at Albano's. How can you be hungry already?"

His lips rise in a saucy grin. "I'm a growin' boy."

I laugh and motion for him to come to me. "You ain't whistling Dixie."

"I don't know how to whistle."

"I'll teach you. Hey, guess what?"

"What?"

"What would you think of your mama being in *Beauty and the Beast?*"

He gapes. "For real?"

Smiling, I nod.

He leaps in the air, thrusting one fist upward. "Yippee!" He races from the room. "I'm gonna tell Aysha."

He's forgotten his hunger. It won't last. "I'll go make them both a snack. Do either of y'all want anything?"

Both shake their heads. They're into the task at hand.

"By the way, Nola, is Aysha sure she doesn't want to share the role of Chip in the show?"

Nola shakes her head. "She's finding she is more interested in what happens backstage than on it. I think she's shadowing her Auntie Willow and likes what she does."

"I think she's onto something."

A rosy blush rises in Willow's cheeks. "I've been letting her play with me, and she has some talent in anticipating what's needed. At five, the kid blows me away."

With Aysha settled, I go make a plate of celery with peanut butter for the kiddos.

A moment later, Willow steps into the kitchen, my script under her arm.

"Did you change your mind about something to eat?"

"No, you left this in the office." She lays it on the counter. "This needs to be your constant companion until it's memorized. I'll give you tonight to study, then tomorrow, we'll start reading lines together."

I wrinkle my nose. "Slave driver."

Her grin rivals Elijah's for sauciness. "You betcha. You're going be great. I'm tickled you have the opportunity to give Sugar Springs a taste of your talent. I think this might be a boon for us." She waggles her eyebrows. "Your friends will come in support of you, while your enemies will come to see you fall on your face, which of course, you won't." She raises both hands, palms up. "Voilà—big audience."

"I'm glad you have faith in me. To be honest, I'm scared spitless. Still, it'll be a chance to perform with Elijah." And Belle is a favorite role of mine.

But this is in our own theatre. Using our own money. I gulp for air.

Willow plucks up her pocketbook from the kitchen counter. "I'm always right. Now, study. I'm going to see Sergio. I'll catch you later."

I debate studying in the front room, but if I sit on the sofa, I'll drop off to sleep. I stay at the kitchen table. As I read, I know the how, why, when, and where I move onstage.

When the kiddos burst in the back door in search of their snack, I point to the plate I prepared for them.

"Whatcha doin', Auntie Marma?"

Aysha's been calling me that since the adoption. "Studying my script, sugar-pie. This part is pretty easy since I blocked the play."

They sit at the table, munching. Aysha swallows. "Why do you call it blocking instead of moving?" She licks the peanut butter off another piece of celery.

"Because three centuries ago, theatre directors used a miniature stage and blocks for the actors to decide where they should be."

"Huh. They were pretty smart." She now nibbles the celery, then grabs her last piece off the plate. "C'mon 'Lijah. Let's go see Bambi and Lickrish."

A quick kiss from each of them, and they're gone.

I spend the next couple of hours making sure I know my blocking. After the kids are in bed, I review the song lyrics. All of those are still implanted in my memory. Music always stays in my brain. Now, to start relearning Belle's lines.

"Lord, somehow, I don't know why, but I feel like your fingerprints are all over this. I'd appreciate some help."

GABE

I'm out in my fields the morning after Jessica and Walter's wedding. Things are coming along well. It's been a few weeks. The spring mixes are ready to harvest for salads, but my tomatoes and peppers will take another couple of months. Still, the garden's progress pleases me. I haven't killed off anything yet.

"Hey, Gabe!" Elijah runs to the edge of the furrowed dirt.

"Hey, little buddy. If you stay between the rows, you can come to me."

With care, he picks his way through. "Guess what?"

I can tell he's excited by the elevated pitch of his voice, so I give him my full attention. "I can't imagine. Tell me."

"Marma is playing Belle in *Beauty an' the Beast*."

She is? "Why the change?"

"Cause Serey had a nackident."

"An accident." The correction slips out without a thought. I hope I didn't hurt his feelings.

"Yeah, that's what I said."

I let it go. "Well, I'm sorry for Serey, but is your mama excited?"

"Yeah. She knows the songs an' the other stuff, but she's a little scared about lines."

"I'm sure she'll be fantastic."

"Yep. Can I do somethin'?"

"Sure." I hand him the basket to carry back to the kitchen. I lay one hand on his shoulder to guide him around the plants, but he doesn't need much help. He's sure-footed.

After putting the lettuces in the walk-in fridge for me, he hugs me and goes out to play. I miss his presence. He's a cool little kid. I'd love to help Beauty raise him.

"Do you think there's any chance, Lord? Marleigh and I are back on a firm friendship footing, but do I stand a chance of winning her? I want to marry her."

A forgotten idea-seed resurfaces in my memory. Now I know what I can do with it. As soon as I finish the restaurant's lunch prep, I go to my office. I need to ask a favor of an actor.

First, I go online to find out what the actor's name is. Then, I ask the Lord to make him favorable to what I want to do. Next, I call Willow. I need her in on this and to give me the dude's phone number.

When I explain my idea, Willow sounds unsure. "Do you think you can really do it?"

"Yeah, with yours and Jackson's help."

When Willow comes over to the cottage, we chat about the plan for close to a half-hour—how we can pull this off.

When she's onboard, we call him. By the time we finish the conversation, I think he's as excited as I am.

Willow claps her hands. She's caught the excitement. "I can't believe we're doing this, but Marleigh is going to be gobsmacked."

"In a good way, I hope." This could backfire. "Willow, this is my last chance with her. Do you think this will work?"

She closes her eyes for a second, then smiles. "If anything can, this will, Gabe."

But what if nothing does?

MARLEIGH

I have to change a few areas of the choreography. I'm not eighteen anymore, nor have I kept up with my dancing once I became an artistic director. However, I figure the kids in the chorus will be thrilled with their expanded numbers, giving them more opportunity to showcase their talents.

I'm as nervous as a cat in a roomful of rocking chairs, but everyone has been wonderful. They've accepted me as a fellow cast member as well as their director. With the help of Nola and Willow, I have the lines almost memorized. Most of them. I hope.

Willow strides to the front of the stage apron over the orchestra pit. "All right, places everyone." We are close enough to opening for her—as stage manager—to take over the show.

I take a huge breath to settle my nerves as I move into place. Elijah, in his role as Chip, waves from the wings. He signals he's praying for me by clasping his hands.

My heart swells.

My confidence grows.

Willow calls for action.

My lips part. Nothing comes out.

It's my opening song, but my mind's blank. I know the song. This is crazy. *Help!* I cast a glance at Willow. I'm ready to bail. Then she nods, the prompter gives one word, whispering through my headset.

My mind clears.

I remember and sing, "Little town, it's a quiet village."

The lapse was a mere moment of stage fright. I finish the song, and the dialogue flows. Exhilaration buoys me. I catch Elijah watching my every move. He believes in me.

I can do this.

We finish scene one with two more line prompts for me. I wish I could say I had every bit of dialogue down, but then I mess up the last scene. It's as if I've never seen the script.

I'm dripping with sweat by the time rehearsal is over. "Hey, everyone, I'd like a word with y'all." I wait for them to gather onstage. "We have ten days left. I promise I'll have the lines down by opening night."

"We believe in you, Marleigh, don't we?" Taylor, who plays Gaston, steps forward.

Prince Adam slash the Beast, joins him. "We sure do. I can't believe you have as much memorized as well as you do."

"Thanks for the support, y'all." I believe in them too. "Together, we'll knock their socks off, right?"

Everyone cheers, stacking hands together at center stage. As one, we shout, "Adventure!"

The past ten days have flown by with rehearsals every night. The cast and crew have gone beyond the usual hours to help me.

Now, it's opening night.

My stomach is a-flutter. I arrive in the dressing room to find red roses in a beautiful vase in front of my mirror.

Could they be from Gabe? My heart skips a beat. I search for a card but there isn't one. Maybe they're from the cast to show support, or they could be from Willow and Nola. They're gorgeous, whoever sent them, but my heart wishes they were Gabe's.

I shouldn't expect them to be. After all, we're just friends. I sigh, knowing we will remain just friends. Still, I can't help wishing ... No.

I need to focus on the show—nothing else. Schooling my thoughts, I do vocal warm-ups while I put on my makeup. The other ladies step into the dressing room one by one, each exclaiming over the roses.

"Who are they from?" asks Mrs. Potts.

Heat rises in my cheeks. "I don't know." A tough admission.

I gather my hair into the style for Belle and pin my microphone in place. Next, I put on my costume. This is the time when I become the character I'm playing, but tonight, I'm having some trouble. Maybe after sound check.

I wait in the wings for Willow to call me. When she does, I recite a couple of lines, sing part of a song, then she gives me the okay—the sound engineer has my volume levels.

I retreat to the hallway offstage. My nerves are strung to the limit. I want to throw up. Elijah, dressed in his Chip costume, runs up to me.

"Marma, you're gonna be so good. I love you." He wraps his little arms around me, and all is right in my world. My nerves calm to a normal level appropriate for opening night.

"Thank you, sugar. You look wonderful. Are you nervous?"

"Nope. At least no more than is good."

I can't help chuckling. "You learned Auntie Willow is right, didn't you?"

"Yeppers." He trots off to his favorite place to wait, in the wings stage left, where he can see everything.

"Places. Curtain in five." Willow's voice warns everyone.

I tiptoe to my spot with my heart pounding, but it's the good kind of stage nerves. Not fear, but nervous energy and the desire to do well.

The first notes of the overture float over the sound system. Slowly, the curtain rises. The house is packed. I'm where I belong. There's one thing missing from my world, but I release him to God.

The overture ends. To thunderous applause, I step into the spotlight and sing. As I do, I search for Gabe, but the light is too bright to see if he made it.

I make a fast costume change for my last scene. So far, I cross my fingers behind my back, I've remembered all my lines. We have one final scene—the one where the Beast becomes Prince Adam, declaring his love for Belle.

If only Belle could be me ... *No, Marleigh. Life isn't a play.*

The music starts. I saunter across the stage, singing. A moment later, facing the audience, I sense more than hear the Beast-Prince step up behind me and sing.

When he gets to his line, "Do you see the change in me, then take my hand," I turn, stretching out my hand.

Something's wrong.

My heart slams against my ribs.

It's not Jackson who stands here. It's Jackson's voice but—

Gabe stretches out his hand to me. Underneath Jackson's singing, Gabe whispers the lyrics.

"Do you see the change in me? Then take my hand."

Elijah scampers onstage. He takes Gabe's hand, then looks up at me, his eyes pleading for me to take the other one.

I look down at my son, his face so full of love and hope. Then, I turn my gaze to Gabe's eyes. They are full of promise.

He drops to one knee. "Beauty ... Marleigh, will you and Elijah marry me?"

The audience bursts into applause. Amid loud bravos, I nod and take Gabe's hand.

Ane Mulligan has been a voracious reader ever since her mother instilled within her a love of reading at age three. Together, they would escape into worlds otherwise unknown. Then, when Ane saw *Peter Pan* on stage, she was struck by a fever—stage fever—and never recovered. So impassioned by story, by first grade Ane was reading at a fifth-grade level, devouring the classics like *Little Women*, by Louisa May Alcott. She wanted to be just like Jo March. However, Ane struggled with ADHD long before they even knew what it was. Still, she didn't let it stop her. Instead of writing her stories, she played them out with her dolls and onstage. Now, Ane lives life from a director's chair—by day at her desk creating her award-winning, best-selling novels, and by night as managing director of a community theatre troupe. She lives in Sugar Hill, Georgia, with her artist husband and a rascally Rottweiler. Find Ane on her website, Amazon Author page, Facebook, Instagram, Pinterest, The Write Conversation, and Blue Ridge Conference Blog.

Recipes

Granny Hamilton's Buttermilk Brined Southern-fried Chicken

Ingredients
1 qt buttermilk (save ¾ C for later)
⅓ cup kosher salt
2 Tbsp sugar
2½–3 lbs meaty chicken pieces (breast halves, thighs, and drumsticks)
2 C all-purpose flour
¼ tsp table salt
¼ tsp black pepper
1/2 tsp sage
1 Tbsp garlic
¾ C buttermilk
Cooking oil

Directions
1. Brining is an important step. It makes the chicken tender and juice. Trust me on this. For brine, in a bowl combine the buttermilk (minus ¾ C), the kosher salt, and sugar. Add all chicken pieces to the brine, making sure all are covered. Chill for 2 to 4 hours. Remove the chicken from brine, drain, and pat dry. Discard brine.

2. In a large bowl combine flour, table salt, garlic, and pepper. Divide flour mixture evenly between two shallow dishes. Place ¾ C buttermilk in another shallow dish. Dip chicken into flour mixture in the first shallow dish, turning to completely coat. Dip flour-coated chicken in the buttermilk, turning to coat. Coat again with flour mixture in the second shallow dish.

3. Meanwhile, in a deep, heavy Dutch oven or kettle, or a deep-fat fryer, heat 1–1 ½ inches oil to 350° F. Using tongs carefully add a few pieces of chicken. (Oil temperature will drop; maintain temperature at 325° F.)

Fry the chicken for 12 to 15 minutes, turning once, until juices run clear when meat is pierced with a fork and coating is golden. Drain on a rack. Keep fried chicken warm in a low oven while frying remaining chicken pieces.

Makes 6 servings

Mimi's Best Cottage Pie*

Ingredients

3-4 cross-cut beef shanks

1 small onion (or ½ large one), diced

olive oil

1–4 cloves of garlic (depends on tastes. Can one have too much garlic? Nay, say I.)

8 oz fresh mushrooms, sliced

1 C frozen peas, defrosted

3–4 potatoes, cooked and mashed

Instructions

Pre-cook the cross-cut beef shanks in a crockpot all day, covered in water with a Tbsp of Better Than Bullion brand Beef Base.

About an hour before you plan to eat, remove the meat from the crockpot, break into small pieces, discarding the fat. Set aside.

Peel and cut potatoes into 2" pieces and boil. When ready, mash and set aside.

Brown the onion and garlic in some olive oil. When it's slightly caramelized (10 minutes or so) add the mushrooms and cook till brown. Add the peas and cooked beef. Cook for 5 minutes.

Put the meat mixture in a baking dish, top with the mashed potatoes and bake for 20–25 minutes at 350° F.

This is an old family staple, a one-dish meal. It's also cheap. Serve it with bread rolls. It's the kind of thing you simply throw together. I guessed at the amounts. You can adjust them to your tastes. Serves 4–6 but can be easily expanded

*Cottage Pie differs from Shepherd's Pie only in the meat. Cottage is beef and Shepherd's is lamb.

April's Gourmet Salad

Salad
16 oz mixed greens & baby spinach
4 baby carrots, sliced thin in coins
1 med red bell pepper, seeded and chopped
4 whole green onions, chopped
1/3 C sun dried tomatoes, drained & chopped
1/3 C golden raisins
4 oz feta cheese crumbles
1/3 C pine nuts, toasted
6 med ripe strawberries, optional

Dressing
3 Tbsp white wine vinegar
2 Tbsp extra virgin olive oil
1 tsp Dijon mustard
1 tsp seedless raspberry or strawberry jam
½ tsp Italian seasoning
salt and pepper, to taste

Instructions
Heat a skillet to medium. Add the pine nuts to the pan. Stir often until they begin to turn golden. Remove to a bowl or a paper towel to cool.

Place greens in a large bowl. Add all other ingredients.

Prepare the dressing: add all dressing ingredients to a small bowl and whisk until well combined. Pour desired amount (a little at a time) over the salad and toss.

Serve immediately.

NOTE: If strawberry jam is used, add 6 ripe, sliced strawberries to the salad.

Author Note

The fictional town of Sugar Springs lies near the southern tip of Lake Lanier in the geological Piedmont area of Georgia.

I dug into research as I pondered why Dylan Sadler wanted the farmland enough to go to such lengths as extortion. While there were gold mines in our area in the past, they wouldn't produce enough today to make his illegal activity worthwhile. There had to be another reason. So, I searched for the geology of Sugar Hill, where I hit pay dirt. Diamonds and other gemstones are found *and mined* in the Piedmont area of Georgia. The Piedmont geologic province, underlain by igneous and metamorphic rocks, forms the foothills of the Appalachian Mountains. The region contains some of the most distinctive landmarks in Georgia and is the source for many of the state's most important raw materials.